WITHIN FIRE

Sonig Varadian

ISBN: 979-8-218-02584-7

WITHIN FIRE

Contents

WITHIN FIRE

ACKNOWLEDGMENTS

Thank you to my friends and family for the continuous support. Thank you to my lovely editor for putting the time and effort into this long process. I also would like to thank my talented illustrator who made the cover art come to life.

CHAPTER 1

As I wake that morning my first thought is how nice it would be if someone called in a stink bomb scare and school got cancelled. Then I get scared, because sometimes my thoughts come true, and that freaks me out.

"Hayden," my mom knocks on my door, "time to get up."
Yeah, time to put on my stupid crappy uniform and go embarrass myself in front of everyone. "Okay."
I've been dreading this day for two months. I drag my feet all the way to British Lit, my last class of the day, as usual, trying not to be seen – which isn't easy, since I'm already 6'1" and I'm only 15. Burr and Burton Academy is a private school in my hometown of Manchester, Vermont, and the pressure to get all A's is really ridiculous. If you get even one C you might as well plan on working at Walmart or Hannaford for the rest of your life.

"Dude," says my friend Vaughn coming up beside me. "Did you check out Lydia's skirt? Definitely not code, but hey, I'm not complaining!" When I don't respond he says, "Hellooo...talking about a hot girl here..."

"I didn't notice."

"Oh right, today is the day. You seem nervous." he says.

"Duh." I say with my annoying tone.

"You need to relax, just don't think about it."
Vaughn Patrick has been my best friend since elementary school,

and no one can figure out why, because we're complete opposites – he's always laughing and joking, and I'm serious. Even the way we look is totally different. I have short reddish-blond hair and his is long, black, and messy. And even though right now we're wearing the same blue blazer, white button-down shirt and red tie, I look like an idiot, and he looks cool. Punkish. All the girls think so, too. They always ask me if he's seeing someone. Drives me crazy. "I'm not like you, Vaughn. I can't relax and let things just happen."

"You never could. Not even when we were kids. You were always nervous about everything."

"I had a right to be nervous, after what happened to me." Vaughn holds up his hand like a shield. "Right, right, the my-dad-abandoned-me thing."

He's not trying to be a jerk. He probably doesn't even realize he's doing it and how much I hate talking about my dad, who disappeared when I was eight. For Vaughn it's like *Yeah, he left, big deal.* He'd feel different if it happened to him. On the other hand, maybe he wouldn't – nothing seems to upset him. When we reach the classroom, I hesitate. Going in is the last thing I want to do.

"Don't sweat it," Vaughn says quietly. "When you read your presentation, it sounded fine. Just chill out. You'll do fine." I nod, knowing that public speaking isn't my forte. There is one thing, however, I really like about this class, and my eyes automatically look for her. Waverly Coulter. As I walk past her desk, I take a whiff of her perfume, and it smells like what I think beaches in California would smell like. Vaughn doesn't think she's that great, but to me; she's the prettiest girl at school, with long curly brown hair, dark eyes, and a gorgeous smile. Of course, her boyfriend, Josh, is there holding her hand and whispering in her ear. He's the new kid, but he's not like a new kid who feels awkward and has trouble fitting in – the first day he was here, it was as if he'd been here his whole life, and everyone liked him right away. Especially her.

Suddenly the lights come on and in walks my teacher, Mr. Reynolds.

"Good morning, children."

"Good morning, Mr. Reynolds." All the kids hate him.

"As you know, today is the day we begin giving our presentations before the long break. Remember, they count for 80 percent of your final grade."

The class grumbles, but there's nothing any of us can do about it.

"I'll be picking students randomly. Let's start with, let's see... Mike Peterson. Please come to the front of the class. State your topic and begin your presentation."

Mike Peterson, number one lacrosse defense, stands, grabs his notes, and heads to the front of the class. Not nervous, he says, "The subject I chose was Robert Frost."

As Mike talks, I try to take deep breaths and calm down, but feel like I could have a heart attack at any moment. The other students shift in their seats, bang pencils, and look bored. Vaughn has his head on his desk. He might even be napping. After what feels like an hour, Mike finishes.

"Mr. Peterson," says Mr. Reynolds, "the presentation was not what I wanted; you deliberately picked a topic that was easy, even for you. Your presentation skill was horrible, and you made everyone fall asleep. You could have done better, and your grade will reflect it. You're a senior for God's sake."

Mike doesn't care as he goes back to his seat, and why should he? Lehigh University has already offered him a full scholarship.

"Hayden Grant, you're next. Please come up and state your topic."

The class turns to look at me as sweat beams down my face. I stand slowly; gather my notes, feeling sick. Vaughn mutters, "Kick ass."

I make my way to the front of the class, I feel like death, like I'm shaking all over and everyone can see. I open my mouth, but no sound comes out. I look at my notes and can't even read them – sweat in my eyes makes my vision blurry.

"Sometime before graduation, Mr. Grant." Mr. Reynolds says. He's a dick.

Not looking at anyone's face, I say, "My presentation is the difference between what's real and what we choose to see."

"Speak up, Mr. Grant – we can't hear you." I wipe my face, trying to stay calm but nothing seems to be working.

Suddenly I'm dizzy, the lights start to flicker ever so slowly, and my hands get really warm. Without warning, my eyelids start to close, and I can feel my eyes darting back and forth, like I'm having a seizure. Next thing I know, I'm on the cold floor, I hear gasps, and Vaughn is shaking me and saying my name over and over. In my head his voice is as loud as a car alarm. I think I heard Waverly's voice, too: *Is he okay?* As Vaughn answers, *he's fine.*

I force my eyes open and notice that the lights are turned off – or did they go off another way? Students are hovering over me, and Mr. Reynolds is saying, "Go back to your seats, everyone!" My brain feels like it's going to explode, but I make myself sit up.

"He needs to go to the office," Vaughn says, "I'll do the honors."

"He's faking," I hear Mike say, "So he doesn't have to do his presentation. What a coward."

"Screw you, dude," says Vaughn. "He needs to chill out. I'll take him to the office." He helps me get to my feet.

"You'll do no such thing. He needs to give his presentation. It counts for 80 percent of his grade! Who the hell shut off the lights, if this is some prank…" Again, he's a dick.
Vaugh pauses for a moment and gives Mr. Reynolds his famous death stare. "You are kidding, right? He blacked out! He could have a brain tumor and you want to make him do some stupid presentation?"

"Don't have that tone with me, Mr. Patrick. I can easily deduct points from your presentation. No exceptions with Mr. Grant."

"Go for it. I can see the headlines." Vaughn says holding his hands up as he's speaking, "Kid dies of brain tumor because teacher refused to let him go to the nurse's office. Fired much."
Students start to laugh in the background.
Mr. Reynolds scowls, and finally nods. "Okay but bring him right back. He's not getting out of this."

"Yeah, okay, dude!" Vaughn says with a hint of sarcasm, as he rolls his eyes and helps me to my feet.
Being practically dragged out, the last thing I see clearly is

Waverly's worried face, I feel myself smile.

"Sweet," says Vaughn. "You got out of doing it, but what the hell kind of performance was that-forget it, I don't even want to know."

I'm still in a daze and don't answer. I'm also more embarrassed than I've ever been in my whole life. What a loser! I'm going to go down for being THAT guy who passed out in front of class.

"Let's get out of here." He mumbles, *sick performance, dude.*

"What? Did you not just witness what happened back there? I have to see the nurse. I think I did something to the lights; I'm slowly going insane – I can just feel it." I start to breathe heavily.

"What, don't be ridiculous. You got nervous; you passed out. You're fine. Let's go home."

"We can't just leave." I say, but I know that's exactly what we're going to do. I'll have my mom call the school or write a note or something. *Yes, I'm a goody tushu.*

"I mean, you're okay, right?" Vaughn asks.

"I'm fine. It's what you said – I got nervous, and I passed out. Let's go."

My house is shabby and run-down, the fence is falling apart, and no repairs have been made since my dad vanished. But the yard is filled with flowers of every color. My mom is a floral designer, and right now she's crouched next to the porch, clipping greenery to go in a bouquet for a client. She's dressed sloppy, torn jeans and her t-shirt has miscellaneous stains on it. She looks up as we approach and says, "Is it 3:00 already?"

"Not quite," I say, but before I can explain why we're home

early, Vaughn says in his breezy voice, "Hey, Mrs. Grant, looking fab, as always!" How he can flirt with my mom is beyond me. She just giggles and tries to smooth some hair out of her eyes.

"How was your day? How did the presentation go? I hope you didn't get nervous."

"He was fine," Vaughn says, not looking at me. "I think he'll get a solid grade."
She smiles, "I'm so glad to hear that. What do you think of this arrangement? Do I need more red or white?"

"It's perfect the way it is." Vaughn says.

"Thank you, Vaughn. Such a gentleman!" I look over in disgust, "Can you stay for supper?"
At last, I speak, interrupting before Vaughn can get in a word. "No, he has to get going." Vaughn glances over. "I do?"

"Yes, you said that you had some things to do when you got home. Remember?" I give him my, piss-off look.

"I did? Oh...okay, yeah. Things to do." Vaughn says, looking at me weird.

"Well, next time." My mom says. I can tell she's holding something back from me.

"Later, dude." I rub my forehead. I can't wait to lie down. I watch as Vaughn leaves, but I know he will get over it.

"Thank you anyway, Mrs. Grant. Catch you later." He says, and heads back down the driveway.
I start to go inside, and my mom catches me off guard. "Wait, I want to hear more about your presentation. Did the teacher like your topic?"

"Loved it." I escape inside, run up the stairs, go into my room and shut the door. Stumbling to the window, I push it open, take a deep breath of fresh air. Then, from my desk drawer, I grab my red lighter and set fire to a piece of paper. I watch as the corners turn black and curl and flake off, carried by the breeze. Mesmerized by the flame, my mind travels to somewhere far away, where nothing bothers me. Just before the heat burns my fingertips, I place it on a dish. A knock on the door startles me and invites me back into my grey and clustered room.

"Hayden? Are you okay? What are you doing?"

I take the dish into my bathroom, flush the ashes down the toilet, and give the room a squirt of air freshener. I open the door. "I'm fine." *Seriously, never any privacy.*

"I thought I smelled something burning."

I pretend that I can't smell it. "Must be coming from outside – I have the window open." She sits on the bed, "Hayden, this has to stop."

"What?"

"This fire stuff. You can't keep doing this; I know you're up here burning things. Plus, there are little burnt spots all over the house, the pillows, the rugs, and on the furniture. You're going to burn this house down." She pauses, "I need to talk to you about something, and I don't want you to get upset."

Just hearing her say that makes me upset, actually, more worried, even though she's been a great mom...but not like my dad, who decided one day to just vanish without a care in the world. I remember he used to read to me at night from a big book about people with mystical powers. Found that kind of odd, but at eight years old, you don't question things. Once, about a month after he left, I asked her where the book was, and she said she'd thrown it away.

"What's up, Mom?" There was an extremely long pause, almost as if she didn't want to tell me.

"Your dads on the way." She said, as she looked away from me. I started to laugh, glanced over, and knew she was dead serious.

"What? Excuse me!" *Oh, perfect, just another thing in my life that I need to deal with. Hello, being a teenage boy.*

"I told you to not get upset." She tries not to raise her voice at me. She knows how hard this is.

"What do you mean, he's on the way? On the way...here? To see us?" She glances at me, not sure if she should spill the entire truth.

"He'll be here soon." she says.

"Jeez, Mom, thanks for the heads-up." At this point, I have no idea what else to say. I'm kind of shocked and can't really process much.

"I tried to tell you when you got home, but you ran off and..."

"No, you didn't tell me anything, you were asking Vaughn to stay for supper... Wait, is that why? Did you want him to be the distraction for me?" She looks at me and that look alone says it all. "I can't believe this. I don't want to see him. He walked out on us, remember! If anything, you should be the one that's more upset than I am."

"Now, Hayden..." I interrupt her.

"He didn't even write to us! Now he just comes home out of nowhere and expects me to greet him with open arms? I don't think so. Where the hell has he even been? Does he even give a rat's ass about us?"

"No one expects you to greet him in such ways. But he's on his way and there's nothing you can do about it."

"Seems like there's not much I can do about anything when it comes to him, huh, Mom?" I don't really mean to hurt her, but when I see the pain that comes across her face, I feel bad. But before I can apologize, she stands and says in a sad voice, "He'll be here any minute, I expect you to behave." And walks out. *Behave! HA! What is she on, crack? After everything that has happened today, this was something that I did not see coming.*

Slamming the door with anger and frustration, I take a deep breath. I start to pace. *Okay, deep breaths, Hayden, chill out. I must tell Vaughn; this is just way too weird.* I dial his number and wait for him to answer. Without saying hello, Vaughn says, "Dude, your mom though..." I shake my head. "Vaughn, first off, seriously? Second, you will not believe this – Connor is coming over." There's a slight pause as I'm waiting for Vaughn to answer. *Hello, anyone there?*

"Who the hell is Connor?" Vaughn says.

"You know – the guy who walked out on me."

"You mean your dad?" Vaughn knows exactly who I'm talking about; he's just being a smart ass.

"He's *not* my dad!"

"Why's he coming over?" Vaughn says, curiously.

"I have no idea, but he's on his way, kind of why my mom asked you to dinner tonight. No offense." There's a loud BANG as I listen to Vaughn breath heavily on the other end. "Where the hell are you?" Before Vaughn can answer me, I hear the doorbell.

"Dude, I have to go." There's another loud bang and I hear Vaughn cover up the phone. I don't hang up hoping to hear something else, instead Vaughn says, "Call me later, dude, and let me know what happens! I gotta jet...Hey, hey don't you dare..." *Something is going on in that house, but I don't have time to ask.* I shrug my shoulders, I know that Vaughn does weird things, but that just didn't strike me as Vaughn material. I go to the window and look outside. Parked in our driveway is a crappy-looking two-door Toyota Tercel. *Figures. How the hell that car even makes it around in this state, is beyond me.* Grabbing my lighter, thinking I have enough time, I set fire to another piece of paper, and breathe in the smoke, trying to calm myself. But right away I hear footsteps coming up toward me. Running into the bathroom, I drop the burning paper in the toilet and flush; at the same time, there's a knock on my door. *Crap here goes nothing.*

"Shit," I shout. "I'm not here!"

"Hayden?" It's *his* voice...the voice I haven't heard since I was eight. I remember the last words, the night before he "left." Of course, I didn't know it was his last night.

"I probably should have said this a long time ago, Hayden, but I think you're a great kid. I'm really proud of you. And I want you to know, I'll always be here for you." At the time I didn't know why he was talking that way. "Always here for me" – what bullshit! He left the next day. "Go away." I say again, but I know it's a losing battle. There's no lock on my door, all he has to do is open, and I'm here, trapped.

And sure enough, he gently opens the door, and it's like no time has passed at all. He looks exactly the same, I swear. He's even wearing that stupid Area 51 t-shirt he got in New Mexico.

"Hayden," he says again. "You got so big!"

He takes a step toward me. Personal space triggers my brain as my hand flies up, halting him. I don't like people being in my bubble, especially people like him. "What do you want? Why are you here?" From behind, my mom says, "Hayden. What did I tell you?" Connor shushes her. "No, it's okay. He's pissed. I don't blame him; I would be too." He takes another step into my room and looks around. "Is that my lighter?" he asks, nonchalantly.

My mom's worried face appears. "I told you he's been setting things on fire." A huge WHOA triggers in my brain. *Hold on, did I just hear that correctly?*

"You told Connor that-is that why he's here?"

"Relax Hayden, your mom is just concerned." I look at him and give him a who-gives-a-shit face.

"So, I burn a piece of paper and suddenly you show up and tell me to stop?"

"Before it gets out of control." My mom says, as I start to laugh. I can't help it.

"Your mom and I just want you to be safe." Connor holds out his hand, but I don't give him the lighter. He slowly brings his hand back to his side. Someone needs to just punch me in the face, so I can finally wake up from this nightmare.

"You know, I got that from my dad. I'm glad you found it and kept it. Do you know what the symbol on it means? *I play along because, there's no sense in me caring at this point and putting up a fight.*

"It's just a lighter with some random triangle with a dotted line and a heavier bold outline." He points toward the lines.

"See how the bottom line is darker than the top line?" I nod. I don't even know why we're talking about a lighter. "Yeah, I see it."

"It's pretty old. I'm surprised it still works." My mom looks at Connor and back towards me.

"I don't want him to have that lighter."

"Who cares about some stupid lighter! Why is he here, what does he want?"
He sighs. I'm sure he wasn't expecting me to cry with joy at the sight of him, but he probably didn't know I could be this nasty. "I would like to explain why I left." he says. *Well, that's a shocker.*

"Honestly, don't bother. I don't want to know, nor do I give a rat's ass."

"Hayden Wade Grant, you don't use that language in this household. Now give your dad a chance…"

"He's NOT my dad! Don't you ever think that's okay." Jumping out of the window sounds better and better. The lights in the house start to flicker, like they did at school.

"You were too young to understand at the time," he begins, "but it was too dangerous for me to stay. Dangerous for you, I mean. I would have risked anything to have stayed."

"Were you wanted by the police or something? There has to be a better reason than that."

"No, not police." He says, without trying to give away any other detail. Not like I would know what the hell he's talking about.
My mom puts her hand on his arm. "I told you, he's still too young to understand."

"Understand what? You dropped out of our lives – what more is there?"

"I didn't just drop out. I've been in touch with your mom this whole time, but very cautiously." I start to laugh uncontrollably and can't seem to stand on my two feet.

"Excuse me?" My legs give way and I drop onto my bed, feeling more betrayed than ever. Because with all that information, it means he didn't leave us – he left me. I look toward my mom's pale face. "Were you ever going to tell me?"

"Your dad told me not to." I start to laugh again. The lights in my room start to flash, but I ignore them.

"Of course! Why should I be included in anything? God forbid."

"I thought it would make things harder if you knew I was still around." Connor says without hesitation. He looks at me, bothered with concern.

"Around? What do you mean? Where is 'around'…Were you dead or something, too?"

"I've been around here and there. Remember my job in the lab? How I used to travel sometimes?" I shrug; don't want to let on that I have any memories of him living here at all. He continues, "Well, those trips weren't what you normally think of as…I mean, I didn't jump on a plane and go to…" My mom appropriately chimes in.

"Let's just say that your dad had business matters to deal with all over the world. That's why he used to go away so much." Her voice is bright, like we're a regular family, talking about normal things. Not learning how to ride my bike.

"So let me get this straight. These so-called 'business trips' did you just forget to come home from the last one?" My mom gets so flustered.

"I told you; it was too dangerous. Being here was putting your life in jeopardy." My dad says, as he's trying to hold things back.

"I heard you the first time, loud and clear. You left for me. I get it. Remind me to nominate you for the Dad of the Year Award."

"Hayden! That's enough." My mom yells.

"It's okay." Connor says again. He doesn't seem upset by my abuse; he just takes it, like he deserves it. He looks at my mom, "Let's give him some time alone to process this." I watch as they both leave my room. I stare up at the wall as my ceiling fan keeps going round and round.

I wait for them to go downstairs before I get up to close my door. I don't call Vaughn; I just sit on my bed and try to figure out what Connor was trying to tell me in so many words. What was the danger? Did it have something to do with his job at the lab? Am I the danger? I never knew that much about what he did for work, I mean as an eight-year-old, those things don't really cross your mind. I always pictured him working with test tubes and lab rats. Trying to maybe come up with a cure for some rare disease. On the weekends we used to go hiking and camping, or we'd go to the playground and shoot hoops while my mom took pictures.

While trying to go down memory lane, I noticed that the lights in the room stopped flickering. I shrugged it off and picked up my lighter and looked closer at the symbol. I'd Google it, but how do you Google a symbol? For some reason, at this very moment I don't see any need to set anything on fire. Which is very strange, because in times of stress, I always do.

I look closely at the darker line that seems to be crossing the triangle and notice my hand feels very warm, and how it's slowly becoming warmer. Not knowing what to do, I drop the lighter. The strangest thing happens, I realize that it's not the lighter that's what's warm, it's my hands. I rush toward the bathroom and quickly run my hands under cold water. Nothing seems to be working, my hands are literally on fire. I scream and when I look back down, my hands are normal.

Distracting me, I hear my mom's voice from outside. "The yard needs a lot of work." I hear Connor respond, "Yeah we need to fix the fence, and paint it." I go to the window. I can't help but notice that she looks happy; maybe happier than I've ever seen her. It's like she can't take her eyes off him. I also notice that he keeps touching her – her arm, her back, even her hair. Memories that I've spend eight years pushing out of my mind, come back. Trips to the beach, when I'd look over and see them kissing...the cards they used to give each other for no reason...the time Vaughn's mom said, "Your parents act like newlyweds still!"

"Hayden and I can start by pruning some of the trees," Connor says, "They're taking over. We should clear out that whole section in the back."

"Don't forget, Hayden has a lot of schoolwork." my mom says.

"We can work on this during the weekends."

"He sleeps late on weekends because he works hard all week. He's a great student. I don't want anything to jeopardize his grades."

"But I think it's important that Hayden and I spend time

together. We need to reconnect." I can see my mom's reaction to all of this.

"What Hayden needs right now is to get used to the idea of you being back. He's hurt and angry. That's not just going to go away because you've come back. He has a lot of things he needs to work through."

Connor crouches and scoops up some dirt. "The soil needs treatment. That's why no grass is growing."

"I haven't had time to take care of anything." She sounds defensive. He stands abruptly.

"Don't forget, it was your idea that I left in the first place." I press my head against the glass window trying to comprehend if I heard things correctly. I hit my head against the window, making an annoyingly loud thump.

"Only because of..." she stops, looking up at my window. She probably can't see me, but I duck out of sight anyway and can't hear the rest of their conversation.

Sitting at my desk, I try to wrap my head around everything. If my mom told him to leave, that means he didn't want to go. He didn't leave us, he was kicked out! But why?

Six p.m. rolls around and our doorbell rings. "Pizza's here!" my mom yells up. Pizza does sound amazing, as my mouth begins to water. I slowly get up from my bed, where I've been staring at the ceiling for the past two hours. Making my way downstairs, I see Connor as he heads toward the kitchen. I can't get over how strange it is to see him, but at the same time it's familiar, almost like he never left. Sure, I'm pissed off beyond words, but I also have to try and mend things, to trust him again or else what are second chances for.

Before digging into my first steamy slice of pizza, I get cornered with questions.

"So," Connor starts off, "You have a girlfriend?" I shrug, really something I don't want to discuss.

"He has friends that are girls." My mom chimes in at the right moment. Even though it's not true, I do appreciate the gesture.

"I still hang out with Vaughn. Remember him?" I'm trying.

"Oh sure, troublemaker, but nice kid," My dad tries to figure me out. "You like school?"

"Who likes school?" I say, as Connor laughs.

"You hate it now," my mom says, "but someday you'll look back and only remember the fun you had."

"Some parts of it are okay," I say, reluctant to feel like he and I are bonding, just in case he has to leave again. "Some of my classes are pretty interesting."

"You like your teachers?" I look at him as I take a big bite of my slice of pepperoni.

"Sure, some of them." Talking about school is so boring. I want to ask my mom why she made him leave, but then they'll know I was listening in, "So, how come you left? Be honest."

My mom nearly chokes on her slice of pizza, but she's quick to the draw. "It was dangerous for him to stay."

"But why? You keep saying that! What was going on -what was so dangerous about him being here?"

Connor looks at my mom for what feels like a few minutes. I know they're trying to figure out how to come up with the perfect lie and make me stop asking questions. Finally, Connor blurts out, "This is going to sound really bizarre, but I want you to keep an open mind. If you can do that, I'll tell you exactly what's been going on." I turn to glance at my mom, she nods her head but doesn't protest.

"I'm all ears, and I'll keep an open mind."

"Good. Hayden, in one month you will turn 16. For most kids it doesn't mean that much, but you're not like most kids."

"What do you mean? Does this mean I'm not allowed to have that huge party I wanted?" My mom completely ignores me, as Connor continues.

"I think you know what I'm talking about." I don't answer. I do kind of know. Over the years I've had so many weird things happen to me like whenever I get angry about something, lights flicker. Lots of times I'll be in my room doing homework and something will fall off the shelf, or tip over. At times the pillow will just fall off the bed, for no reason. Or stuff on my desk will rearrange itself. I'll go into the bathroom and when I come back out, things are in different places. My computer, at times, would turn off or my TV would have a mind of its own. Lately there have been burn spots all over the house, but I've never mentioned any of this.

Connor sees, by the look on my face, that he's right. "You ever feel like you have some kind of...gift?" I shrug, very confused at what he's trying to get across.

"I'm not sure what you're talking about."

"Well, I'm telling you that, you do. And when you turn 16, you'll see even more evidence of it. And at times it'll feel uncontrollable. That's why I came back – to help you understand it. Otherwise, you may end up hurting yourself.

"Or someone else." My mom says.

I start to feel sick and stop eating. "What are you people talking about? Are you on something? This is nonsense."

"I don't want you to be scared. I went though it as well, once I turned 16, I underwent an apprenticeship with a Master Warlock." I choke on my own saliva. I pause for what seems like a good two minutes.

"Excuse me, a what? Hold on, if I'm getting this correctly, you're telling me I'm a warlock?"

"Kind of, yes. More like an altered warlock." I bust out laughing and jam another slice of pizza in my mouth. "You have to take this seriously." Connor says.

"I know what a damn warlock is. We're talking like Harry Potter or Merlin here...Good one Connor, good one." I shake my head and take another bite of my pizza. "You are hilarious, and mom, you went along with this bullshit?"

"I'm not joking, kid. Plus, Harry Potter isn't real. There aren't a lot of them around, but you could know one and not even realize it, because they look like regular people.

"Sweetheart, we're trying to tell you something serious, and we're very nervous about it." I can see my mom's reaction and know when she's telling me the truth.

"Holy shit, you're being dead serious right now. Wait, so you're telling me that I'm a...

"Warlock." Connor reconfirms.

"Right a 'warlock' and you want me to believe that? So, what, I have to use my powers for good and not evil?"

"Hayden, this is no joking matter." My mom looks directly at me.

"You people must be on molly. I mean I know Vermont is like the drug capital of the world here, but mom seriously, you're not buying this shit?"

"Watch your language, Hayden." Connor looks up toward me.

"Hayden, I'm not lying to you. You're a warlock and you need to be careful. You're like me."

"Like you? I'm nothing like you." I take another bite of my pizza. It's hard to register everything when he comes home after eight years and spills this information on you that he's also a warlock. I play along with his little game.

"What is your power?" *This should be good.*

"I was fascinated with light..."

"The point your dad is trying to make," My mom interrupts. "Is that sometimes the powers can get out of hand. That's why he's come back. To keep that from happening."

"Wow, congratulations Mom, you won the award for best convincing performance. You guys are meant for each other, ever think of an acting career? Here I thought you were telling me some joke...Alright, say I do believe you, which I don't. If you're so interested in helping me with my powers, then why did you leave?"

"I know things are hard to comprehend, but I'm telling you the truth. I'm not joking, nor do I care to be joking. I thought if by leaving, it all would stop. My dad forced me to develop my powers and bad things happened. I wasn't going to do that to you. Your Mom and I felt that if I wasn't here, maybe you wouldn't develop these powers." It still isn't processing that I'm some sort of a warlock or whatever.

"I'm making cookies." My mom says suddenly, as if that will fix things. "Who wants some?" I look at her, laugh, and make my way back toward my room without looking back. "You guys are seriously mental."

I'm in my room around 10:30 p.m. doing homework, even though there is no way in hell that I can concentrate. Connor appears in the doorway, concerned.

"Your mom and I are going to bed." He tries to smile, but it's very awkward.

"Okay." Connor lingers.

"You'll believe me in time." Connor says in return.

"Yeah, whatever." I say.

"For now, just think about what I said to you tonight." I hear my mom call good night and moments later their bedroom door closes.

I finally get to bed around midnight, but wake up a few hours later, after what seems like a nightmare. My hands are on fire, and in my nightmare all I can think about is, "I can't do anything if my hands are on fire" I can't read a book, I can't use the computer and I won't be able to hold my cell phone. When I wake up, my hands are in excruciating pain, and I smell burning flesh. I turn on the light, and my hands are bright red, but after a few seconds the pain starts to go away. My hands are back to normal, so it must have been a nightmare. I fall back asleep, or so it seems. All that runs through my head is, "I'm a warlock...a freakin' warlock."
Next morning arrives and I wake up, not remembering much of

what happened, but I came to realize that not only am I not in my bedroom or bed, but how in the world did I get outside.

CHAPTER 2

Dream state is usually described as a condition of altered consciousness in which someone does not recognize the environment and reacts in a manner as if in a dream. Current state, outside on my front lawn, fully clothed and unaware of my surroundings. *First things firsts, I have to wake up from my dream state.* I slowly open my eyes, forcing to see my surroundings, kneeling on the concrete ground, knowing that at any moment someone could spot me. Enraged, I smack my knuckles hard against the concrete walkway, only to realize that I am in fact not in a dream state. Bleeding, I wipe my knuckles on my ripped jeans and slowly make my way back inside. Tiptoeing into my room, trying not to be seen. I quickly wash my hands and pour water on my face, because I can't imagine what really happened last night and the thought crosses my mind, that I may never know. Quickly getting dressed, I look over at my computer and realize that it's the weekend. I lay on my bed staring up at my ceiling fan, watching it rotate until my eyes start to close. What seems like some time, I hear faint sounds coming from the kitchen.

"Hayden, breakfast is ready. Come on down." I hear my mom yell from the bottom of the stairs. That smell of delicious bacon emanates throughout the house. The best fatty smell in the entire world. "Coming!" I grab a clean shirt and make my way down the stairs, when I hear the sound of breakfast dishes clinking. It's a sound that I never usually hear. For a moment, I thought that Connor coming back was a big dream or nightmare, but then I see him sitting at the kitchen table. We've never really been a breakfast family, my mother and I at least. Usually, I'm rushing for my first class with sometimes a bagel in my mouth, while Vaughn's waiting for me by the sidewalk.

"Morning, Hayden." Connor says while dunking last night's chocolate chip cookie into his coffee. My mom shakes her head at him.

"Are you okay?" My mom examines me, "You look like you haven't slept."

"I'm alright." I respond, monotoned. There's no way that I'm going to tell her, let alone anyone what happened last night. Heck, I don't even remember. Could you imagine how that would play out, "Oh by the way, last night I was sleepwalking, and I ended up waking up on our front lawn, ripped pants and all. But don't worry, everything's just great." I can just see the look on her face.

"Well, you sure, you have bags under your eyes." *See what I mean?*

"Mom, I'm fine. Does it really matter what I look like? I was up doing homework and stuff."

"Alright, just make sure tonight you get some sleep." I smile at her, but I know she's acting this way because he's back, for how long, I'm not sure. I take a piece of bacon and grab a hot cup of coffee. Feeling awkward as they both stare at me, I grab my coffee and make my way toward my room. Sitting on the edge of my bed, I reach for my phone and call Vaughn.

"Yo, fool. What's going on? Haven't heard from you." Sometimes I wonder about Vaughn. He's got multiple personalities at times.

"Everything cool with you? I'm chill. Just going through the motions." I had no idea what I was going to tell him. Felt a bit awkward.

"I'm good, you know me. So, spill, what's he like? Is he staying, why the F did he leave?" He slurs out five million questions at once. "I'm literally curious, so c'mon, spill it."

"Here's the thing – I'm not really sure why he left, it's kind of a mystery, if you ask me. I guess my mom thought it would be easier on us if he left for a while. But apparently, he's back now." I had to tell him something. *What else would I say, he's a prick and doesn't care about anything. Oh, and by the way I have special abilities like, Harry Potter.* Vaughn would start laughing if I ever told him the truth.

"So, what the F does that mean – is he actually staying?" I really have no idea what to say.

"Not sure, but on the plus side, I might be getting his old car." I hear Vaughn breathe slowly on the other end. "It's a Tercel." That's when I hear him start to laugh.

"Dude, really. A Tercel!" He can't help but laugh.

"At least it's a car...Anyway my mom has this whole day planned out, but cool if we catch up later?" I wait for his response. I know he can tell that I'm lying to him, but sometimes you have to do that to your best friends, to hide the truth. "Dude, you still there?"

"Yeah, still here. Don't get the Tercel, nab another car if you can. We can talk later though." I can tell something is off with him. I hear another loud bang from his end of the line. "Shit, what the...I swear I will...Hayden I gotta go. Later dude." I hear the click. I stare at my phone, not knowing what to do. I contemplate calling him back, but in that second Connor comes into my room.

"Hayden, listen I know that things are a bit weird right now, but I was wondering if you wanted to go to the dealership with your mom and I." I shake my head as I just said something similar to Vaughn, maybe I do have some sort of mystical powers. "Think about it. We're going to leave soon. It would be nice for you to come."

"Umm...sure, I will be right down." Sometimes, the unexpected happens and you don't know what to do, so you just go with it. I'm wondering if this is his way of easing back into the whole warlock shit.

On the way to the dealership, my mom looks over at Connor, who's driving. "I can't believe you still drive this thing."
"I'm having second thoughts about giving it to Hayden. I'm not sure it's safe anymore. Might be time to trade it in." His eyes meet mine in the rearview mirror. I quickly look away, I'm completely petrified knowing that only a few minutes ago, I told a lie to Vaughn about the Tercel and now this. He continues, "Maybe when we look for my car, we can look at one for you as well."

"Awesome, thanks!" Now if I just get a Beamer. I can picture myself driving into the parking lot at school as Waverly sees me. She's holding hands with Josh, her loser boyfriend, who rides his bike in. I glide into a spot, and she says, *Wow, nice car.* Then she breaks up with him, and we go for a ride, and everything happens just like it was meant to...

"WATCH OUT!" my mom yells. I come back to reality as my dad swerves to the left to avoid hitting the oncoming car, and then quickly swerves right. My seatbelt is lodged tightly around my chest, preventing me from moving. The car radio turns on ever so softly, fading in and out, kind of like static. I think I hear a faint laughter, and moments later the Tercel slams into the guardrail. I'm thrown against the front seat and hear the sound of metal crushing and glass shattering. Next minute, I hear the pop of what's supposed to be air bags, but this car didn't have them. I watch in slow motion as my dad is ejected from the front seat through the windshield. Silence. My mind goes blank, and the car gets darker and darker until, I'm out cold.

I come to a few seconds later, my eyes fluttering open. The horn is blaring, and my mom is screaming, "Connor, Connor!" She's trying to move her body, to see what's happening but she can't move as the seatbelt is stuck. The horn goes silent to my ears, as I unbuckle my seatbelt and lean forward. My mom's face is covered in blood, and I look out to see a large metal piece sticking out of my dad's side. I take in a deep breath and know that my dad's probably not going to make it. This gut feeling sets in as I know something isn't right, almost like this was directed toward my dad.

I scramble out of the car and open my mom's door. *Oh God, shit there's blood everywhere.* I manage to reach into my pocket and grab my crappy cell phone as my hands are shaking uncontrollably. I quickly dial 911 as I glance over at my dad's motionless body. I look toward my mom and my hands start to heat up, very slowly, I look into her eyes as a single tear falls down my cheek. "Everything's going to be alright, hang in there, Mom." My hands are now extremely hot and without thinking, I take my hands and place them on the seatbelt and watch as it slowly burns off the fabric and setting my mom free. Startled, not having much time to really react,

I hear the sirens as cops, ambulances and fire trucks pull up. Paramedics get out from the back and the front with gurneys running toward us. One of them takes hold of my arm and does a double take, "Kid, were you in the accident? Do you know who these people are?"

I nod. "Those, those, they're my parents. I managed to get free. What…What's happening to them?" I can only muster up a few sentences because my bodies in shock. I glance over where my dad is but can't see him as he's surrounded by paramedics. The paramedic checks my vitals to make sure I'm okay, but he looks at me funny and says, "Were you in the car or did you happen to be on the same road?" *What the hell is he talking about?* I look at myself to make sure that I'm understanding everything. There's nothing wrong with me, at least I don't think so. "Hello kid. Were you in the car? Because you don't have a single mark on you." I'm still a bit delusional. *He's right; I don't have a single scratch on my body. My shirt isn't torn and I'm walking around as if I just witnessed the accident. The blood that I'm covered in, isn't mine.* I slowly start to sway back and forth until I hit the ground, fainting on site.

The ride to the hospital is a blur. We arrive quickly; and at this point I've come to, and I watch them running my dad toward the double doors, in which I may never see him again. Not allowing me through the doors, I pace nervously in the waiting room, hoping that someone comes out to tell me something. I glance back and forth at the double doors that keep opening and closing until, finally a nurse comes toward me.

"Grant?" She looks at me intensely. All I can see are her lips moving, but no sound comes out. I can't open my mouth to say anything in return, so I just nod. The lights in the room become so bright that I can't quite see what's happening, as I feel her push me toward a seat in the corner of the room. "I'm going to take you into the other room so we can check to make sure everything's alright." I don't answer but follow her to the examining room. We enter one of the rooms and she places me on the seat, when I hear the familiar sound of the wrinkled paper touching my bottom. *I hate hospitals.* I squint looking up at her name tag. Ann. Before I can say anything, her finger is moving from side to side, as she checks my vision.

"Do you feel any pain here?" I shake my head, no. She runs a few more tests, leaves me some hospital clothes to change into and then slowly walks toward the door. "The doctor will be in shortly." Before I can ask her about my parents, she's out the door and I'm left in a small 2-by-4 sized room. I can't stay here for any longer, so I slowly open the door, creeping outside towards the hallway and tiptoe away from the room. The hallway is surprisingly empty. I make my way back toward the double doors when I'm spotted by another nurse. *Shit, I've been made.*

"You seem lost, who are you looking for?" I tell her and she guides me to room 321.

I take in a deep breath, swallow any saliva that's left in my mouth, and slowly turn the door handle to the right as my handshakes. I hear the faint beeping noises and slowly walk in. The curtain makes it hard for me to see anything, but I keep hearing the beeps of the monitors on full volume. At the corner of my eye, I spot the tubes and the bags full of fluid. My hand still grasped firmly to the door handle; I pull it open just in time as I puke all over the floor. I feel a warm hand on my shoulder and look up as the nurse rubs my back and takes me back towards my checkup room. She hands me a bag of ice to place on my head. I'm so incredibly embarrassed, as not only did I puke in the hallway, but my ass is completely exposed from the ridiculous gown I'm wearing. Nurse Ann hands me a clipboard full of paperwork, which I need to go over. I take in a deep breath. All I really care about at this moment are my parents, but no one seems to be giving me a straight answer. She's telling me to look over all the paperwork just in case, but all I hear are mumbles, then I see her handing me a pen. She slowly walks away, and I have no time to react. Pacing back and forth I do the only thing that comes to mind, I pick up my cell phone and dial Vaughn's number. I start to rapidly tell him where I am and what happened, when I hear nothing on the other end but just a very loud bang and then silence. Very puzzled, I glance at my phone to see if I was the one who hung up on him. *Screw this, I can't deal with this BS.* I walk out of the examination room, and into the waiting area as I call my mom's sister (Beth), who I haven't seen or heard from in probably six years. Hoping it's the same number; I dial her up and wait. Finally, after what seems like ages, she answers.

"Hayden is that you?" she says, with a bit of a harsh tone to her question. "Why are you calling?" Love to know that she loves me back.

"We've been in a car accident, a bad one." I can barely hear myself think after saying the words out loud. I wait. Still waiting for an answer. "Did you hear me?"

"Who's we? Are you okay? What's happening?" I hear a piercing noise on the other end and quickly move the phone away from my ear. I touch my ear and shake it, because I just went deaf for about a few seconds. Slowly bringing the phone back toward my ear, all I hear is static. "Aunt Beth, can you hear me? Someone there?" I shake my phone, as if that's going to help. I hear nothing from the other end. "If you can hear me, we're at St. Patrick's Hospital." I hang up the phone, trying to figure out if I should call back again. Thirty minutes or so goes by as I'm sitting in the waiting room, trying to figure out what my next move is, when I see Vaughn in the corner walking toward me.

"Dude, what happened? You cool?" I'm silent for a good minute before I answer. "I'm cool yeah, it's my parents that aren't.

"How'd you know what hospital to go to?" Sometimes it baffles me how Vaughn just knows things.

"Easy dude, I'm a pretty good hacker and traced your call." Right. Forgot to mention that minor detail about him. The reasons why he's such a troublemaker; he's got a good bad boy look and he has a scary way of getting around computers. Comes in handy at times, but I never really asked how this all happened and frankly, I'd rather not know.

Vaughn doesn't ask me any more questions, but just sits in the waiting room with me. Roughly 30 minutes go by, and I see an older lady running through the entranceway, not caring who she pushes over. Aunt Beth, ladies and gentlemen, woman that I haven't seen in about six years. She spots me and without hesitation, grabs me and pulls me into a massive hug. Trying to breathe in between her squeezes, I get a word out, "Aunt Beth, you're crushing my frame." She lets go and takes a good look at me. Almost as if she's analyzing my every move.

"Well, you haven't really changed a bit. More pimples and your voice is deeper." My face turns a different shade of red. I open my mouth to say something corky or just anything in general when I get interrupted.

"Mrs. Beth, you might not remember me; it's been a while but I'm..."

"Vaughn Patrick, of course I know who you are." She smiles. "You look so handsome." Seriously! I shake my head, why would I ever get a nice compliment.

"When did he arrive?" I fathom an answer, but then realize I'm not sure if she's talking about Vaughn or my dad. "Hayden, are you listening to me?" I keep glancing back at Vaughn, then to her.

"Dude don't make things awkward. Answer her." Vaughn smiles and looks at Aunt Beth.

"He arrived midday yesterday, if you're talking about my dad." She takes a seat and folds her hands one on top of the other. Rocking back and forth, she's kind of making me nervous, so I sit down beside her.

"Why the hell would he come back after all this time?" Before I can get two words out, the doctor comes into the waiting room, clipboard and all and the look on his face says it all.

"Hayden Grant?" I stand up, but my Aunt Beth beats me to it and walks over to the doctor.

"I'm his Aunt Beth, what's happening?" The doctor starts to explain what's happening to my mom, but I zone out when I see a dark shadowed figure coming from the corridor. The lights start to flicker, and I feel a cold chill. I feel an even colder presence near me and then I jump. Shaken, I turn around to see Vaughn's hand on my shoulder.

"Dude, where did you go?" I look back toward the corridor that's fully lit. I rub my eyes to make sure that I'm not hallucinating. But naturally I am, because why would I see something so ridiculous.

"Sorry just spaced out. What's Dr. Mitchell saying?"

"Your mom has a serious concussion and her brains like swelling or something. Just listen, man." The doctor continues his verdict.

"She's unconscious but stable. We're going to monitor her and if necessary, induce a coma. It's not rare, but also not common. That might just give the brain a chance to heal."

Aunt Beth pulls the doctor aside, so naturally Vaughn and I can't hear the conversation. "A coma, there must be something else you can do."

"It's our best bet to saving her life." Dr. Mitchell says softly. "For now, all we can do is wait and see what happens." He excuses himself and leaves us alone to ponder. Before I go back to my seat, Dr. Mitchell looks at me curiously and turns back down the corridor.

Eleven p.m., the standard clock in the waiting room hits. I can tell that Vaughn's getting antsy. "I don't know how you do this, but is it cool if I take off?"

"I didn't expect you to stay much longer. So yeah, talk soon and thanks for coming." We exchange a bro hug, and he starts walking out the door, when Aunt Beth intervenes.

"Where are you going? You boys are going to stay with me tonight." Vaughn and I exchange looks. Why would Vaughn need to stay with her, he's got a home.

"Oh Mrs. Beth, if it's alright, I would like to see my family tonight. I'll be back in the morning." Aunt Beth looks at me, then back at Vaughn.

"I have a better idea. Hayden, you go with Vaughn and come back in the morning." Vaughn's eyes perk up, as if he's mortified about something.

"Oh yeah, umm, yeah, that should be cool." Vaughn gives me an awkward look. I'm not sure what's happening, but I don't say much. "Where will you be staying, Mrs. Beth?"

"Don't worry about me, I'm going to be making arrangements for Connor's funeral and taking care of your mom, like Connor should have years ago." I can't understand what exactly happened between my aunt and my dad, but I don't ask. I follow Vaughn out of the hospital in silence. He stops me in the middle of the street. I look up, as he sees my face.

"I can't believe that he's gone. I literally just got used to him being back, and now he's gone." I feel like I'm going to tear up, but then I see Vaughn's face and look puzzled.

"You can't come to my house." I look at him, not sure what my face looks like to him. "Okay?" I say.

"Vaughn, what's going on? You've been super weird over the phone lately. Is Jack back?"

"I said you can't come to my house. Let it go." I watch him walk away into the darkness. I have no idea what just happened, but the only thing I can do is walk back inside the hospital. The double doors open, the waiting room is now empty except one seat; taken up by my aunt, who is snoring away. I sit next to her and start to doze off. I wake up to look at the clock on the wall that now says 4a.m. Aunt Beth is awake with a magazine in her hand. We both look at each other, but before she can scold me, another doctor comes through the double doors.

"Hi, I'm Dr. Brown, I've just been in to see your mom."

Aunt Beth interrupts me again, "How is she?"

"Unfortunately, the swelling has gotten worse." He sees my worried face. "We're doing the best we can." Some time passes as Aunt Beth, and I can't really catch any sleep. Eleven a.m. rolls around, I'm so tired that I can't stand up any longer. I sit down to catch my breath when the doctor comes back into the waiting room. I look up and look back at Aunt Beth, who is fast asleep. The doctor comes up to me.

"Just wanted to inform you that her vitals are improving; would you like to see her?" Aunt Beth wakes up immediately and nods her head ready to see her sister. We follow him through the double doors and into the ICU. The doctor slowly opens her door, creaking a bit until I see my mom's face. Swollen, bruised, and wrapped in bandages. Fresh stitches across her forehead and cheek, brings tears to my eyes. I can't help it seeing her like this, her mouth covered by an oxygen mask while several machines are beeping at once. She honestly looks dead, she's so pale. *I think I'm going to be sick.* I run to the nearest restroom and throw up. I have never seen my mom or anyone for that matter this way before. I go back to the waiting room and take deep breaths. Few minutes later, Aunt Beth comes out giving me a hug and asking me if I'm alright. She looks at me, as she's picking up her purse and putting on her light coat.

"Let's go home and get you some proper food." I look at her, and then back down the corridor where they're keeping my mom.

"I'd like to stay here if that's possible. There are doctors and nurses on call all the time, so I won't be alone. Please, Aunt Beth." She looks at me and knows that there's no hope in convincing me to go with her.

"Alright, but I will be back in the morning and check in with me every hour." I nod and watch her leave the hospital. I go up to the counter and ask if there's any way I can stay in the same room as my mom. I quickly fall asleep but only to wake up what feels like minutes after to my mom's voice. I can see her oxygen mask on her chin.

"Hayden, is that you?" I smile and drag my chair next to hers. "What happened?"

"You don't remember?"

"No, where's your dad." I'm not sure what to do at this point. She can't remember things, so telling her that he's dead, would only make her condition worse. But I have to give her something.

"We were in a really bad car accident and things happened." A look of horror crosses my mom's face, as if she already knows what happened. She turns her head as I see tears falling down her face. She's about to tell me something when her eyes close and her heartbeat starts to race. The machine is going crazy, making loud noises. I see the call button near her bed and press it. A few nurses arrive rapidly checking her pulse. *Why did I even tell her anything? I knew this would happen.* I decide that it's best I leave the room and let them help her without me being a distraction.

Tiptoeing through the hallway, I end up looking for the scary sign that says, "Morgue." Stumbling upon the sign, I look at the double doors, but am hesitant to push them open. It's by far one the creepiest places anyone could step foot in, besides a cemetery. Something about walking around people's bodies is just weird. I decide that maybe it wouldn't be as terrifying if I call Vaughn and have him on the other line.

"Hey man, how you are holding up?" He says with genuine

concern.

"Could be better, you know." I whisper into the phone, hoping no doctor or nurse can hear me inside the morgue.

"Any reason you're whispering?"

"Yeah, well I'm kinda in the morgue at the moment. Don't want to be caught down here." There's a slight pause in our conversation, I'm thinking that he somehow hung up on me, yet again. I hear him breathe.

"Bad ass Hayden has arrived. Don't go anywhere, I'll be right there." Before I can respond, I hear a click. *Well, here I am in a scary hallway, which smells like death. Am I nervous? HELL YA! But as Vaughn said, "Bad Ass Hayden" is in the house.* The lights start to flicker, and the power suddenly goes out. Leaning up against the cold wall, I take in a few deep breaths, when the double doors down the hall swing open, like something out of a horror movie, right before the guy is going to kill you. It's so dark, that all I can see are the emergency lights flickering on and off. I close my eyes, take a deep breath, and feel my hands heat up. I open my eyes and realize that they're giving off light and heat. The heat in my hand rises to the point where it's excruciating. My vision starts to blur, I become dizzy and slowly hit the cold ground with a thump. In the distance, I see something, but everything fades and becomes dark.

"Hayden! Dude, can you hear me?" My eyes open slowly, I see Vaughn standing over my body. He's got a toothpick in his mouth and smacks my face, to make sure I'm fully aware that he's present.

"What happened?" I get up, slowly as everything is still fuzzy. I look down at my hands, seeing that they're back to normal. *Yup, I'm def going insane.* Vaughn smiles, chews on his toothpick, and helps me to my feet.

"You ready for this?" Vaughn's smiling as if he can't wait to do something illegal. I see him open the door to the morgue. I nod, as we both push the door open at the same time.

Looks like any other morgue, well at least ones you see in the movies or TV shows. Open doors everywhere, metal tables and things on the table lined up for the examination process. I get a bit queasy, but I have to suck it up so I don't look like a pussy in front of Vaughn. We both stare at each other, then split up to search for Connor's name tag. Vaughn walks over and drags his hands along the metal doors, where the dead are lying. He pauses and looks over at a name tag.

"Dude, come check this out. Bradley Frever. Does that name sound familiar to you?" I look at the name tag, try to think but can't seem to figure it out.

"Nope, not ringing any bells."

"I swear we had some corky dude in our class, with that same name." I've zoned him out, because in the metal container next to this Bradley dude is Connor Grant.

"Vaughn!" I yell. "He's here." We both look at the writing, to make sure that it's really his name.

"What are you waiting for, open the damn thing and let's take a look-see." I don't know how Vaughn does it has no fear whatsoever. We both grab the handle, opening it very carefully. We stare at each other. There he is, eyes closed, body white with scratches all over. I've noticed that since I grabbed the handle, I've been holding my breath. Vaughn sees me, pokes my shoulder, and I let out all the air in my lungs.

"Holy shit. Why...how-oh God, I think I'm going to hurl."

Vaughn says, as he's looking into my dad's open eyes.

"You and me both. Shut the door. SHUT IT." Vaughn is definitely going to puke. Right before we both close the door, I see something in the distance, something strange. I look at my dad's right hand, between his thumb and index finger.

"Vaughn, do you see that?" Vaughn, still holding his mouth, replies, "See what?" I touch my dad's hand, and as I do, the symbol disappears.

"Dude, what game are you playing at?" Vaughn shoves the door closed, almost taking my hand with it. I scratch my head, puzzled, because I've seen that same symbol before. The air gets super chilly, as I breathe out and see white coming out of my mouth. Vaughn looks at me, then sees his breath, white in color as well. I see something dark in the distance. My body starts to shake uncontrollably, I hit the cold ground hard and don't move. Vaughn looking down at my lifeless body, quickly shakes me and slaps me in the face. Jolting up, like I've been zapped with 1,000 volts, I see Vaughn's face, in terror.

"What the F is going on?" I shake my head, as I have no idea what just happened. "You started shaking and then, BAM you were on the ground out cold."

"Yeah, I'm fine. Nothing to worry about. Let's get the hell out of here." Vaughn looks at me, then down at my hand, where he saw something. We exit the morgue, checking to make sure that no one saw us. We tiptoe back up toward the main hallway, Vaughn stops me.

"Back there, before we left the room, your hands were well..." My eyes dart open. *Shit, did he see my hands glow?*

"My hands were what?"

"Nothing, I just thought I saw your hands give off light, but that's insane." I awkwardly smile and say nothing.

"It's the morgue, its giving you and me weird thoughts." He smirks and we start walking toward the lobby. I turn around, looking down the hallway, and suddenly see that same dark figure. My hand starts to itch, as I look down, engraved in between my thumb and index finger, is the same symbol as Connor had. Brushing it off, I head toward my mom's room. Vaughn says his goodbyes, looks over at me with a weird look, and disappears. I close my mom's door, pull up the chair in the corner and drift into a deep sleep.

The next morning is upon us, as the doctor comes in around 7a.m. "Your mom is doing pretty well, considering." I smile at him, thanking him for keeping a close eye on her. Aunt Beth arrives an hour later, with bagels and orange juice. Thankful for the morning pick-me-up, she asks me how I'm doing. I give her the basics.

"The funeral is arranged for tomorrow, I know it's short notice, but I called a few of your mom's friends. I just don't really know much about your dad's friends. Is there anyone you would like to attend?" I stare into the blank hallway, coming to, I nod and tell her I'd make some phone calls.

That afternoon, my mom slowly comes to, but in and out. It feels like a lifetime ago that we were in our kitchen having pizza and talking about warlocks. I'm startled as the side of my leg starts to buzz. Reaching into my jean pocket, my phone vibrates loudly. I answer it, not even looking at who's calling, thinking that it's only Vaughn.

"Hi Hayden, it's Waverly." It takes me a few minutes to comprehend who's on the other line. "I just heard about your mom and dad. Is there anything that I can do?" *How did she find out about my parents? Odd.*

"No, I'm okay for now. Thanks for calling."

"You're welcome. I'm only a phone call away, if you need to talk to someone, or I can come over." I've had so many fantasies about her, talking to her, hanging out with her. My heart skips a beat whenever I'm near her. I start to feel butterflies in the pit of my stomach and smile.

"Thank you for checking in on me. Means a lot." We say our goodbyes and I hear her hang up. I take in a deep breath and can't help but feel giddy despite it all. I walk into the hallway, with the grin on my face that I haven't had in a long time. In the distance, however, I see someone that looks exactly like Connor. I do a double take, squint my eyes to make sure I'm seeing straight, and look up again. An extremely thin, short man walks toward me.

"Hayden! I'd know that face anywhere. You look just like him." *Who the F is this guy, and I look just like whom?*

"Sorry, should I know you?"

"I would expect that response. I'm your dad's older brother." I look at him, as I now see the resemblance. "I'm your Uncle Lincoln." I just nod, because as of two seconds ago, I never knew he existed.

"Nice to know that I have an uncle at this point in my life. But sorry, I don't know you."

"You were too young to remember. I used to be at the house a lot, but your dad and I had somewhat of a falling out." I just listen and nod my head. He looks over into the room my mom is staying at. "How's she doing?"

"She seems to be on the mend." Short and sweet answers, Hayden.

"That's very good to hear." I interrupt him.

"I'm sorry, but I don't understand why you're here." Lincoln looks at me with a weird face.

"I'm here to pay respects for my brother."

"Right, I understand that. How did you even know what hospital we were at?" Before I can ask another question, he shushes me and walks toward my mom's room.

"A boy your age, shouldn't be left on his own. What are you...15 now?" I'm puzzled, has he been keeping tabs on me, when I don't know a single thing about him? "You should come stay with me."

"Ha, yeah no thank you. I don't know who you really are. Sorry, but not staying with some stranger who claims to be my uncle. I'm all set." I turn and walk away before he gets another word in. I sit down near my mom and watch as her chest moves up and down. Lincoln steps in.

"If you need anything, feel free to call me. Hayden, don't forget, just because you don't really know me, doesn't mean we're not family." He hands me his business card, like I was some client. He starts to leave.

"Funeral's tomorrow if you feel like being a part of this family in some way. Maybe that's a good way to pay your respects." I walk away before I can listen for his answer. My body shivers as I sit back down in the chair, something about Lincoln gives me the heebie-jeebies.

Tomorrow arrives, the day of the funeral. There are about 40 people showing up and giving their condolences. I, of course, don't recognize half the people, but I simply don't care. As the priest is doing his thing, to send my dad to a happier place, my aunt reaches for my hand, squeezing it. As she's squeezing my hand, I zone out and go back to the day of the accident. *What did you swerve from? How did we end up in the guardrail? What was the static noise I heard right before my dad was ejected from the seat? Was it laughter on the other end? Was it my powers that did all of this? What are my powers?* Aunt Beth lets go of my hand, and I come to the cemetery. Tiny pellets of rain start to fall on my forehead as I look up towards the sky. Aunt Beth pops open her umbrella as the fog is creeping toward my dad's resting place. She walks away handing me the umbrella. "I'll give you guys a moment," as she walks away with the rest of the crowd. I kneel on the ground, getting my suit pants wet and dirty. A fresh dirt pile stares in front of me. *Well, Connor, I guess this means goodbye for real this time. Just one question for you, why did you tell me that I have special powers that come at 16, and then leave me like that? Was this some sort of a test? Did I fail? Am I really a warlock, or was that a joke?* It's pouring now, as the sides of my umbrella drip, making my suit sleeves damp. I look back to see if anyone else is here, when I see Vaughn, who is leaning against the tree with no umbrella.

In the far distance is my uncle, we exchange nods as I make my way toward Vaughn. Still getting that weird vibe from the hospital, I take one more look at my uncle. Vaughn sees me looking and walks toward me. A massive gust of wind sweeps my umbrella and leaves me soaked, my gingerish hair, flat against my face. Nothing seems to be going right, but it's just water.

"Who would have thought we'd be at your dad's funeral." I look at him and laugh. "Trying to ease the tension." Vaughn says.

"I know. I shouldn't be laughing. I don't know where things are headed now. What's going to happen? My dad's dead after seeing him for like .3 seconds and my mom's currently in the hospital. What if I lose her, too?"

"Don't worry, man, she's going to be just fine. She's in great hands." He pats my back.

"Thanks. I'm just super worried about her." We stay there for a few minutes and head back toward Vaughn's car. "Is it cool if I crash at your place tonight?"

"Yeah, shouldn't be an issue." I look at him because last time I asked, he wanted me nowhere near his place. In the distance I hear my aunt and Vaughn's mom talking. They keep looking at the both of us, like we did something wrong.

Before we get into Vaughn's car, I see him again. Vaughn is about to ask me something but he gets interrupted.

"Hayden!" I roll my eyes.

"Thought you wouldn't show." We both look intensely at each other. "Glad you changed your mind."

"It was the right thing to do for him. I'm also sorry for what you're going through. It must be hard knowing what your dad has been through and then watching him leave you." I can't react in time, when he embraces me in a very awkward hug. "I'm going to stay a bit longer, to pay my respects as you would say." Vaughn looks at me, back at the mysterious guy, then back at me.

"Okay, who the hell is that? Creep."

"Believe it or not, that's my uncle. Never knew I had one until yesterday. Isn't that super great." Sarcasm noted.

"Interesting. Sounds super sketchy to me." I nod and agree with him. "Think about it for a second. Your dad comes back, right, then he…and that's when you first meet your so-called uncle. I bet you they weren't close at all. Dude I'd be wary of that shit."

"You definitely bring up a good point. Right now, I'll just give him the benefit of the doubt, since he apparently lost his only brother." There's a silent exchange as we make our way towards Vaughn's place. I know that there's something weird about my uncle showing up, but at this very moment, all I want to do is rest. We drive down the many streets back to my house, so I can pick up a few things, when Vaughn pulls the car over to the side.

"Why are you stopping?" I can see Vaughn's serious face now.

"How did you end up with no broken bones, or scratches on you? Just seems a bit odd."

"To be honest, I'm not quite sure. All I remember is my mom yelling and then we swerved and hit the guardrail. I passed out after." I pause. "Can we not talk about this right now?"

"Just was curious." He peers over at me, as we're both in silence the rest of the ride. I know he's not convinced.

"Can you just drop me off at home? I think I'd rather be alone tonight."

"Sure, whatever works for you." He glances at me. "You sure you're going to be good?"

"Yeah, all good." We pull up to my house. Empty and pitch black. I get out of his car, slam the door as I hear him roll down the window.

"You sure?"

"Yeah, I'll be fine. Thanks for the ride." He waves. "Wait, make sure your mom doesn't call my aunt asking about where I am." Vaughn nods, agrees, and speeds away. I make my way inside the house, up the stairs, and into my room about to pass out. I'm lying face down on my bed, breathing in the feathered pillow, when my phone buzzes. *This better not be Aunt Beth.* It keeps buzzing, as I really don't feel like answering this call. I decide to pick it up, knowing it's my aunt.

"Yes, hello?" I hear a girl's voice speak.

"Hi Hayden, it's Waverly again."

"Oh, hey, umm hi. Whad up?" *Whad up, really?*

"Was calling to apologize that I didn't make it to your dad's funeral." I'm puzzled and takes me a few minutes to respond.

"This is Waverly Coulter I'm talking to, right?"

"Yes, Hayden. It's me." The phone falls from my hands and slides under my bed. I fall out of bed, trying to reach it. Fumbling to reach it, I quickly say hi again. *Smooth moves.*

"Listen, I know you don't want to talk to anyone right now, but maybe it's better if you did." I breathe heavily. "I'm just making sure that you're alright, that's all."

"Thank you, that means a lot." My palms are sweating, I have those butterflies again in my stomach.

"I also wanted to say that when my parents passed away, I didn't know what to do and I know what you're going through." I had forgotten about her parents.

"Waverly, I didn't..." I hesitated. "I'm sorry."

"It's alright. I just thought you would want to talk about it with someone who knows what you're going through.

"Sorry to pry, but who are you living with?"

"My brother, he's been taking care of me since it happened. Just lately he hasn't been around."

"It's very nice that your brother takes care of you, but where has he been?" I realized that I was again prying and asking too many questions. "I'm sorry, that was a bit forward."

"That's okay. It helps to clear your head a bit. My brother has a weird job and a new girlfriend now." She started to laugh on the other end.

"What does he do?"

"Don't laugh, please." She says. I agree and let her continue. "My parents used to be software engineers, when they passed my brother took over. He's consumed in fixing things, it's a bit weird."

"Nah, sounds like a cool profession. Not many people can say that they fix cool things for a living. Does it bother you that he's never home?"

"Yes and no, I've been on my own for a bit now, that it doesn't seem to faze me when he doesn't come home. But thank you for being concerned."

"No prob. Waverly, can you do me a favor?" I take a big gulp of my saliva but end up mumbling what I said to her.

"Sorry, I didn't quite hear you." I take another gulp.

"It's been really nice chatting with you." We both say bye to each other, and I hear the click of the phone on her end. I'm very shocked to hear from her, of all people. The girl of my dreams, coming into play. I walk toward my bathroom, and with everything going on, it's the happiest I've been in a long time. I walk over to my bed, lie down looking up at the ceiling and crack a smile again. *The girl of my dreams, actually cares about me. She's not consumed with Josh.* My eyelids rest for what seems like hours, but I know that I can only sleep for a few hours at most. Around 12:30 a.m. I finally fall asleep, only to wake up again at 3:20 a.m. I look at my clock, which is by my bed, and for some reason I feel like something is going to happen. I have this gut feeling that something is after me because of what's been going on. Tossing and turning in my bed, I find a comfortable spot on my right side. My eyes are wide open, as I stare into the distance. My clock turns red when it hits 3:21 a.m. I hold my breath because my clock has never turned red, let alone any other color. *Hayden, time to wake up. I need to wake up.* The only thing I can do is get out of bed, grab the nearest blanket and wrap myself in a cocoon. I pace back and forth, from the window to my door. Stopping at my window, I glance outside and notice something strange in the distance – that same shadow I saw in the hospital. I rub my eyes to make sure that I'm not hallucinating. Looking back toward the street, the shadow is gone. *I must be seeing things, snap out of it.* I let out my breath, in which I didn't know I was holding, and make my way back to my bed. As I'm just about to head back, I turn around one last time and realize that my window is now slightly opened. Starting to close it, it seems stuck on something, so I pull with all my might – nothing happens. I give up, when all of a sudden, what seems like a massive gust of wind flies my window open and smacks me hard in the forehead, knocking me to the floor. Takes me a while to get up and before I close the window, I hear something in the house. I yell out, "Who's there?" and squint in the darkness, knowing that whatever that thing was in the street, was long gone by now. Scared, and holding on to my blanket tightly, as if it's going to protect me, I make my way back onto my bed. I curl up and try to get some sleep. Even though, this all might be in my head, I fall asleep and try not to think about anything. Oh, and I forgot to mention, Happy Birthday to me!

CHAPTER 3

The morning arrives, sun beams on my face as I struggle to open my eyes. Welcome to being 16, and to top it all off, I have the worst headache in the world. Rolling over, not wanting to get out of bed, I check the time as it flashes 9:45a.m. *Shit, I'm sooo late.* Monday morning and already I've missed my first class by two hours. *Why didn't Vaughn wake me up? Did I miss something over the weekend?* I quickly get dressed, grab my books, throw on my stupid uniform, and make my way downstairs. Grabbing probably what is the last stale bagel in the house, I reach over to get my mom's keys without thinking. As I start to head outside, the house phone rings. *Do I get that? Who has a house phone anymore...oh wait, my family does.* I stay back and answer the phone.

"Hello, Grant residence." Just trying to be professional since it's not my phone.

"Hello, is this Hayden?" A man says in a deep voice that I don't recognize.

"Yes, this is him." I wait for a response.

"Hayden, this is Principal Jacobs." Weird, why would he be calling me, "I heard about the tragic accident with your parents. I'd like to give my condolences. I've spoken to all your current teachers, and I think its best you take some time away." Wow, it's like a dream come true, but knowing I probably have to give that stupid presentation today...

"Thank you, Mr. Jacobs. However, I do have this presentation for Mr. Reynolds and I'm pretty sure he would fail me at any opportune moment."

"Correct, Mr. Reynolds did mention your presentation, but the fact is that he's got a stick up his ass." I laugh. "Excuse my language, that was very inappropriate of me. Once you come back to school, we will make the arrangements for you to present your work to him." I give him my thanks and hear the click of the phone. Well, wow, I mean can you imagine what would have happened if I didn't answer the phone. Maybe 16 isn't such a bad age after all.

***

Meanwhile back at school, Vaughn and Waverly are sitting in Mr. Reynolds' class. They hear a faint click as the loudspeaker chimes on.

"Could Mr. Patrick please report to the principal's office?" Everyone in the classroom oohs and ahhs. Vaughn looks confused.

"This is odd; I haven't done anything bad for a week now." He smirks, looking up at the box.

"Ohhh Vaughn, you're in trouble." Erik, a classmate of his calls out.

"Piss off, Erik, don't make me hurt you." Vaughn jumps toward Erik, who falls off his seat. Vaughn laughs out loud and shakes his head, like that was too easy. Walking through the double wooden doors, he approaches the principal's assistant. She directs him to the office. Vaughn knocks on the door, as the principal grunts at his appearance.

"Long time, Mr. Patrick." Vaughn doesn't smile.

"Call me Vaughn. Why people use professionalism is beyond me."

"Vaughn, thank you for coming by. Seems like your days of trouble are somewhat over, thank goodness for that. There's only so much my staff can clean up after you teepee'd the hallway." Vaughn smirks. "Will you gather Mr. Grant's belongings from his locker? I'm afraid he will not be coming back this semester." Vaughn gives him the confused look.

"Semester...why?" Principal Jacobs doesn't answer. "So, are you like, kicking him out?"

"I think as his close friend, you should go clean out his locker and not question me." Vaughn has the, "are you for real" look on his face. "I'm assuming all your nonsense pranks are over. I would hate to see your semester be finished as well. It's my responsibility to look after my students. Hayden is a gifted young boy, and after tragic losses, it's hard for students to return. So if you would please gather his things and exit my office that would be great." Vaughn doesn't have time to respond. He walks out the door.

"What a douche." He hits the locker and remembers that he forgot his backpack in the classroom. He slowly makes his way back and enters the room with a big thug, taking his seat. Waverly looks in his direction, and leans over, and whispers, "Are you alright? What did he want?"

He leans toward her desk, "He wants me to gather Hayden's belongings. Principal is a douche."

"Shit, you know who, is looking at us. Here, call me after class and we can figure something out." Vaughn looks at her and smiles. Mr. Reynolds calls on him.

"So, Mr. Patrick, you think that you can talk in my class just because you were called to the big man? It sure seems like you have more pressing matters with your classmates, so please enlighten me on what is so damn fascinating that you can't share with the class." Vaughn looks at him, with his devilish punk look.

"Well, Adam, may I call you Adam? I don't think that this person would like me to share their secrets to the class." Vaughn doesn't give a shit about what Mr. Reynolds says or does. Mr. Reynolds, not liking Vaughn's response one bit, ejects him from the classroom. Waverly, not being so careful, chimes in.

"Wow, he's trying to help a friend, who's gone through a lot, and this is what you do in return?" She quickly regrets what she says, covering her mouth.

"Waverly, this is disappointing. You can join him then if you choose to speak out in my class. Zero for the day." She looks at him, and while rolling her eyes, grabs her belongings, and walks out the door in disgust.

"Vaughn, wait up." Vaughn slows down and waits for her in the hallway.

"He's such a bastard. I actually thought he was getting nicer, but that's clearly not the case." She catches her breath. "Hey, so since we're both, you know, kicked out of class, would you like to possibly take a walk with me?" Waverly says without hesitation.

"No offense, but are you just being nice to me to get closer to Hayden?"

"That's not the reason why I'm being nice. Jeez, Vaughn, you haven't changed." He shrugs his shoulders and makes his way toward Hayden's locker.

"Well, this is probably the first time we've spoken since like 10th grade. You're one of those – how should I put it, 'popular kids'...or as I would say it, bratty girls. You are, after all, dating Josh, the loser, who happens to be the captain of the lacrosse team."

"That's a little harsh, don't you think?"

"You can take that however you'd like." Waverly rolls her eyes.

Vaughn bangs on Hayden's locker, trying to figure out the combination. "This damn combination is pissing me off." Waverly smirks. "What's so funny?"

"You are! Seriously you're the best well-known high school hacker, and you can't even open a locker combination." She laughs. "It's kinda cute." He smirks and ignores her comment.

"You know, Mr. Reynolds needs a taste of his own medicine. That guy is such a dick, I'm surprised he's still employed here," responds Vaughn while still fiddling with Hayden's locker. Waverly is suddenly silent as there's a tap on Vaughn's shoulder. "What, Waverly?"

"I'm a dick you say, well Vaughn, it's nice to know that my students think so highly of me. Just for that, you're no longer welcome in my classroom, and you just failed my course." Vaughn watches as Mr. Reynolds walks away.

"Well, there goes my streak, looks like I'll be getting expelled."

"He can't do that to anyone. Freedom of speech doesn't exist here apparently. Ugh, he's such an asshole." She smiles at him.

"Agreed, at least I've said my piece." She pats him on the back. "I guess you know me better than anyone." They both giggle.

"You could say that. Like old times."

"I underestimated you, Waverly." She gives him a half smile.

"Don't be so quick to judge." Finally getting the locker open, he reaches in and grabs Hayden's leather jacket and a couple of his books. He closes the locker and starts walking away toward the courtyard. "Vaughn, wait!"

"Should I be used to you yelling out my name now?"

"Ha ha, real funny. I was wondering if you could give me a lift home – you know, since we've both been kicked out of classes." She gives him her "I can't resist" smile.

"Sure, I guess. Same house?"

"Yup. Thanks." Vaughn leads the way to his car, a bit puzzled why she's asking for a ride. They both get in without saying a word for a good 20 minutes, as Vaughn drives down her street.

"I have to say, this is weird. I'm driving down the same street and dropping you off at the same house that we used to make out in." There was a long pause.

"Yeah, I know." She pauses, too. "That was a while back ago, things have changed. We should have never stopped being friends though."

"If I recall, that was not my choice. You made it clear you wanted nothing to do with me after."

"You don't know anything; it was tough times." She says, angrily.

"Right, and I bet you're still not going to explain it to me." She rolls her eyes. "Guess I wasn't what or whom you really wanted."

"We were 15 years old. You know nothing, just because you were my make-out buddy, doesn't mean anything."

"Well then, Waverly, say how you really feel. Cause I thought I was a damn good kisser."

"Don't do that. You act all tough and mighty, but deep down I know how you felt."

"So, you know everything there is about me? Right, finding out that not only are you making out with me because I'm the 'bad boy' of high school...but then I figure out that you had fallen for someone else. Sweet, brownie points for you."

"You know sometimes, you can be such an ass..."

"Sorry sweetheart for relaying the truth. Hurts, doesn't it?"

Waverly doesn't respond. Instead, she gets out of the car, slams the door, and steps out. But before leaving, she hunches down to talk to him through the open window.

"To think I actually had true feelings for you." Vaughn looks out toward her. "Goodbye, Vaughn." He doesn't respond and peels away without making sure that she's safely inside. Driving down the street, he pulls a quick left turn and stops in front of Hayden's house. He gets out of the car, slamming the door, with Hayden's belongings and walks toward the front door. He bangs multiple times.

***

"Hayden, answer the damn door. I know you're there." I open the door.

"What's up your ass?" I wait for Vaughn's response, but nothing's said. "Alrighty then, so did you want to go back to the hospital with me?"

"Sure. But here is your stuff from your locker. Had that lovely talk with our principal today." I thank him, drop the stuff on the floor and shut the door behind me. We both hop into his car in silence. Vaughn is clutching his steering wheel and I know something is wrong. Before I can ask him, what is really going on, he speaks up.

"I drove Waverly home this afternoon. Oh, and we both got kicked out of Mr. Reynolds classroom." I look at him and can't help but laugh.

"What did you do now?" I say. "Actually, never mind. So, you drove Waverly home, huh? How was she?" Vaughn looks at me.

"She's fine, stubborn as usual. Just super weird that she's talking to me again." I look toward him. "She wants to like –

reconnect with me and whatnot. It's freakin' weird."

"Well, I mean, maybe she's just trying to mend old wounds." Vaughn gives me the look, the look that says, "phew, Hayden doesn't know about us." Naturally, I had no idea at the time.

"Maybe, who knows?" Vaughn looks in the back seat. "Do me a favor, grab that box in the back for me." I look back and see this weirdly shaped box. It's heavy but I grab it and place it on my lap.

"What's this?" I examine it, not sure what to expect.

"Happy Birthday, Bro."

"You remembered. Thank you!" I'm shocked that of all people, he'd be the one to remember.

"Not every day you turn 16, dude. Well, open it." I smile at him and rip open the box. The box is completely empty except for a small box inside. "You better like it, I paid a shit-load for it." I grab the small box and slowly open it, afraid of what's inside. My eyes light up as I'm so shocked to be getting the one thing I've wanted since middle school.

"How did you get this? Or afford it, I should ask?"

"Don't worry about it. I know how much you dig it." I smile and give him the bro hug.

"I've been waiting to get my hands on this for ages." I hold up the burned corners of the perfect comic book.

"Nothing smells better than a first edition of the 1942 Adventures of Superman. Did you know it was the first edition published by Random House?" Vaughn laughs at me, as he knows how geeky I get when it comes to comics. "Wow, Vaughn, this is incredible. This piece is worth like $1,000. I don't know how you did it but..."

"Happy 16th birthday man. Cherish that because you're not

getting anything else for another five years." We both laugh and I place the comic book right back in its plastic case. We arrive at the hospital moments later. I've haven't felt this happy since, well I can't really remember when. But now that feeling has diminished as we both enter the main double doors of the hospital.

We head toward my mom's room. I knock ever so slightly and walk inside. She's fast asleep. Not wanting to disturb her, we both walk back out, and make our way to the shitty vending machine that says "fresh hot cocoa," right, 'cause that's so damn fresh. Just as we suspected, our cocoas were, in fact, shitty. We head back toward my mom's room. My usual chair is still placed in the corner of the room. Vaughn grabs another chair from the lobby and drags it into the room. My phone suddenly starts to vibrate. I quickly jump as I reach into my pocket. I look at the caller ID, my heart starts to flutter, and I show the phone to Vaughn.

"Interesting...get it, dude." He says. I take in a deep breath and push the answer button.

"Hey Waverly." I say, attempting to sound cool, but feeling a bit nervous again.

"Hi Hayden, how are you?" I look over at Vaughn. He rolls his eyes. "I heard you're not going to be at school this semester."

"News travels fast, I guess. Vaughn, I'm assuming, filled you in." I cover my hand over the speaker to get Vaughn's attention. He leans in and whispers to put the phone on speaker. We both step out into the hallway.

"Seems like you and Vaughn are on the same page. I saw him today." I make eye contact with Vaughn. He yawns and rolls his eyes.

"Yeah, I heard." Vaughn takes the phone from my hands.

"Dude, what are you doing?"

"Relax," I muted her. She can't hear us. "Listen, don't mention me and her shit. I don't want her being all nosey and whatnot." Not sure why he's being like this, but I play along.

"So, what's up?" I ask her, after Vaughn hands be the phone.

"Just wanted to check in, see how you're doing." I'm about to answer when she says something again. "Listen, I know things have been distant with you and me, Vaughn as well. The past always creeps up to the present and I don't want things to be weird after Vaughn and I." I look at Vaughn, he looks at me. He grabs the phone out of my hand and clicks the off button.

"What the…what was that for? What the hell was she talking about, weird things after you and her."

"Listen man, it was a long time ago and I didn't even know you, like, dug her. So, I mean cut me some slack." I look at him and still can't grasp what he's talking about. "God, we used to hook up and shit. Happy."

"Why wouldn't you just tell me that?"

"I don't know dude, 'cause you like love her or something and knowing that I kinda tapped that."

"First off, gross, and second of all, I'm your best friend, why wouldn't you tell me?"

"I don't know, just it's the past and today she just opened the can of worms and honestly I don't want to deal with that shit. Why don't you ask her why she's calling you and not spending time with her loser boyfriend, Josh." Vaughn brings up a good point.

"We can talk about this later. I'm not letting this get to me on my damn birthday."

***

Vaughn walks to the other end of the hallway to give Hayden some space and to grab more cocoas. He looks down the hallway, takes out his cell phone and, dials a random number.

"Scorpion, it's Beta. Do me a favor, can you do some research on a symbol for me." The person on the other line breathes in. "Triangle, dotted line in the middle, and a heavy bolded outline." Pause in conversation. "That's it, find out and get back to me." He hangs up the phone, looks around the hallway, and makes his way back inside.

CHAPER 4

The sunlight from the blinds peeks its way inside, waking me up from what was a semi- perfect dream. I realize once my eyes flutter open, that I'm back in the grey hospital in an uncomfortable rocking chair and officially 16 years old. I slowly start to get up, when I see Vaughn on the other side sleeping in another uncomfortable chair. I sit by my mom, whose eyes flutter open. She smiles at me.

"Hey Mom, I've been so worried about you."

"Hayden, you look like you haven't slept in weeks. I'm so happy to see you." I try not to tear up, but a single tear falls from my eye.

"Do you remember anything?" She looks at me, and then sees Vaughn on the other side, passed out. She gestures for me to come in closer. I lean in.

"Always remember, whatever happens, this was all for you. We both love you and want you to know the truth. You are a gift, and everything we've done is to protect you. If I happen to go to another place, promise me that you will be careful and use your gifts to help others." I pull back and look at her with confusion.

"I don't understand. I get that you both think I'm a warlock. But what are the gifts?" She just looks at me, smiles, and slowly closes her eyes. "Mom!"

"Trust your instincts, Hayden. You are more powerful than you know." Her eyes close. Vaughn wakes up and looks toward me.

"Dude, you, okay?"

"Yeah, you know me." I look back toward my mom, still trying to piece together what she just said. Vaughn gets up, struggling from the uncomfortable folding chair and walks toward me. I smile and look back to him. "I'm going to head home and try to get some sleep."

"Let me at least give you a ride." We both hop into Vaughn's car, and don't say a word the entire ride back. We pull up to my shabby house, quickly glancing at one another. Vaughn doesn't pull away and just sits in his car. I open the front door and close it slowly behind me. I get that something happened between him and Waverly, but I'm more distraught that he wouldn't just come out and really say it. I walk towards my house. Vaughn, in the meantime, takes in a deep breath as his phone vibrates in his pocket. He hears a faint breath on the other end.

"Beta, you need to be careful. He's not what you think he is. Trust your gut and make sure you are protected. Don't be hunted."

"Hey, what about that symbol?" There's nothing on the other end and click. "Ass."

Meanwhile, I walk into the silent house and go straight to my room. It seems like I haven't been home in months. Again, just to reassure you that I'm technically not allowed to be alone in a house without a parent or guardian. Honestly though, who has time for that shit. I head straight to my room and start to realize just how tired I am. Closing the door and throwing my stuff on the bed, I take off my pants as my black and white polka-dot boxers are visible. *Don't laugh; I don't have to be creative when I'm picking out boxers.* I immediately crash on the bed face first, without taking off my white shirt. I drift into a deep sleep. They say when you haven't slept in a long time that you start to have vivid dreams, or your imagination seems to wander. I'm not sure how true that is, but in my case, all I can think about is the good ole times. So naturally I start to dream about the younger times.

Vaughn and I used to play in the front yard all the time. I think it was some sort of tradition with us dudes, but then again, we were younger and stupider. *"Stay out of the street, kids!"* -My dad calls out from the porch. *"Stay right where I can see you."* Vaughn giggles, and answers dutifully, *"We will, Mr. Grant!"* A few minutes later my mom calls, *"Who wants chocolate chip cookies?"*- Vaughn, who always got teased for his voracious appetite, shouts, *"Me!"* I giggle, running toward the front door, pushing Vaughn aside to get to the cookies first. Before we both make it to the door, a beautiful girl comes riding down the street on her bike, dressed in a pink and yellow dress. She stops in front of the house, smiles, and gets off her bike. She makes her way toward the picket fence and waves. Vaughn runs over to her, *"Hello there beautiful, the names Vaughn."* Hold on, I quickly have to say that it didn't matter what age Vaughn was at the time, he always had a suave way about him. I slowly walk toward the beautiful girl; I hear her whisper her name. I get closer trying not to be shy, but I'm, of course, too late. She hops on her bike, looks back, and winks at me. I watch as her curly hair bounces off her back and she disappears around the corner. *"Wow, what a gal, huh, Hay? I mean I know were only eight but..."* I can't answer him. Vaughn grabs my arm, *"Race you to the cookies."* He runs past me, *"What was her name, Vaughn?"* He looks at me and smiles, *"Waverly."*

I open my eyes and slightly smile, as this was the first good dream I've had in a long time. Sitting up and glancing around my room, I realize that I'm home alone. I grab my phone that's on top of the drawer and call Vaughn. It goes straight to voicemail, meaning he turned it off, which he never does. With everything that's happened since I've turned 16, it got me thinking, I probably shouldn't be alone in my house. But alas, I actually like the quiet and not having to deal with adults. I start to pace back and forth in my room, when I hear a faint creak from the floorboard that I just walked over. Curious, I walk over it again. I think to myself, *I never heard this before.* I try to pry the wooden floorboard open, completely struggling. Out of pure anger, I kick in the wooden panel making a decent-sized hole in the floor. Reaching inside, I pull the board up and find what looks like an old chrome box. Slowly lifting the box from under the panel, I lay it on the floor just staring at it, not knowing what to do next. On the sides of the box are multiple symbols that I've never seen before. Turning the box over, I try to imagine what this box contains, or in fact if it's even something that I should have found. It was hidden under the floorboards for a reason. I look closely and see that there's a tiny slot, just enough for a key to be placed. This is not something out of a graphic novel, like *Locke & Key.* The keys aren't haunted or anything. But knowing that I don't have anything to open the box with, I try anyway but nothing, not even a budge. Starting to feel angry now, I throw it on my bed and begin pacing up and down trying to come up with a plan. I just stare at it; like that will do anything really. Finally, after what seems like hours of staring, I lie down on my bed as my eyes flutter to a close, thinking about the box and its contents.

Around 3:20 a.m. my clock starts to buzz. Hearing the piercing sounds, I turn over and wake up to something in my room that's emulating a bright red light. Rubbing my eyes, making sure that I'm not just seeing things, I look over to find that the box is glowing. Puzzled at what to do next, I get out of bed and return to the glowing box. Picking it up, I'm jolted with a sharp electric pain, followed by a severely loud, piercing bang. Letting the box drop to the floor, the bang gets louder and before I can reach to cover my ears, the box gives out a pulse, setting the room into a vibration field. The pulse sends my body across the room, hitting my door with a big BANG. The box is still glowing red, blood drips from the side of my face, and I notice the symbol on my finger is also glowing. Did that just really happen, or am I still dreaming? *Wake up, Hayden. WAKE UP.* I slowly come to the realization that I'm actually fully awake and this box is still glowing red, while throwing me across the room. Crawling toward the box, because why wouldn't I...I faintly hear a noise coming from downstairs. Looking at the box once more, the red glow starts to fade. Again, I hear the same noise coming from downstairs and without hesitation, I grab the glowing box and open my bedroom door. Gently I open the door. "Who's there?" Of course, no one responds. I'm freaking myself out with all this nonsense. I promise, I don't really watch that many horror movies. But this is right out of a Stephen King kind of novel. Oh, and I'm not sure if I believe this as well, but sometimes people think their houses are haunted. I can't really figure that part out yet. A few seconds pass and I come to the crazy realization that I'm just seeing things because I haven't slept. I amble toward my bed, taking the box with me. The minute my hand touches the side of the box, where the symbol is, it pulses again, throwing me across the room. I don't move and am left sprawled on the floor.

I wake up on the floor, holding the box in my hand, which is now open. *Damn this box, I just had to go and find something like this.* I jump, startled as the box flies out of my hands, and before it hits the ground, my hand flies up, stopping the box in mid-flight. It's now floating over my bed. I take in a deep breath and realize, holy shit, I'm actually doing this. I also take in another deep breath and realize that maybe my dad was right all along; I am some kind of warlock or something out of this world. Slowly moving my hands down toward the bed, the box moves with it and settles on top of my bed. My hands now relax, and the box gives off yet another pulse. My body suddenly flies, hitting the bureau. I clearly underestimated my capability for my so-called powers. *What the hell is this box and why is this all happening? Is it connected to me or my family? Also, why are you throwing me around? It hurts!* Moments later, the entire house is silent, like someone pressed the mute button. I can't even describe it to you. I rub the outside of my thumb, as it's starting to hurt a little. I still have that weird symbol, but don't really think about what it means or how it got there. The moment I rub the symbol, a white sort of cloud appears in the corner of my room. I swear I feel like I should be in another universe for all this weird shit to be happening. Not knowing really where this so-called cloud came from, I walk toward it. *Yeah, Hayden, great idea, walk toward a random cloud in the middle of your room. Smart points go to NO ONE.* I slowly reach out to this cloud, making sure that my mind isn't playing tricks on me. It's real alright. Giving off a cold sense, I decide to walk through it. *Seriously, why the hell would I do this? Thoughts, anyone?* So here I am walking through this so-called cloud in the middle of my room, in which I clearly created with my powers. It honestly feels like someone should slap me in the face because I see all these horror movies and yell at the TV when some idiot is about to walk or go where they're not supposed to. That is how a viewer is watching me now. "No, you idiot, why are you doing that, when you know something evil is on the other end."

So here it goes.

I walk through this cloud, or whatever it is, in the middle of my room. It's so cold that all of a sudden, my body shakes and a loud noise pulse through my brain. I'm zapped and the white cloud becomes grey, and I'm now taken to what looks like another time. I walk out of the cloud, look around, and everything seems to be the same.

In what seems like a few seconds, I realize that I'm back in my room, but it all looks and feels very different. What exactly, I'm not quite sure. My posters on the wall are gone; my bed is no longer there. In fact, the entire room has been turned into an art studio. I'm so confused, and in the corner of the room the cloud is still there but seems to be fading fast. I walk out of the room and make my way downstairs. I hear commotion coming from the kitchen, I tip-toe to make sure no one hears me. My mom is in the kitchen singing to herself with her headphones plugged in. In the corner is Vaughn reading a book and smiling at my mom. *What the hell is going on?* I walk into the kitchen and say just that. "Umm, what the hell is going on here?" I look at them both in the eye, but they don't move. I wave my arms, making sure that they actually can see and hear me.

"Hello, can you hear me?" I go up to my mom. "Mom??" Nothing, it's like I don't even exist. Vaughn looks over in my direction and it seems like he can see me.

"Oh, thank goodness, do you mind telling me what the actual f is going on?" I wait, and he doesn't even acknowledge that I'm there. Something weird is happening. Vaughn starts to talk.

"Mrs. Grant, do you think maybe we can try and get out of the house today?" He looks at her with a sense of sadness.

"I don't think it's safe, and I'm not ready to go back out there. Things are even more dangerous now more than ever."

"We have to try and do something. We can't just sit here and watch this place crumble. I made a promise and I have to follow through. It can't end this way."

"Look at it out there, Vaughn. It's dark, it's dense, and more so, it's scary.

"So, what, you are just going to sit in your kitchen and pretend that nothing happened? That Hayden didn't..." My mom interrupts Vaughn.

"Don't you dare speak his name. Just don't." She slams the cabinet and walks out of the kitchen. Vaughn looks over at her and walks over to the kitchen table and pours himself another cup of coffee.

"Cheers to another useless attempt in saving this place." I'm about to approach him, when the cloud takes me in and sucks me into another spot entirely.

A few minutes later, I arrive at what looks like Waverly's front door. The cloud still following me, fades a little in the distance. Waverly comes running out of the front door. She's clearly on the phone, talking to someone. I can hear the entire conversation. I'm not sure how this is all happening.

"Vaughn, calm down. There has to be a way to save him. You of all people would never give up." She says over the phone. I hear him answer her.

"We've tried everything! You couldn't break it; I couldn't break it and now look what has become of this place. The sun never comes out, it's always gloomy and there's that gaping black hole in the middle of the freakin' universe." He starts to breathe heavily on the other end. *WAIT, what is going on? Who are they talking about? Why can't she see me either?*

"Come over, Vaughn, we can talk about this in person. I don't feel safe over the phone anymore." She hangs up and takes in a deep breath. "Why are you doing this?" The scene fades out and the cloud takes me to yet another location. This time, the middle of Red Hill Forest. Red Hill Forest is and will always be the one spot that I went to with my dad. Our sacred space, if you can say that. The cloud dumps me into the middle of the forest, which is now no longer a forest. It looks like someone dropped a bomb in the middle of it and never reported it. The cloud fades away again, and in the distance is both Vaughn and Waverly. They are taking samples of the black goo that is the forest now. I walk toward them, seeing what exactly they are up to.

"Would you have ever thought this would be our lives now?" Waverly looks over at Vaughn. A tear falls from her face. "Things were never supposed to be like this."

"We could have never predicted this. We had no clue. If you would have told me that in three years, our town would be this..." She falls to the ground and Vaughn rushes to her. "I don't get it either, but we have to try. We just have to!" He hugs her tight and kisses her on the lips.

"I love you." She says to him.

"I love you, too. We will get through this." I'm so confused. But before I can even figure out what's happening the same damn cloud picks me up and drops me back to another location.

"Okay, whatever you are, you really have to stop this. It isn't funny anymore." The cloud spits me out back inside my house. My mom is in the basement.

"Alright, Mom, I'm going to ask you one more time. What the hell is happening here, and I need answers." Clearly thinking that she would answer me again, she starts to cry. She's throwing away boxes of things that have my name on it. She starts to cry even more so when a mysterious man comes out from the other room. I have no idea who he is, but he looks familiar. He approaches my mom and hugs her.

"Don't do this to yourself. We didn't see the signs and we couldn't help in the end." He says.

"This is all my fault." My mom responds. "Things wouldn't be this bad if we just showed him."

"No one saw the signs, so please stop blaming yourself. We are all to blame."

"Easy for you to say, Kyne." She says and then I piece together who he is. Waverly's older brother. I can't seem to get any answers from what is going on, when the same cloud comes but this time splitting everyone in one room.

"Vaughn, you had to have known the signs." Kyne says. Vaughn looks over at Waverly, then back at Kyne.

"I did see them, early on. But I didn't know what was happening and how I could have predicted any of this. You think I would have known this would have happened. I was a little preoccupied with my family and well me. It was three years ago. Don't you remember?"

"Of course, I remember. We all remember and can never forget. Mrs. Grant, are you going to be alright?" Kyne says.

"I will pull through and go outside to face whatever has yet to come." She answers.

"Waverly, will you do whatever it takes?" Vaughn asks her.

"Yes, I promise to do whatever it takes." Vaughn looks over at Kyne.

"It's you and me, against..." He takes in a deep breath. "You ready?" Kyne says.

"Never ready, dude, never." The conversation goes mute as the room gets dark and it's just me and this cloud in my basement. I'm sitting on the basement steps, trying to piece together everything. I see something come in from the other end of the room. Face blacked out; it starts to talk.

"Well, look at you defying the laws of magic. You think this gives you a free pass into the future?" I look behind me to see if this figure is talking to someone else.

"Wait, can you see me?" I look toward this figure, but still can't see his face.

"Who else would I be talking to? You are the one with magic, are you not?" He creeps in closer. "You realize that this is all your doing. You can't just do whatever you want because you have powers."

"What! I don't understand, what am I doing? Where am I? Who are you?" He starts to laugh. "Stop it. I said stop it!" I get so angry that the house starts to shake, like an earthquake.

"Welcome to the year 2023. The year that our universe as we know it, crumbles. Don't say I didn't warn you." He disappears.

"Wait, you can't just leave like that." I scratch my head. "2023, how is that even possible. Its only 2019." I walk away from the cloud and head toward the kitchen. I start to look around and realize that not only is everything out of place and different, things look more modernized. I glance over at my mom's workspace and notice that the year is 2023. But where am I? Why does everyone seem like they're gearing up for the next apocalypse?

I see the same cloud again, but this time it's turning black. I try to walk away from it, but it sucks me up yet again to one more final destination. I hear sounds from the distance.

"We honor those who have braved their way into this world. You went up against true evil to conquer the unthinkable. Here is the time we say thank you and never have to say our goodbyes for the ones we lost. So please instead, let's raise a glass to remember just how precious life can be." The man and a few others, drink to remember, but who exactly passed away? In the distance I see, Waverly, Vaughn, Kyne, and a few other names on headstones right next to my dad's. Before I can even comprehend, I'm taken back to the basement with the mysterious man's voice.

"Change the past, to change the future. Only you can do it." He fades away in the distance. The cloud takes me in one last time and drops me hard back into my room. I look around to make sure that I'm actually back in my room. I pinch myself, just to make sure that this wasn't all a dream. Things seem to be back to normal. The box is now closed and sealed, my hands are another shade of white and I'm drenched in my own sweat. I hear my cell phone vibrate. I pick it up.

"Dude, is everything alright? I've been trying to reach for you days now."

"Days, what are you talking about?" I put the phone aside and walk to my window. It's still dark outside. "What exactly do you mean by days?"

"Just that, Waverly and I have been calling you for the past two days. You didn't answer so we thought you went to the hospital. Went there, and no sign of you. Waverly and I decided to go to your house. The door was locked shut and no way in. Not even to your secret entrance. So, tell me, where the hell have you been?"

"I've been in the house the entire time, but something happened to me. You wouldn't believe me if I told you anyway. I think there's something wrong with me, Vaughn. I need help."

"I'll be right over." I hear a faint click, as I hold my phone to my ear. Something is very off and I'm not even sure how to describe it. I quickly head to the bathroom, splash cold water on my face and make my way downstairs. Things look the same as they did before. Calendar reads 2019, at least that's what I'm seeing. I sit down at the kitchen table, and don't seem to move an inch. I just look around wondering if somehow, I'm still in the other place. I hear the doorbell.

"Come in." Vaughn starts to laugh. "Oh right, it's locked." Opening the door, Vaughn and Waverly greet me with a hug.

"You look like shit." I nod to thank him. "So, fill me in, what is going on with you?"

"Hayden, you seem like you've seen a ghost or something." Waverly says.

"Honestly, it's nothing, I think I just was really tired and overslept these past few days. Really, everything is just fine. Do you guys want a cup of coffee? I just need to make a quick phone call." Before they can answer me, I run to my room and they don't seem to follow. I close the door to my room and try not to hyperventilate. I grab my lighter and start to set a piece of paper from my desk on fire. I breathe it in and it seems to calm me down again. It's like my gateway drug. In the corner of my eye, I spot my uncle's business card. Not quite thinking straight, I dial his number. The phone rings twice, then someone picks up on the other line.

"This better be an important call, because I don't want to listen to you for more than two minutes."

"Okay, well I will try to not piss you off in the next two minutes. By the way, it's your so-called nephew, Hayden." I take a deep breath, not knowing what to expect.

"Oh, I'm sorry, nice to hear your voice. I thought you were someone else. How are you holding up?"

"I'm sorry to bother you. I'm alright. Just was curious how close you were to my mom and dad. They just never mentioned you before."

"Things are going to be harder, and your mom definitely knows me, we just never really saw eye to eye. You can blame your dad for that one. Is there something I can help you with, though?" I'm about to tell him about the so-called cloud that I apparently "portaled" through, but I don't want to sound crazier than usual.

"Oh no, not really. I just came across your business card and decided to call you. Say, what do you do anyway?" Small talk, when I know that I called him for a reason. Mostly to not be downstairs and be asked a million questions about where I've been.

"I work, of course. There's nothing you need to know. If you ever need anything, just contact this number and please say your name before saying hello. Okay, kiddo?"

"Oh yes, my apologies." *What a douchebag.* "I'll make sure to mention my name, if I happen to call again."

"Perfect. I wanted to come by the house sometime this week to talk to you, if that's cool? I'm sure Aunt Beth is taking good care of you. I also want to visit your mom in the hospital but not sure what her room number is. Can I come by Monday night?" I haven't told anyone that I'm currently living alone, since at my age it's kind of illegal. No one's really asked anyway.

"Oh...umm...yeah sure, Monday night works." I hear a click on the other end. *He freakin' hung up on me. Seriously!*

I go downstairs, trying to shake off the stupid phone call I just had. Waverly and Vaughn are still sitting at the kitchen table. At least they helped themselves to some coffee. I open the fridge to find it bare, as it should be. *Right, I don't food shop...wish my mom was here.* I slam it shut, frustrated, and walk away as my stomach growls at me. Maybe some fresh air will help with my terrible headache and my rumbling stomach.

"So, are you just going to pretend that we don't exist?" Vaughn yells at me.

"I'm sorry, there's a lot going on in my head right now that I can't even explain." Waverly grabs my arm and pulls me in.

"We can't help you, Hayden, if you won't let us in." She does have a point. "Let's talk outside; maybe some fresh air will help. Right, Vaughn?"

"Yeah, sure, whatever works." We all make our way outside.

It's a mild drizzly evening but a great way to clear my head. I open the front door and walk outside, not grabbing an umbrella, because it's only drizzling. But naturally the minute I step outside, it starts to down pour. We all run toward the side of the house, where there's a covered section that my dad was working on for a while. I stand there looking at them, waiting for the five million questions.

"So, what is going on?" Waverly says, in her sweet and innocent voice.

"Honestly, you both wouldn't understand. There are things about me that is just nuts." I say, thinking about how now I'm officially crazy and thinking that maybe I am a warlock. I could see from Vaughn's expression that he wasn't too pleased with me.

"Either you tell us what the hell is going on with you, or we walk." Waverly gives the, "seriously" look to Vaughn. "I'm not taking things lightly anymore. Clearly there is something going on. If you can't confide in your friends, then we can't help you."

"Fine, yes, you do have a point. But if I tell you what's been happening to me, do you promise not to laugh or look at me different?"

"Why would we look at you differently, Hayden? That's not something that friends do." Waverly says, then looking toward Vaughn. "Isn't that right, Vaughn?"

"Yeah, yeah, friends don't do that. So what's it going to be?"

"So, first off I have to show you something." Before I can even start to show them my so-called powers, Vaughn's phone rings. He reaches into his pocket, gives it a look and rolls his eyes.

"Shit, I have to take this. Hold that thought." I shake my head, because if he thinks that I'm the one being weird, then I can't explain his behavior. He walks away from us.

"Hayden, is it something between you and Vaughn?" She looks concerned. "I feel like you've been distant with one another." I start to laugh, and I really don't mean to. She's dead silent.

"Oh, well, I mean things have been a little tense between us. It's been tough with my mom and dad, and then he's been all over the place with his phone calls. Not to mention, the times that I call him, and it goes right to voicemail. I honestly have no idea what's going on with him. He tells me that he wants me to be honest and to fill him in on what's happening with me, when I don't even know what's going on in his life. May I ask you why you are all of a sudden back in our lives?" I take in a deep breath, wow, I've been holding that in for a while.

"What do you mean that he's been all over the place? This is the first time I've seen him on the phone, and we were just together." She looks at me as if she wasn't supposed to say that. "What I mean is, I haven't really noticed him on the phone. He's always worried about you and asks me how you are doing."

"You didn't answer my question, Waverly. Why are you all of a sudden interested in being in my life?"

"I know that we haven't been close in a while, and that is partly my fault. I've had a lot of other things going on in my life. The moment I saw you again this year, it just made me wonder if things would have been different between us. I don't really know what I'm trying to say. I just know that I care about you, and I want you to feel safe and comfortable around us." I honestly have no clue what to say to that. Is she just saying all this to shut me up? Does she have a secret that she doesn't want to share with me? Girls, man, why are they so confusing?

"Fine, if that's how you want to answer, then sounds good." Before she can respond, Vaughn comes strolling back. And by the looks of it, it doesn't seem like he will be sticking around.

"Yo, so I have to go, but this isn't over. I want to know what is going on." I shake my head.

"Well, it works both ways. Seems like you have a secret agenda that you don't want us to know about! Anyway, nice chat. I will see you guys later." Without looking at them, I go back inside and lock the door, pissed off. Vaughn and Waverly look at each other. She walks over to him.

***

"Okay, what the hell, Vaughn?"

"What? I have a life, too, you know." Smirking.

"You don't have to be a dick about it. We've been trying to open up to him so he can tell us what's going on, and you do this."

"What the hell did I do? Oh sorry, did I by accident answer my phone and not do what I was supposed to do?"

"Who were you talking to?" She asks.

"Does it matter? Also, it's none of your business. Why don't you go home and make out with your boyfriend, Josh. You seem to LOVE spending time with him." Vaughn is now just pissed off in general.

"What's your problem? I get that we have a history, but wow, just wow. You know what, I don't have to put up with this. If you don't want to be a friend, then just don't even bother being in my life."

"Do you not get it, Waverly? You and I are something special. The way things have been going, it feels like the only thing that's stopping us is HIM." He comes really close to Waverly. "Tell me that you don't feel something? Tell me that if I put my hand on your cheek, that you won't push it away." Vaughn does just that, he takes his hand, placing it on her cheek and he's right, she doesn't push him away.

"What am I supposed to do? Push you away and forget the weird times we had together. I don't know what I want. I know that right now, I can't do this. We need to focus on Hayden. He seems to be going through a lot and the fact that we are doing this, it's not right."

"It's right, just not right now. So, when you are ready to actually share your true feelings, I'll be doing my own thing. Answering any phone call I want, and frankly being more of a friend to Hayden than you have ever been." He leans in, kisses her on the cheek, and walks toward his car. Without hesitation, he turns on the engine, puts it in drive, and peels out of the driveway.

"DAMNIT!" Waverly stomps her feet, and starts walking back toward her house, when she realizes that she left her bag inside. She turns back and knocks on Hayden's door.

***

"Hayden, I know you don't want anything to do with me right now. I just left my bag inside, may I just come in and get it." There's a long pause. I open the door.

"I can get it for you." She looks at me up and down; I didn't realize that I had taken off my shirt.

"Oh, umm, I can just...it's okay, I can wait." She takes a deep breath. I start to laugh and invite her in.

"Only for your bag, I don't want you to ask me anything." Well, obviously that didn't go over too well, as she's staring at me intently. She immediately asks me something.

"May I ask you for a favor?" She says, as I take in a deep breath not knowing what she's about to ask me. "Is it possible for me to see your tattoo, I'm just curious."

"Oh, my tattoo, sure." I'm surprised she even noticed it.

"I'm sorry, is that weird?" She crinkles her forehead. "It's just in a spot where I wouldn't normally notice." I nod and tell her that everything is alright, and it isn't weird.

"What does it mean?"

"It means hope. I got it freshman year of high school, even though technically I'm not allowed to. Vaughn and I lied about our age." A warm, tingly feeling passes through my body, as she keeps touching the mark. I close my eyes, when I feel her hand move closer to the side of my body, near my ribs.

"What does the other one mean?" I turn quickly and stare at her.

"Huh, what other one?" She doesn't know how to respond. "It looks like some kind of weird writing on your rib line, but I can't quite make out what it says."

"I don't have a second tattoo, Waverly. Stop kidding around." She doesn't say a word as I make my way toward the mirror. I turn to the side, and right there in plain sight is the other tattoo. Touching it, I flinch as it turns red and the pain becomes excruciating, almost like the tattoo is being inked this very second. I cringe. I grab my shirt, putting it on slowly just in case my newest tattoo decides to have a mind of its own. I sit back down, pondering. "Sorry, this must feel all weird for you." She looks into my eyes. "There's been a lot going on lately that I haven't really been able to talk about with...well, anyone." She puts her hand on my shoulder, but quickly retracts.

"How about I let you be, and you can figure things out. I'm not that far away and if you need me for anything, please don't hesitate to call me." Waverly adds. She looks back at me one last time, and walks out the front door. Okay, yes that was a little awkward, but thank goodness she spotted that.

New tattoo. I wonder what that's all about? Warlock shit? Dad's new way of telling me something from the grave? I guess it's safe to say that I'm a warlock now, but to what end? Should I really be telling anyone? Honestly, I don't even know where to begin. My thoughts turn blank. I decide to call it a night.

The next morning approaches, and without knowing why, I dial Waverly. I take a deep breath.

"Good morning, umm, I can't explain this." I grin. She's silent on the other end.

"Hayden, oh hi, good morning. How are you feeling?" She asks with concern. I expected her to say, well, nothing really.

"I'm good, actually, just wanted to hear your voice." There's a slight pause as we both don't know what to say next. *Oh, Hayden, you are such an idiot.* I break the awkward silence.

"How does pancakes sound, my house?" I smile, as pancakes are one of my essentials in life. "I'll make some and you can come over, if you'd like to. Unless you rather go to school?"

"Yeah, school, umm I mean I should go…" I can tell in her voice, that she's thinking about not going. So many things are running through my head at the moment. *I'm literally here asking the girl of my dreams to come over and have breakfast with me!*

I head downstairs and start making pancakes, just in case she feels like actually ditching school and coming over. A few minutes go by, and I hear a knock on the door. *She came!* She walks into the kitchen, sets her coat down, and we both eat in silence. About 20 minutes goes by when she looks down at her watch.

"I have to go now, are you going to be okay?" *Of course I'll be okay. But I'm not going to tell her that things are really weird for me at the moment.*

"Don't worry about me. Thank you again for everything." She's about to say something when I start to clean up. I look at her and we both head toward the door. I watch her walk to the bus stop. We both wave, a bit awkwardly. I can somewhat make out a smile, when Josh comes running up to her and hugs her, planting a kiss on her cheek. I roll my eyes and walk away, back toward my house. *Seriously, why is she with him?* I get to my house, and as I approach the door, a very odd feeling comes across me. Almost as if there's a presence besides me in the house. My feet are planted, and I don't move as fear approaches. It sounds like someone breathing heavily behind me; scared to look back, I feel a hand grab my shoulder. Instincts kick in, I turn, grab their arm, and force them hard to the ground as a pulse of my magic keeps them placed. I look and notice who grabbed me.

"Waverly? What?... don't scare me." She struggles, getting up.

"What the hell was that? Shit, I think you broke my arm." I take a look, knowing, perfectly well that she's completely fine.

"What are you doing, I thought you got on the bus to wherever you were headed to in a rush?" She rubs her arm.

"I saw you stop in front of your door and from the bus it looked like something was seriously wrong. I just wanted to make sure you were okay." I smile but then look inside my house.

"Don't you have Josh to comfort?" I immediately regret every word. "I'm sorry, that was harsh. I'm sorry."

"If you don't want my help, I'll leave you." I apologize again, taking slow steps toward the open door. "Should we call the police?"

"No, why would I need the police? Just felt a weird presence." I start making my way inside, when Waverly grabs my arm. I know that my mom isn't back from the hospital; therefore, it's someone else.

"Hello? Mom...MOM!" I tiptoe around the front hallway and hear a noise. Waverly grabs my arm tighter. I turn the corner, inviting myself into the kitchen.

"We shouldn't be here, Hayden." I agree with her but something about this seems odd. I suddenly have magical powers, can't control them, and now things are happening randomly.

"For all I know, it could just be my aunt. She does have a key." I scratch my head in disbelief. But there is no way that she could have gotten in without me seeing her. I wasn't that far away from the front door.

"What if it isn't her?"

"I'll have to take that chance." Waverly grabs hold of my arm again and squeezes tightly. "Hello, is anyone here?" I hear a creak coming from upstairs. "I know someone is here, show yourself before I call the police." I pull Waverly toward the stairs; she holds me back for a few seconds before I start making my way upstairs. I stand at the top of the landing and feel a very slight chill pass by me. "Something's not right."

"You can say that again." Waverly says in her sarcastic voice. I tiptoe toward my room, pushing the door open ever so slowly. My door seems jammed as I notice a bunch of papers floating around and stuck under my door. I push with force, as I'm invited back into my messy room. Posters are ripped and tossed on the ground, sheets are scattered, and my computer is cracked in half.

"Holy crap!" Waverly grabs my hand and looks around. "Someone was looking for something here. Hayden, I think we should call the police."

"Okay, now I'm freakin' pissed off. You think you can come in here and toss things around and scare me. You're WRONG." It's also about 30 degrees in my room, as I notice that the window is wide open. "Waverly, can you do me a favor and close the window for me, and under no circumstances are we calling the damn police. I've had enough drama for a lifetime; I don't need them finding out that I'm living on my own."

"Hayden, I'm scared, please let's get out of here." I hold

Waverly's hand tight and walk toward the window to close it myself. I looked around the room to see if anything's missing. My heart's pounding so fast that you could hear it. I'm in complete shock as I don't understand why this is happening. I know that someone is here, but not sure if they are real or just something that's haunting me again.

"Let's leave, Hayden." I look at her.

"We can't leave; I need to know what they were looking for."

"You're scared just like I am, I can see it. Please, Hayden, let's go."

"Waverly, PLEASE, I need to find something tangible." I reach under the bed, my hand moving side to side, searching for anything missing. I pop back up almost hitting Waverly in the face as she looks down.

"What! What!" I say, registering her scared face.

"You scared me that's all."

"Oh, I'm sorry." I say, clearly not focused on her and how frightened she looks.

"Is anything missing?" She looks around.

"It doesn't look like it; I wonder what this thing was really looking for."

"Thing?" I glare at her, realizing that she probably thinks I'm crazy. "You have to report this then, Hayden, it's the right thing to do."

"The right thing to do is figure out who did this in the first place." They had to be looking for something..."

"Hayden, I have a question."

"Sure." I say, kind of annoyed.

"How are you so calm about all this?" She brings up a valid

point-I don't know how to answer that.

"I guess I have to be." I have to be honest with her. "If I tell you something, will you promise not to say anything?"

"Of course, your secret is safe with me. Let's just talk about this outside." We walk down the stairs and out the front door, so she feels safer. I don't even notice that she's holding my hand.

"Hayden, what is it?" She grabs my other hand and looks me straight in the eyes. I'm officially sweating now as I have to tell her my secret, unless I lie to her.

"Promise me." I say.

"Of course, Hayden, I promise." I take in a deep breath and start to explain to her.

"A couple of nights ago I had this really weird nightmare or what seemed like one anyway, and in this nightmare, I saw a cloud-like shadow in my room, and I think it's trying to tell me something. I don't really know what that meant but it really took me by surprise, and now this. Things are happening out of the blue and it all started when my dad came back." She reaches toward me and hugs me. I breathe in her aroma, but she pulls away.

"Hayden, your dad has nothing to do with this. It's just a really big coincidence. There's something off, though, I can feel it."

"Feel it how?"

"You know how sometimes you can sense things that are just going to happen? Well, that's what I'm talking about." Sense things...I think she's just saying all this to make me sound less crazy. "Listen, Waverly, thank you again, but this is really bizarre, and it seems like I have to figure things out for myself. If you don't mind, I would like to be alone."

"There is no way in hell that I'm leaving you alone, Hayden. No way!!" She looks at me with her puppy-dog eyes. *Yeah, I'm not buying into that. Nope, not going to look into her eyes again.* She looks at me again. "You just thought something was in your house and, telling me you saw some cloud and whatnot, and you want me to leave?" She does have a point. But me being me, I do what I do best.

"Waverly, I just want to be alone to process everything."

"Learn to process with someone around because, I'm sorry, unless you drag me out of here, I'm not leaving you alone. Don't argue with me." Something in my body starts to happen, and I usually don't get like this but man oh man am I angry. It's never happened before and all of a sudden...

"LEAVE ME ALONE!" My hands start to burn up and then something really weird happens. My hands are on fire. Literally on fire, no puns intended here. I turn around quickly so she doesn't see how much of a freak I really am. I start to run away from her.

"Waverly, I'm sorry, I...I, you need to leave me alone." I slam the front door practically in her face and run into my bathroom. Hyperventilating I try to take in a deep breath and run my hands under cold water. I'm freaking out. Sweat is pouring down the sides of my face. It's like I ate something really spicy, couldn't handle it, and then bam, my mouth is forever on fire. I know you know what I'm talking about. So yeah, that is currently happening to me, except I'm actually burning. The weird thing that I should point out, well besides the whole thing where my hands light up like a damn Christmas tree, is that it doesn't hurt. Does that make sense? I hear a loud thump coming from downstairs, and before I can see who it is, I hear the front door slam and Waverly's heavy breathing as she's running up my stairs. She bangs on my bedroom door, as it creaks open. I quickly put my hands behind my back. She approaches.

"I thought I could handle all of this but clearly, I can't. You and I are very different people and when we were younger it was a lot easier..." She keeps talking but I can't hear anything that's coming out of her mouth because I'm preoccupied with my freakin' burning hands. "So, I wanted to tell you that I never stopped liking you." That's when my ears perk up and I'm looking at her. I notice my hands are changing back to normal.

"Wait, you what?" I say, not quite grasping the information.

"I like you, Hayden, always have. I've just been a fool for not putting two and two together." I'm fidgeting, but she doesn't seem to notice.

"Waverly, I can't do this right now; I have more important things to worry about than your feelings." *Crap, I just royally messed everything up. Wow are you a big idiot or are you trying to lose the one girl of your dreams. I'll go with both. Ugh.*

"I just told you that I have feelings for you ever since we first met, and you shut me out." *This is the reason why girls are just so complicated. They never get it. Or is it the fact that guys don't really understand women. Vaughn would know all the answers to this; he seems pretty with it when it comes to that department.*

"Waverly, you know how much I care for you, but I have things that I need to handle. Plus, aren't you with Josh anyway?" *Crap again...what is my problem.*

"For once in your life, Hayden, tell me the truth..." *Well shit, now what am I supposed to say?*

"Waverly, I really have nothing to say at the moment. This honestly has nothing to do with you, but I have to figure some things out. I really don't want you to take that the wrong way." I yell out in pain all of a sudden. I look down and my hands are bright red. It feels like I stuck my hands on top of a stove and left them there. I'm about to run back toward the bathroom when, IT happens. She leans in and kisses me. Our lips meet and for that split second, I've lost all control of my body and I realize that my hands are on her face. No longer burning and I'm so calm. *This is the moment I've been waiting for since, well, FOREVER.*

"That was, well, overdue." Waverly looks directly in my eyes and the only thing I can think of is Josh. What the hell is wrong with me? That's the first thing I think about. Sure, Hayden, think about how when Josh finds out about this little kissing action, how he will beat you to a pulp. *Did that just happen? Can you reassure me that it actually happened, please!* Leave it to me to ruin the moment, again.

"What about Josh?" I ask without thinking. *Doh!* She looks toward the floor, as if pondering her next statement carefully. Silence. I take in a deep breath, look toward her beautiful face and open my mouth ever so slightly. She starts to speak.

"If you need me, you know where I am. Please don't do anything irrational, call me or Vaughn. I have to go." Before I can say anything, she's exiting my bedroom, and I hear the front door close. I stand in my room, not moving. *What just happened? Did I do something wrong? Was the kiss that bad? Or was it that good?* I ponder for a few minutes, as I pace back and forth in my room. Even though that was the most confusing thing in the world, I'm smiling from ear to ear. She kissed me, ME! I finally stop pacing and come back to somewhat of reality because all this happened for a reason. Someone was in my house, in my room, looking for something. But what? Things like this never happen to me, but I've noticed that ever since I turned 16, things have been very weird. I also feel different. Not saying hey I just went through puberty in like five minutes and now I feel like a man. No, it's more like, there is something going on that I can't really seem to explain. I need to clear my head. I leave everything the way it is and walk out the front door. *Shit, of course I never got my license so I can't really go anywhere. Ugh, cab it is.*

The cab pulls up to my house in less than 20 minutes. "Hobert Hospital, please." The cabby doesn't say a word and drives me right to the hospital. All I really want to do is rest my head on the windowsill and close my eyes. Mom would always know the right things to say. I nod off for a few seconds, when I hear the brakes of the cab. I pay him and walk toward the revolving doors. My mom's room is up a flight from the entrance, down the scary hallway, and the last door on the right. I slowly pull the door open to find my mom wide-eyed. I hate seeing her in this condition.

"Hi. You're awake. How are you feeling? Are you okay? Where's Aunt Beth?" She smiles at me. Something I've truly missed.

"I told her to go back home and get some rest. I have all the help I can get here at the hospital and you, of course." I shake my head in disapproval.

"Mom, you shouldn't have done that, she's your sister."

"Sometimes sisters don't get along, as you would think." She looks away for a brief second. I know her and Aunt Beth never really saw eye to eye.

"Hayden, I'm glad you're here, I need to talk to you." She's got that look, the really eager-to-tell-me-something look. I pull up a chair and wait for what she has to tell me. Holding her warm hand I look into her baby-blue eyes, the same ones she passed on to me. "What's on your mind, Mom?"

She smiles, something I've missed for a long time. "Honey, there's something I need to tell you about your dad. It might come to you as a shock, but please don't be alarmed." I wait.

CHAPER 5

As she begins to speak, I notice a certain glow and happiness in her eyes. I've never seen her like this before. Fresh grief stabs me, as she mentions my dad's name again. She continues with her story. "Your dad was the most handsome man I've ever seen. We first met at the corner grille; I was a waitress back then, 23 actually. Sparks flew since that day, and the next thing I knew, your dad proposed to me. It was romantic, the way he proposed. Rose petals on the bed, and he knelt down on one knee, and popped the question. I probably held my breath for longer than I should have. Then came our wedding, which was amazing. My family combined with all his, showed up to give us the best wedding I could have asked for. I remember it like it was yesterday." Her eyes began to tear up as she held my hand. "Your dad started to speak, *'I love you with all my heart, but there's something I want to tell you before you truly are mine forever.'* "I looked into your dad's eyes and sometimes when I look at you, I see him again."

"You don't have to tell me this if it's too painful, Mom." She smiles at me.

"No son, I have to share this story with you."

"So what did he say? I already know that he was a warlock and all, what else could there possibly be?"

She continues her brief story. "Well, I told him, *'There's nothing that would make me not love you forever.'* " My mom sighed. "Our favorite song came on as he glided me to the dance floor. He held me so close, and I could tell that he was afraid to tell me something."

"What was he trying to tell you, Mom?" I said, with a little impatience in my voice. She continues.

"Your dad kissed me as everyone started to cheer and clap. He said very calmly," ...she paused and took a deep breath. "I'm a warlock and someone's trying to kill me." "He said to me during our wedding." I look at her with a bit of shock.

"...someone wanted him dead, for being a warlock?" I said, with some hesitation. She ignored me and continued her story.

"Now at the time finding out what he was, caught me off guard. I mainly had the same reaction as you did. Finding out, though, that someone wanted his head on a platter, is what really got me scared." HOLD UP...*Why is my mom telling me this now, when he's dead already?*

"Did you ever find out who wanted him dead?" I whisper to her, thinking I should at least ask.

"No, I never did because after that night, I spent every waking moment with him. I was afraid that someone was actually going to come in our house and kill him. It was terrifying living this way. There was something about your dad that was different from all the other guys I dated. Not because of the warlock thing. I just knew."

"What do you mean?" Now I'm fascinated to learn more about my dad.

"Well, he could always get tickets to my favorite play every year, when it was sold out. He would somehow get me into my favorite restaurant for my birthday. I just imagined it was good luck, but it kept happening all the time. I got extremely suspicious, and that's when I started noticing certain patterns. When he finally let out the secret that he was a warlock, the thought clicked in my head."

"Well, what happened next?" Of course, I need to know the ending and where she's getting at.

"Back at our wedding I asked him if he was really real. He

stopped dancing with me and told me…. *'If I wasn't real, how are we doing this? I couldn't lie to you anymore. Do you still love me?'* "I began to dance with him again, and I told him that I would love him regardless, forever."

"I'm confused, why are you telling me this story? Is there something that I'm missing?" I look at her, making sure that she's not avoiding something crucial. She looks into my eyes, continuing her story.

"See Hayden, even though your dad kept the biggest secret of all, I didn't care. I accepted what he was and later found out that I was pregnant with you. But I've always been worried that someone would be after us and kill him because of what he was." A tear falls from her face. I can't help but be sad for her, but at the same time, I'm a little upset she didn't tell me all of this beforehand.

"That's why he left us, and you didn't tell me that I had his powers? Is that what you are getting at?" I'm honestly not sure where this story is going.

"I was scared. Things weren't right once I found out what he was. Things started to happen out of the blue. Your dad never meant to hurt anyone, I kept telling him that. That poor family, it stuck with him forever. I loved him and I still do."

"Hold up, what are you talking about?" Now I'm officially confused. My mom's face turned a sheet of white. Her blood pressure started to rise. As I tried to comprehend what was happening, I got shoved aside from the nurse.

"She needs something to bring her blood pressure down. Son, I strongly suggest that you leave and come back later. She needs rest." I couldn't move. My mom just dropped a bombshell, and then left me hanging with the biggest question of all. Who was my dad really?

I needed answers, and this was going to bother me. She looked up at me, pushing the nurse's arm aside.

"HAYDEN, you have to understand that your dad never meant to hurt them. You have to believe me when I tell you that." Another tear falls from her face.

"Mom, what are you talking about? What did he do?" She looks at me, scared, and then passes out. The nurse shoves me out of the room. It all happened so fast, as I was being escorted into the hallway. Great, now I was trapped in this endless hallway and not getting the answers that I needed. This was going to sit in my brain, forever. I had no other choice, but to grab a cab and head back home. So many thoughts were circling in my head. *What was Mom saying that he never meant to hurt anyone? What the hell is going on?* I arrived home, confused, I opened the front door, locked it behind me, and walked into my messy room. Laying on my bed, I can't even comprehend what my mom was trying to tell me. Or in fact, why she was telling me all this. I start to doze off, when I hear a big bang coming from downstairs, that jolted me out of my bed. I quickly get up and start to tiptoe down the stairs, scared. Doesn't help that my stairs creek every time my foot hits it. Getting to the bottom, I take in a deep breath and listen. Of course, the noise is coming from my basement. Literally, nothing good ever comes from the basement. Stupidly, I head down there anyway. I need to figure out what this noise is. Not sure what exactly I'm looking for, I glance at the back window, which is currently wide open. It's doing that thing, where it's smashing against the wall, making it really feel like you're in a horror movie. I just keep looking at the window that is flapping back and forth. I remember that same window flapping in my future visit. My eyes fixated only on the window, I trip down the first stair and tumble down, hitting the cement floor, hard. I slowly get up, holding my side. I trip again, but this time over a large cardboard box labeled "Hayden's Memories." *'What the hell, Hayden!'* Curiosity piques my interest. I lean down and grab the box, dusting it off. Not really paying attention, I start to walk with the box open and a piece of paper comes flying out, landing on the dusty floor. I stare at the paper for what seems about five minutes, before I decide to pick it up. It's written on old parchment paper, which is something that you never see these days. I shouldn't read it, but after all, it was in my box.

September 1, 1992

My Love,

With everything that has been happening, I wanted to make sure that you of all people understand that I didn't do anything. Sure, people are pointing to me, when they clearly saw me in front of that house, but only you know the truth. I would give anything to go back in time to fix things. I love you no matter what happens to me, and we shall be together again. Make sure that Hayden gets what I got for him. I left it in the cardboard box, and when he is ready, and old enough, I want you to give it to him. Promise me that our son will have a normal life. After all, that is why we made the choice for me to leave. See you soon and love you from the bottom of my heart.

Connor

What the hell was that all about? I probably re read the letter about ten times, before I actually looked at the cardboard box. Again, that question kept lingering in my head...what happened in 1992 that was so tragic? Enough to have my mom tell me some of the story. Most importantly, I wanted to know what was in this humongous box. Screw this, I opened the box. Seems like an ordinary box, with random things inside it. Found another lighter and old bow and arrow set, and what looked like a practice target. How it all fit inside this box, is beyond my comprehension. I honestly don't know why, but I started to laugh uncontrollably. Why in the world would my dad leave this box for me, and not to mention a bow and arrow set? I feel like I missed a huge chunk of my life. Was this really going to help me in the long run? I'm confused, are you?

"I can't believe after all this time; this box has been sitting here in the basement. With a weird lighter, and a bow and arrow set." I say aloud to myself. Basically, I do what any 16-year- old kid would do, I test out the products. Maybe it has some special power that I can use. I am a warlock after all. I put the straw target on the other side of the basement and walk back to pick up the bow. Holding the bow, I place an arrow on the rest, and pull it back toward my mouth. *Okay, Hayden, sure you know what the hell you're doing.* Seems natural enough. "Well, here goes nothing." I release the string and watch as the arrow flies across the basement and hits the target.

"Wow, that was very interesting. Didn't think I would be this good my first try." I start to laugh again, because honestly this is so ridiculous. I drop the bow and arrow on the basement floor, when I hear that same noise again. The basement window is wide open again, as a breeze seeps through, causing me to shiver. A few minutes pass by when I head back up the stairs. I ignore the faint sounds, because I keep telling myself that this is an old house. Walking up toward my bedroom, I weirdly enough have the urge to clean. So, here I am cleaning and then the thought comes to me...where has Vaughn been all this time? Should I give him a call?

I ponder. Instead of dialing his number, I for some reason, call Waverly. I immediately hang up. "Stupid, why in the world would you call her? I'm calling Vaughn." I dial his number. I let it ring for a few times, nothing. That is so unlike him, to the point where I'm getting a little worried. I place my phone on the bed, and seconds later it starts ringing. I pick up the phone without looking at who was calling.

"Hello?" A sweet voice answers.

"Hey, Hayden. It's Waverly."

"Oh hey, how are things?" I feel awkward talking to her now. I honestly wanted to talk to Vaughn. But it would be very rude if I hung up.

"I'm doing well thanks. I wasn't sure if you wanted to talk to me again, after everything that happened. Are you cool to chat?" She says. Really, is she asking me if I'm cool to chat? What is this? What's happening?

"Yeah, all cool. I found an old letter in my basement today, and just was very nice to see a letter my dad wrote to my mom." Again, why am I telling her all this?

"That sounds great, Hayden. Listen I wanted to ask you something." Oh boy, nothing ever good comes from that.

"Sure, what's up?" I say, waiting for her response.

"Have you heard from Vaughn at all?"

"Actually no, I was meaning to call him today. Wait, why do you ask?"

"I was just curious; I feel like he's been off lately." Right, because she knows him so well.

"That was random." I say rudely.

"Yeah, forget I asked. What was in that letter?" I don't answer her right away.

"Can I ask you a question now?" I wait until she answers. Then I ask my question. "Do you believe in warlocks and witches?" Another long pause.

"I mean, depends on if you're talking in books and stuff like Harry Potter. But if you're asking me if I think they're real...well, probably not." She starts to giggle over the phone. "That was random, too." I take in a deep breath, hoping that I can change the subject or something.

"I was just curious, too. I have a lot of thoughts running through my head lately. Just was something I was thinking about."

"Hayden, are you okay?" *Oh great, now she probably thinks I'm crazy and need help. I don't need any help.* Stupidly, I start to make that noise when the line goes dead, like in the movies. You know what I'm talking about?

"Hello? (chhh) Waverly, shit can you hear me? I'm sorry; I can't hear you (chhh)." I'm such an ass for doing this to her, but I have no other choice. I made things super awkward, and I can't go back. I hang up. I can't believe that just happened, but some things I just have to do. The only person who will understand me fully, is Vaughn. Where the f is he? I pick up the phone and dial his number again. By the third ring, I'm getting really worried; it's not like him to NOT answer the phone. Just as I'm about to call his ass again, the doorbell rings. I drop my phone in pure fear. I start to descend my stairs. The doorbell rings again, and I can't manage to open the door, until I hear a voice on the other side.

"Hayden, I know you're in there. Will you open the door please?" Waverly says from the other side of the door. DAMNIT, why is she here?

"Can you come through the back door?" I run toward the back opening it ever so slowly. I see her with her cute pink dress on. I take in a deep breath and try to smile without giving her the satisfaction of knowing I'm happy to see her. She's waiting for my invite, like some vampire on the prowl. I grab her shoulder and shove her inside the house.

"Ouch, what was that for?" she says, rubbing her shoulder.

"Sorry, I don't want people knowing that I'm here." She's puzzled all right, but I ignore it. We both look at each other and stupidly my mouth opens without my brain thinking about it first.

"Why aren't you with your boyfriend, Josh? I'm sure he's wondering what you're doing here talking to someone like me." I immediately want to take it all back, but naturally that's not how things work.

"I came here to talk to you, Hayden. Josh doesn't need to know my every move." I try to smile but can't. She makes me so nervous.

"Would you like a glass of water or something to eat?" I open the refrigerator and realize that it's completely empty. I slam the door and sit down near her.

"Okay, we need to talk. Face to face this time." She says, without hesitation.

"Oh, umm sure." What else am I going to say?

"You've changed. I get that you've been going through a lot with your dad passing away and your mom with her current condition. But what's going on with you?"

Okay, where did this come from? This wasn't part of the plan. She's not supposed to ask these questions about me. I kind of was thinking about grabbing her and planting a soft kiss on her lips and seeing where things would go. Then Josh pops into my head. Wow,

I'm just a really confused boy right now.

"First off, I appreciate your concern for my health and all, but if anything, you're the one who's acting weird and different. The last time we physically spoke, was in middle school. You chat with Vaughn more than anyone else I know."

"I know that we've lost touch, but I feel like we know each other more than anyone else does." *What THE HELL is going on? I have no idea where any of this is coming from. Let alone why she's even talking to me about this. Maybe she's someone trying to kill me; does she know what I am? No, no, she can't know what I am...I asked her. Get a grip, Hayden.*

Her hand reaches over the counter, and lands on top of mine. For a split second my heart flutters. I'm such a girl sometimes. I jolt a bit, and she takes her hand off mine.

"I need to tell you something, and it's been bothering me for a while. So, I just need to come out and say it." She looks at me dead in the eyes and doesn't say a word. "You're making me nervous when you don't answer."

"Oh sorry, processing. You can tell me anything, Hayden." Maybe I shouldn't tell her.

"What I tell you now, you have to promise not to say or repeat it to anyone else. Promise?"

"Of course, I promise." Okay, here goes nothing. I'm about to tell her what I am, when my phone rings.

"Hold that thought, I need to take this." I walk away from the table and answer the phone. "Where the hell have you been, dude." You can hear the frustration in my voice.

"Dude, totally forgot to mention I went to this epic haunted camp and..." He keeps blabbing but all I can think about is her.

"Yo, Hayden are you even listening to me?" I clear my throat.

"Oh yeah, I'm listening, sorry. Can you swing by, we really need to talk?" We both hang up and I walk back toward Waverly.

"Would you like some tea?" I say, being polite because I have to kick her out again.

"No, thank you. So, what was so important that you were going to tell me?" Shit! I can't tell her now. I have to give her something else to think about.

"I was going to tell you that..." I can't lie to her. "I love you." *Holy shit.... really Hayden!!!* She looks at me, not saying a word, gets up and walks toward the stove.

"I'll have that tea now." Yup, I went too far.

The doorbell rings, thank goodness I know who it is this time. I tell Vaughn to come through the back door. He waltzes in like he owns the place.

"Got any food? I'm starving. Dude, so this camping place was the sh...oh, Waverly, what are you doing here?"

"Hi, Vaughn nice to see you too. Hayden invited me over."

"Umm, actually you kind of just came over." Waverly gives me the "are you serious" kind of look. Vaughn is giving me the evil eye stare. Yup, clearly, I missed something.

"Vaughn, would you care for some tea?"

"Enough of this bullshit. Waverly, what are you doing here? Hayden, what the hell is going on?" I look at her, then back at him. SHIT, what do I say? "You know what, I don't really care. Waverly, congrats cheating on Josh. Hayden, I'm surprised that you have the guts to actually talk to her." Okay, now I'm pissed off.

"Vaughn, what is your deal? We're all friends here." Vaughn storms off and pulls me aside.

"For starters, you haven't spoken to her since what, middle school?"

"Is everything okay? What's going on?" I need to ask.

"Nothing is going on." He storms off back into the kitchen, leaving me hanging. *Great, just great. What did I do wrong?*

Waverly looks at Vaughn as if they have been keeping something from me. Vaughn just doesn't seem to care about anything, and here I am going to say something that I probably shouldn't say. Here it goes.

"I'm a warlock!" I wait. Seconds pass, but they don't seem to say anything. Waverly starts to laugh. Vaughn surprisingly doesn't.

"You can't be serious?" She laughs even harder. "You know that's just a bunch of fairy tale garbage, right?" I don't crack a smile, and stare at her with my eyes wide open.

"Dude, this is freakin' awesome. I kind of had a feeling you were keeping something from me all these years."

"Holy crap, you're serious? Hayden, there is no such thing as warlocks. It's just stories that people make up for their kids and whatnot."

"I knew you wouldn't take me seriously. Never mind, forget I even said it." Her hands place on mine again, but this time I take them away quickly. Vaughn looks at us.

"I didn't mean to laugh at you, Hayden. Just warlocks…" She can't finish her sentence.

"Wav, how can you not believe in them, when there's one literally standing in front of you? I think it's the coolest thing I've heard yet. Hay, how come you never told me sooner?"

"To be honest, I just recently found out. I mean I knew there was something off about me, and when my dad told me I was shocked just like you."

"This is freakin' awesome!" Vaughn continues to say. Waverly is still silent.

"Hayden, I don't know what to say."

"Well, start believing it because that's what I am, and that's what my dad was. He was about to tell me something before the accident. He told me that I was a warlock, and that he never wanted this life for me." She gets up from her seat and gives me a hug. She starts to whisper in my ear, "I believe you, honestly." Vaughn smiles at me and gives me a wink. Just at that moment, the doorbell rings again. *Jeez, what's with the doorbell today?*

"Are you expecting anyone?" Vaughn says.

"No." I head toward the front door and peek to see who it is. To my surprise, there's a six-pack of beer on the ground. I open the door.

"Dude, who is it?" Vaughn says as I pick up the six-pack. I'm about to close the front door, when I see someone a block away, looking at me with binoculars. I slam the door, freaked out.

"Beer, sweet. From whom?" I just stare at the beer.

"Hay, it's just beer, relax we won't get caught."

"Someone is watching me, from this house across the street." I say.

"Get real, who in the world would want to spy on a nerd like you?" Vaughn laughs.

"Real funny, dude." I take a few steps back from everyone.

"Hayden is everything..." Waverly stops mid-sentence and looks at Vaughn, who then looks at her.

"Am I missing something?" I say, curiously.

"Huh?" They both say at the same exact time. I shrug my

shoulders and lock the door.

We all stand in the kitchen drinking the beer, we're definitely not old enough to drink. Not sure why we are drinking it, for all I know it could have been poisoned from the dude across the street, spying on me. I can't take the silence anymore; Vaughn beats me to it.

"Waverly, so nice to see you back in the picture. I must say, it's a little odd, don't you agree, Hayden?" Vaughn smiles evilly.

"Okay, I don't know what's going on with you two, but enough's enough. Vaughn, there's something you need to know that's been happening besides the obvious." I say with a bit of anger in my voice. Clearly, I do not like where Vaughn's head is at.

"There's more than what you just said?" Vaughn states, as he looks at Waverly again.

"Yes, I think there is someone after me." I respond. Waverly looks at Vaughn yet again. "Okay, clearly there is something that I'm missing. So, you better tell me right now." Vaughn looks over at Waverly and then back at me.

"Don't Vaughn, please." She says, nervous. I look at her intently.

"Don't what? What is happening?" I'm very confused and getting a bit annoyed.

"It's really not a big deal. It was a long time ago, and it's in the past." He smirks as he's giving his non cholent answer to me. Vaughn looks over at Waverly, but before she can interrupt, he blurts it out. "We had sex and dated while you were still head over heels for her, also made out like a week ago. Plus, I think we might have a little chemistry left."

"Screw you, Vaughn, he wasn't supposed to hear that." Waverly stomps her feet in protest.

"I WASN'T, huh? I mean, Vaughn said something about liking you, but…So you were going to keep this all a secret from me? Oh, you just happened to have sex with the girl of my dreams and then was like, oh yeah, we shall never tell Hayden this. Screw you both." I'm getting overly heated and notice my hands are as well.

"Vaughn, why did you just ruin everything." She says.

"How the f did I ruin it. I just told my best friend what has been happening between us, you should be happy that it's out in the open now." He smiles a little and then looks toward me.

"I'm not happy at all. We have no chemistry by the way, so don't even think that we do." She looks away from Vaughn.

"Oh, so you didn't want to kiss me in the car the other day?" He reacts to her statement.

"The other day? Ha, you wish. I wouldn't kiss you if you were the last person on the earth." Waverly is now yelling directly at Vaughn.

"Keep telling yourself that." Vaughn says with a smile.

"Both of you GET OUT!" I start yelling, I can't even understand how or why this just happened. "I literally told you both that I'm a freakin' warlock and all you want to talk about is how you have the hots for each other. Get the hell out of my house." Vaughn looks at me, realizing that he did actually hurt my feelings. Waverly has no idea how to respond to that. They both leave the house.

"Make sure you both make out in the car, since that's what you clearly wanted to do." I slam the door, pissed off. I forget to lock it after they leave. Without hesitation, I grab my phone and call the one person I'd never imagine I'd call.

"Hey, kiddo!" My uncle says.

"Guess you have Caller ID." I say.

"Yup, got to love this new technology. What's up?" I hear a weird noise in the background but ignore it.

"Just needed someone to chat to. My two friends are fighting and kind of dropped a bomb on me. Not sure why I called you, though."

"I'm glad you did. Listen kid, if these two friends need to hash things out, then let them. Seems like you needed a break from them anyway. How's mom doing? I should have come back to the hospital, but pretty sure I'm not welcome there. Being your dad's brother and all." Uncle Lincoln says.

"I'm sure she'd love to see you."

"What room is she in? Maybe I will go later today." He takes in a deep breath. Not sure if it's just my instincts or not, but something doesn't seem right. "So, can you give me her room number?"

"Sure, I think it's 243. Make sure you use the elevator on the west wing. Don't ask."

"Thanks, kiddo. I'll stop by later tonight." He says, I wait for him to say something else. "Okay cool, I'll see you soon, Hayden." I hear a big crash noise on the other end, and I'm about to ask what's going on, when the line goes dead. *Okay, well that was very odd.*

I walk around the kitchen, when I walk toward the living room Vaughn and Waverly are sitting there. *"Great, I didn't lock the door apparently."*

"So, I know that you kicked us out, but we didn't want to leave you on, you know, bad terms." Waverly says.

"Right, what she said." I shake my head because that's so typical of Vaughn so say.

"There's really nothing more to say. You clearly have some

feelings that you both need to sort out, and I don't want to be involved. Waverly, I told you something, and you didn't seem to care. I spilled that I'm a warlock, and all you guys can think about is getting into each other's pants."

"It's really not like that. Sure, we used to like each other but I'm with Josh and there's nothing going on." Vaughn smiles at Waverly.

"Enough, I don't care anymore. Don't give me the BS Josh thing. I know you don't like him. So, if we're done here, I'd like to go back to the hospital to see my mom." Silence is upon all of us, but they don't seem to leave my side. A few hours pass, when the doorbell rings again. I walk toward it, peeking through and see that it's my uncle. Vaughn and Waverly are sitting on opposite ends of the couch.

"Hey, how's mom doing? Come in." I say.

"She's doing great, she was shocked to see me, but happy." Uncle Lincoln starts to talk about her condition.

"How long has it been?" I feel like I'm asking too many questions, but I haven't seen him, well, ever.

"It's been a long time." He looks toward the ground, as if he's been hiding something. I can see Vaughn looking at him with a glare. Vaughn usually has that instinct about certain people. I'm just to upset with him to even care.

"Would you like some tea?" I say, to be polite.

"I'd love some, thank you, Hayden." He walks into the living room to be hosted by Waverly and Vaughn. I look at Vaughn and know that something is wrong.

"You must be Lincoln." Waverly smiles. "Nice to meet you."

"Likewise. You must be the famous Waverly I've heard so much about." Waverly looks toward Hayden, blushing. "All good things, my dear."

"Mr. Grant, tell me, how do you know so much about Waverly, when you've never really been in Hayden's life?" Vaughn says, without hesitation.

"Call me Lincoln, Vaughn." He smiles at Vaughn. Something is definitely weird.

"You didn't answer my question. Also, how do you know who I am?"

"Hayden's dad used to talk to me about all of you. It is how I know each of your names." Vaughn doesn't buy it, but before he can say another word, I chime in.

"Why does it take a death in the family for me to finally meet you?" Waverly and Vaughn look at each other simultaneously as they slowly get up to leave the room. Even though I know Vaughn wants to hear every single detail.

"Hayden, there are some things that I'm not proud of and I would like to think of the happy times your dad and I had. As you might know, I was his best man at the wedding, when I heard that they had a son, I wanted to be there front and center. It was the happiest day of his life besides the wedding, knowing that he had a baby boy."

"I never knew that you saw me when I was younger. You were at my parents wedding, my dad's best man? Honestly, I didn't even know I had an uncle until now. Why did my mom and dad keep me from you?"

"I don't think your mom and dad wanted me in your life, it was hard times." My lip curls in suspicion.

"I just wish I knew that I had an uncle; life would have been a lot easier for me."

"I realize that son, and I'm here for you now no matter what." We both smile at each other when Waverly and Vaughn walk back in.

"So yeah, you guys up for watching a movie?" She didn't know what else to suggest.

"Yeah, movie night sounds good." Vaughn agrees with Waverly, for once.

"Uncle, you up for a movie?" I had to ask, not to make things even weirder.

"Let's do it!" I open the drawer full of movies; Waverly can't believe how many we have. Little does she know that most of these are Vaughn's that I never returned. Politely, I ask Waverly to pick the movie. She chooses *X-Men*. Halfway through the movie, my phone rings. I roll my eyes, because it's at one of the best parts. I ask Vaughn to grab my phone and answer it.

"Oh, that must hurt." Not paying attention as Wolverine plunges his hands of metal into Rogue and Waverly lets out a yelp. Vaughn picks up the phone and hears breathing on the other end.

"Hello, Hayden's phone. How may I assist you?" I look over at Vaughn's childish expression. He's always wanted to answer the phone like that.

"Hello, this is the hospital calling." Vaughn holds the phone away from his face and gestures to me to come quick.

"This is Hayden." I hold my breath waiting for the response.

"This is Doctor Carter; I have some news about your mom." I hate where this is going.   "She was doing great until a few hours ago, her body became very agitated. We've given her something to calm her down, but so far it hasn't helped." He continues to talk.

"Wait, what do you mean agitated, what happened?" I leave the room; I don't want everyone staring at me. "How could she be fine one minute and then not the next?" The doctor continues to talk. I listen but can't seem to grasp why this happened in the first place. "I'll be right over. Thank you." I hang up and walk back into the living room.

"Hayden, son, what's happened?" Uncle Lincoln says, without getting up from the couch.

"Mom's just not doing well for some reason. I thought you saw her, and everything was fine?"

"She was great when I saw her. She was talking and walking around. I brought her some food and everything."

"Well, something happened. I'm going back to the hospital. If you don't mind, I'd like you all to leave." Uncle Lincoln, Waverly, and Vaughn get up. Vaughn gives Lincoln the stink eye.

"Wait, we're coming with you." Waverly says and walks out the door with me and Vaughn.

"No offense, Uncle but you can see yourself out. I want to see my mom." He looks at me without hesitation in his voice, just merely looks at me and then walks out the door.

We are all packed into Vaughn's car, when Vaughn, of course, has to say something. "Dude, I'm sorry but your uncle is weird. He gives me this weird vibe, and doesn't it seem weird that the minute he visits your mom that something happens to her?" Vaughn has a good point. I just can't seem to put two and two together. I want to just see my mom, and that's it.

Arriving at the hospital in less than five minutes, I barely wait for the car to stop, when I open the door and run toward the entrance. The nurses outside are yelling at me, but I'm not paying attention. The double doors open, and I enter, with Vaughn and Waverly in tow.

"Doctor Carter, I'm Hayden Grant. You called me, how's my mom?" He looks at me, worried.

"She's still in her room, but please keep your distance." I don't let him finish as I charge into her room and take hold of her hand.

"Mom, Mom look at me. What's going on?" I gaze into her baby-blue eyes.

"Why does it turn and turn. It hurts like a knife; he comes and leaves a trace..." She keeps babbling nonsense. Waverly takes hold of my hand, and I see her grab Vaughn's as well.

"No. No. No dark night, make it disappear. Stop." I start to tear up looking at her in this condition.

"Son, you need to leave the room now. We need to calm her down." I don't move and neither does my friends.

"Blacknight, beware. He comes when you least expect it and then takes it all away." I can't control myself and start to scream at the doctor. He plunges a needle into her veins, and she immediately passes out.

"Hayden Grant, we have no choice but to take her to a mental institute. We will have to put her in constraints, she hit a nurse earlier."

"Constraints...my mom's not a loony! She doesn't belong there. I know my mom and she would never..." I'm yelling so loudly that the entire hospital staff turns to look inside the room. Vaughn looks as he never seen this side of me before.

"She's not a loony; they just need to make sure she's alright. Let's take a step outside," Vaughn says. He knows how to calm me down. Waverly follows.

"I don't understand how this can all happen in a blink of an eye." Vaughn looks at me and then back down to the floor. "What? You have that look on your face. Spit it out."

"It's just odd to me that your uncle appears back in your life. Then he tells you that he went to see your mom, not a few hours ago. Acts all weird in front of us, not to mention I had a weird vibe. Then all this happened? C'mon, I can't be the only one who thinks this is very weird?"

"I agree with Vaughn, I didn't want to say this, but your uncle gives me the creeps." Waverly says, trying to be polite.

"I know there is something about him that I just can't seem to grasp. Maybe he's a warlock as well."

Vaughn looks over at me, pats me on the shoulder and directs me to his car. "Let's get out of here."

"We're going to get to the bottom of this." Waverly says.

I look at Waverly, "Thanks, guys." She smiles at me and squeezes my hand. I get into the car. Vaughn and Waverly are outside the door.

***

"You think it's him, don't you?" Vaughn nods his head in agreement.

"There's just too much of a coincidence. He's bad news, Waverly. I can just feel it.

"Usually, your hunches are on point."

"Yeah, that's what scares me. We need to keep an eye out on Hayden." She agrees, gets in the car and they all drive off back toward Hayden's house.

CHAPER 6

I'm quiet during the ride back to the house. Waverly takes my hand gently saying, "I know how you feel." I look down at my hands that are trembling and hold in my breath before I give her an answer.

"You must know what I'm going through; you lost both your parents. How did you deal with it?"

"It was very hard, but luckily my brother was there for me. He took care of me when I really needed it. Time just slowed down when my parents died. I lost track of everything, including my friends. It was my mistake to distance myself from you and Vaughn and my other friends. I just wanted to be left alone. You have friends that care about you and will help you through this process."

"I'm thankful for that, and I'm glad that we re-connected but really why? It's torture for me." Waverly doesn't have enough time to answer me because, well, I think I just really caught her off guard, I do that sometimes to people. Vaughn is in the driver's seat, and I can tell that he's rolling his eyes at me. He doesn't say a word. We pull into the driveway, get out, and make our way toward the front door. I've never really felt like this before. I wasn't really an emotional guy, sure, I have some sort of ADD but who doesn't. The minute we all enter my house, all I can really focus on is the comfy couch staring at me. I see in the corner of my eye Vaughn heading into the kitchen, naturally. *I swear every chance he gets to eat, he will.* I smell the popcorn popping, while Waverly heats up some hot chocolate, for her or us, I don't really know. She's something new in my life and I can't grasp if that's a good thing or not. Then there's my uncle, the person who's never been in my life, but for some reason he's been more present than my dad had. That should say something. Vaughn comes back with popcorn, eating half the bowl while entering the living room. For some reason, I get up off the couch, head into the kitchen and grab the hidden bottle of Jack Daniel's.

"You guys want a drink?" Vaughn doesn't even respond, as he places the popcorn on the table and runs into the kitchen.

"Hayden, you know you shouldn't be drinking. It's illegal." Waverly says all innocent. Vaughn can't help but laugh at her.

"Waverly, please. My mom kept this here when she was having a bad day. Actually, kind of seemed like it was always a bad day. One drink won't kill me or you for that matter."

"Vaughn, how can you encourage him to drink?" Waverly says only looking at Vaughn.

"Did you not witness what happened today? Us guys, that's what we do, we don't go into our rooms and cry our eyes out." Vaughn says, sternly. Waverly is appalled as she looks over in my direction. Like I have anything to say to that.

"This is not a way to drown your anger. If you were smart, you would put that back. We can head over to my house, if you want to get away from here and clear your head." At this point, all I'm hearing is "blah blah blah." I take a couple shot glasses out and start to pour whisky into them. She rolls her eyes and walks away.

"Down the hatch." I take the shot; it burns ever so slightly as it goes down my throat.

"Holy shit, that is smooth. Hit me again." Vaughn cracks me up. "Our so-called sober partner in crime, ladies and gents." Vaughn raises the shot toward Waverly. She is about to say something, when

I chime in.

"I guess with everything going on, I don't care if it's illegal, so forgive me. Yes, we'd like to go to your house after we finish this bottle." Oh shit, I messed that up completely. She gives me the evil eye, looks at Vaughn, who is laughing in the corner. Looks like the ladies always win. I look at the bottle and slowly put it back into the cupboard, with a sad face.

"Pussy." Vaughn whispers to me, as he takes his last shot of whisky. Minutes later, we leave my house and walk toward Waverly's, which is only a few blocks away. Vaughn doesn't say a word and just follows us.

"My brother doesn't seem to be home, so all clear. I do, however, want to take you downstairs, so you can see his office. I think you'd like it, especially being a warl..."

"Warlock, you can say it. I know it's weird but get used to it." Vaughn puts his hand up, as if he's in class about to ask a question.

"So, if you truly are a warlock, then show us your powers." I look at him. *SHIT.*

"It doesn't really work that way. I can't just summon my powers whenever its convenient for you."

"Well, how truly convenient." Vaughn replies with sarcasm. He whispers to me again. "Dude, you know that she kind of wants you?"

Whispering, I say, "What!" Vaughn laughs and starts walking down the stairs.

"Boys, are you coming or what?" She yells from the bottom of the stairs. Finally making it downstairs to her brother's office, Vaughn stops dead in his tracks and tries to look around. The room looks like a dusty office that hasn't been touched in centuries. Pitch black as if right out of a horror movie, the only light source is from a tiny hanging bulb. Our eyes try to adjust to the darkness. Waverly pushes hard on what looks like the wall, and a door swings open.

"Holy shit...this is amazing. I never...wow." Vaughn can't contain himself; he's so excited about this so-called secret door that just magically opened. I have literally no words.

"Yeah, pretty cool, huh?" She smiles at us. "It's his own fortress of solitude. He never lets me down here, so we better make this quick." I melt a little more for her, as she mentioned my favorite comic book character. *It's Superman, if you didn't get that.* I've never seen anything so massive before, literally everything in this room is filled with gadgets. It's something a normal human would never have, which then makes me a bit curious and suspicious. The look on Vaughn's face also tells me that he is very suspicious.

"There are things here that are just...bloody brilliant." I say, with a slight English accent.

"Wait, hold up here. What is that?" Vaughn points to what looks like a pistol.

"Yeah, I know, tell me about it." Waverly doesn't seem to be fazed.

Vaughn continues to talk out loud. "I mean look at this stuff. Silver bullets, rock salt, a 35mm camera, night vision scopes, tape recorders with microphones, and a torch. He even has a thermometer, a compass, wind chimes, and a huge spotlight. Is he a freakin' ghost hunter?" Vaughn looks in my direction, because I literally have the same question.

"What he said, there is no way in hell that someone who has all these things, is just a collector. He's a hunter, isn't he?"

"You guys remember when we were kids and used to pretend that there were ghosts living in the living room?" Waverly says, with a straight face. Vaughn and I can't help but laugh.

"Ha, that was real? I know that ghosts exist but didn't realize that you can hunt them." Vaughn chimes in.

"I feel like we're in an episode of *Supernatural* and that we need to prep for the next demon apocalypse." I look at Vaughn...

"Since when are you into demonology?" I wait for his reply. "I'm serious, dude."

"I have an interest in these things. Don't ask." Vaughn says, without looking at Waverly or me. Waverly of course looks over puzzled.

"To be honest, this is nothing compared to what's behind his secret door." She says.

"SECRET DOOR?" Vaughn and I both say at the exact same time.

Without thinking, Vaughn says, "I think I'm in love with your brother." I laugh at his response. "No seriously, I think I'm really in love with everything in this room."

"Don't jump to any conclusions; he thinks he's one of the ghost hunters you see on TV."

"*Supernatural.* I told you guys. Oh man, if I could live in that show, it would make my year." Vaughn is so happy; I've never seen him like this before.

"And here I was going to say *American Horror Story.*" I say out loud, without even thinking about it.

"Dude, that show's not even scary, just freakin' weird." Waverly ignores us.

"Ever since my parents, you know, he just does this for a living and now I never see him."

"Whoa, slow your pretty little roll. Your brother is a legit ghost hunter?" Vaughn thought it was all a joke, but the look on Waverly's face says it all. "So, this whole time, when I was referencing *Supernatural*, you were just holding your tongue?"

"What was I supposed to say...oh hey, my brother is an up-front for-real ghost hunter?"

"YES, maybe lead with that next time." Vaughn and Waverly continue to argue.

"This is awesome!" the only thing that comes out of my mouth. She nods her head in disagreement.

"I guess it's cool, but it has its ups and downs." She says, looking down at the ground. "Having a brother that is obsessive with hunting makes it hard to be a family. If that makes sense?" She's trying to pick the lock to open up another room.

"Do you need help with picking that lock?" Vaughn says, because I know he knows how to pick any lock.

"Got it. Thanks, though." She smiles at Vaughn.

"That was hot...I mean." He looks over at me. I just brush it off. She opens the secret door. I'm completely flabbergasted.

"Where in the world did, he acquire this?" I say, with my eyes wide open.

"Holy smokes, this place just gets better and better. Hayden, are you seeing this?" I've literally never seen Vaughn so giddy in my life.

"It's like a dream come true." I say, trying to fit in with Vaughn's apparently newly found obsession.

"He doesn't know that I know about this secret door, let alone his toys. Honestly, I have no idea where he even got all these things. Let alone, that." Vaughn and I look at one another, yup, boys will be boys. I hate to say this but I'm hard. I know, such a weird thing to say. Actually, we both are right now.

"I want one, can I touch it?" Vaughn says, without thinking. I burst out laughing.

"Nice one, Vaughn. Wait, I want to touch it, too." Waverly shakes her head.

"Boys." She laughs. "Be careful...if you lose it, he will murder me." We both walk toward it and slowly open the see-through silver box. We take a deep breath, and then let it out quietly.

"I seriously can't believe I'm holding the...I mean the cap-n-ball revolver. I've got to say, this is genius." Vaughn is just, how can I describe it, he's in heaven stroking this revolver.

"It's a nice gun, just please be careful." Waverly didn't realize she was holding her breath the entire time Vaughn was holding the gun.

"Can I hold it now? Stop caressing it, Vaughn." We both laugh and he hands the gun to me. It's the most beautiful thing I've seen. Well...second best thing. As I'm holding it, something starts to happen. My hands get really hot and start to hurt. Then my head gets this crazy amount of pressure and I start to get dizzy. Something strange is happening and Vaughn starts to notice.

"Umm, Hayden, are you alright?" Vaughn tries to take the gun out of my hand. Waverly is screaming in the background.

"Get it off, what's happening? Vaughn, I can't see anything." I fall hard on the ground, as it feels like someone threw a massive rock at my head and I was bleeding. Vaughn tries again to grab the gun, but he can't. I'm shaking like a mini seizure. Waverly is now in the corner crouched down, not moving a muscle.

"Hayden, don't do that." She starts to cry. "There are bullets in there."

"What...who the f** leaves it loaded? Why would you give us a loaded freakin' gun? What the hell were you thinking, Wav?" Vaughn's super pissed off now. "Hay, are you okay?" Vaughn finally takes the gun away from me and my palms go back to normal. I slowly get up off the ground.

"I don't understand what just happened." I finally get to my feet.

"What kind of bullets are in here?" Vaughn opens the compartment and takes them out. The bullets are red hot, and he drops them to the ground. I walk right over to them and examine them.

"Hey Wav, what does this mean? There's a symbol that I've never seen before embedded in the bullets. Not that I've seen a lot of bullets.

"I...I...I'm so sorry, I should have known that this would happen. Please forgive me, Hayden." I honestly don't know why she's apologizing to me. Vaughn looks at me and then back at the bullets and gun. His thinking face is on, which is very rare.

"I think I know what's going on." Vaughn says, "also, Wav, your brother recently used this gun. There's a bullet missing, and it smells like residue. Come here and check it out." We both go close to the gun and look to see that, he's right. "See the hole next to the last bullet?"

"I don't know if that's a good thing or not?" Waverly says, as she glances in my direction. I'm still holding onto my head, as it's pounding.

"How much do you think they are?" I say without really paying attention to their previous conversation. I walk right past her and look at the bullets again. I stupidly pick it up and immediately drop it to the floor. "OUCH FOR THE LOVE OF."

"Stop doing that, please."

"That shell is extremely hot. Waverly, that's not a good sign at all. I think I know what is happening."

"Hayden, are you alright?" She asks.

"No, why the hell would you think I'm alright." I say in a harsh tone. "Okay, Vaughn, what do you think is happening?"

"Well, it's just a theory of course, but I think that your brother shot something recently and since Hayden is well 'supernatural' that I think he's the one who can actually feel the heat of the bullets."

"Why do you say 'supernatural' in quotes?" I say, curious.

"Hayden, seriously, you literally just told us that you're a warlock. If that's not something supernatural, then I don't know what is." Vaughn has a good point. I guess I just never put two and two together.

"Hold up, so you're telling me that my brother recently fired a bullet at something supernatural? I feel like I would have known." Waverly does not look up at us.

"Right, because he's got a secret room for a reason. Not sure he thinks you know what he does, Wav." Vaughn does have a point. "Waverly, you haven't been home in a while, right?"

"Yes, I've been around you boys. I don't know, maybe it's best that we just go back upstairs and pretend nothing happened. I just don't want to cause trouble and put you both in danger. Especially now that Hayden's a warlock, or whatever."

"Waverly, may I ask you a question?" I say, as I look over at Vaughn.

"Go for it." Vaughn's all ears now. I'm sure he's dying to know what my so-called question is. He's got that look.

"Do you find that your house is well...weird in some ways?" She gives me a puzzled look.

"Umm, I don't think so. I mean sometimes I hear noises coming from here, but I just brush it off because it could be just my brother coming in late." Vaughn starts to smile and keep in a laugh. I brush it off and start walking upstairs when Vaughn responds.

"All these questions are leading to what exactly, Hay?" I just look over in his direction, but don't answer. "I mean seriously, you didn't know what a warlock was before all this, I'm assuming?"

"Okay, yes I admit, I had no idea what a warlock really was or what that meant for me. But the minute I told you both, you just laughed in my face, like I was joking."

"I mean, what did you expect? Do you realize how ridiculous that sounds?" Waverly shakes her head in agreement with Vaughn.

"Ridiculous, coming from a basement full of hunting supernatural's. Can we just go back upstairs already?" At this point I'm not having any fun and want this all behind me.

Vaughn shrugs his shoulders and places the gun back in its silver box. Waverly closes the heavy door as we tiptoe back up. You know, just in case her brother shows up and sees us snooping. *That would be just my luck. I can picture it now: Oh hi, we were just in your basement looking at your gun. Fine thing you've got there, oh don't worry, I just dropped it because it was hot and I'm the only loser who can actually feel the heat. I'm Hayden, by the way. I'll be leaving now—Yeah, that's how it would go. HELL NO!*

"You guys can't mention this to anyone, with all your powers that you have, or whatever, you can't risk him knowing." Waverly says, with a hint of worry in her voice.

"Risk anything? I can't even hold a gun without having my freakiness come out. I'm a 15-,shit, 16- year-old boy, who's trying to live a normal life. Then all of a sudden, my dad comes back, drops a huge bomb and tells me I'm a warlock. Honestly, your brother is the least of my worries." At that minute, I wish I didn't go off in a rant and just closed my mouth. I know they are both looking out for me, but what else should I have done? I continue, though. "Then my uncle out of nowhere comes into my life, asking me all these rando questions. My mom goes kinda mental, like what the hell am I supposed to think?" Waverly reaches her hand out.

"Don't worry Hayden, you'll get all the answers in due time, I promise. Just now you need to focus on the things you really need." I have no idea what she is really getting at, but I guess it's the thought that counts. Vaughn finally chimes in.

"Yeah, dude. You never know what can happen. So, you have to be cautious, just in case."

"In case of what? What's out there that's so dangerous, so far nothing has happened expect for a nightmare that I don't really remember. I witness my dad's death and my mom's near death, but you know, I don't even get hurt. Oh, then the best part is that I think I traveled into the future and saw the outcome of something happening. If you knew you had special powers, wouldn't you want something to hold onto that would keep you safe?" Vaughn shakes his head from a distance.

"Hold up, you went to the future? Are you more than just a warlock? Like, what the hell are your powers?" Vaughn curiously asks.

"How the f should I know. But yes, it seemed like I was in the future, because everyone was weirdly talking and didn't even know that I was in the room."

"What was happening in the future?" Waverly asks, curious.

"Why does that even matter right now?" I'm getting pissed off.

"For f sakes, Hayden. You think you're all high and mighty over here and we're just trying to help you figure things out." Vaughn says in a pissed-off tone. Guess I rub off on him.

"You have no idea what it's like to be me and go through this all alone. You get everything, Vaughn. All the girls love you; you don't get called a freak, and the only person who you thought could love you is dating some tool."

"WOW, I hope you are not referring to me, Hayden. That's a load of shit." Waverly doesn't even know how to react anymore.

"Ha, that person is dating a tool, I will give you that. Lighten up, if I had powers, I would be all about that and getting back at those stupid people who made fun of me. Grow some balls, this is something cool."

"Both of you, shut the hell up. I'm standing right here. I'm here to help you, but if you are going to talk about me as I'm standing here, then forget it." Waverly walks away.

"Right, I keep forgetting that we're just friends. Oh wait, are we really just friends or are you coming back to tell me that you slept with Vaughn and then now you just feel sorry for me?" Vaughn is in utter shock at my behavior. "Aren't you with Josh?" She looks down toward the ground. "My point exactly. I'm leaving and if you know what's best for you, Waverly, stay away from me. I'm a freak of nature. You don't want to be around someone messed up like me." Vaughn walks over to me and slaps me in the face.

"Don't talk to her like that. She cares so much about you; it makes me sick."

"Oh right, why don't you shove that pole further up your ass because it's so clear that you and her have a thing and apparently still do. So, piss off, get in her pants like you do with every other girl who's got their skirts hiked up. I'm leaving." Vaughn and Waverly are so shocked, that they don't even see what's happening. But in seconds, they look up.

"Hayden!" Waverly yells. "HAYDEN!"

"What?" She points at my entire body, which is now surrounded by red flames.

"WTF. Hayden stop it." Vaughn backs away.

"I swear I'm not doing this on purpose. I just got really pissed off."

"Dude, has this happened before?" I look over at him and remember the box that made my hands turn red and I was sucked into the future.

"Once, but it wasn't something I knew was happening. Maybe I just need to calm down." Before I can even say anything else, my body feels weird and I'm no longer in the room. I've gone someplace else.

"What the f just happened? Where did he go?" Waverly looks over at Vaughn.

"Did he just disappear? Wait, did he just time travel? I'm seeing things, right? This is so fucked up."

"Vaughn, calm down. There has to be an explanation for this." Waverly says, without really thinking.

"Yes, he got so pissed off at us that he freakin' time traveled. Probably someplace where we don't exist. Did you not listen to all the shit he was saying?"

"Oh, I heard all the insults coming toward me. I can't believe this actually happened. What do we do? Wait, are you seriously in love with me?"

"OMG seriously, Wav, don't be all cocky now that he's not in the room. Just because you're a pretty face, doesn't mean a thing." She looks at him very oddly. "Don't look at me like that. I like you, sure, but who doesn't? Hayden is in love with you, any moron can see that, but apparently you go for the jocks that have their pants on so tight, because let me tell you Josh..." She starts to walk away from him because she knows he's right. "He looks like he stepped out of European spray-tan magazine. His pants are so tight that I swear he has no balls."

"Enough! I don't need you telling me who I can and cannot date. We have more pressing matters at hand here."

"Sure, your highness." Vaughn bends down to her to a bow. They both look into each other's eyes.

"Was it even real?" She asks Vaughn.

"Was what real?" He kind of knows what she's asking.

"You and me? Did you ever care for me or was it all an act?" Silence. Vaughn comes close to Waverly, their faces very close to one another. They both take a deep breath.

"Vaughn...I..." She says.

"I get it, but just so you know. I loved you." He leans in and kisses her on the cheek. They both pull away and gaze into one another's eyes. Vaughn's hands are caressing her hair and down to her lips. She starts to moan when he reaches for her shirt. She stops him and pulls away.

"Stop, we can't do this. Hayden just disappeared in front of us. We can't do this."

"Can't or won't? Are you afraid of me?" Vaughn says, still looking into her eyes.

"Honestly, I'm afraid of what might happen. I like you but..."

She starts to tear up. "This is so wrong." Vaughn doesn't say a word, walks over to grab his coat and goes up the stairs, closing the door behind him. A moment passes as Waverly touches her lips and realizes that she's in a very bad spot. She starts to walk up those same stairs and closes the door. Vaughn is about to walk out the door.

"Vaughn, wait please."

"What? You've made things really clear. Plus, we have Hayden to find and figure out where he ended up going. Or I should say what timeline. How f'ed up is that?"

"You're a really good friend and I respect you; I would like it very much if were just friends." She says.

"Screw you, Waverly. Go find Josh or whatever and deal with it. Clearly you can't decide what guy you want to screw over. You know what we call those types of people.... teases. That's what you are." Vaughn walks out the door, slamming it in her face. She stares at the closed door, and immediately opens it again.

"Stop being such a pussy and tell me what you want from me?"

"What I want from you? Seriously, am I the girl in this scenario. I want you, Waverly. But you have been juggling guys left and right. Friends it is." She runs toward Vaughn, grabs his head and kisses him on the lips. He pulls away, looks into her arms and kisses her back. They fade out into the distance.

***

Meanwhile, I've just realized that I'm no longer in the company of my friends.

"What the hell...guys, this isn't funny." I look around and can't seem to grasp where exactly I am. "Okay, this isn't funny." No one answers me. I walk outside and realize that I'm at my house but my dad's in the front yard talking to some kid.

"Listen, you have to be careful with certain things. Just because you're a kid still doesn't mean that things can't happen to you." Then out of the front door, comes my mom with lemonade and snacks.

"Okay you two, let's take a break and go back to working on the fence later. Hayden, come outside and help your dad out please."

"Wait, if that kid isn't me, then who is it?" I know that I can't be seen, yet again. So, I continue to listen in to their conversation.

"Mom, can we go play?" I say, but I look like I'm about seven.

"Only for a few minutes, and please you both be very careful." She hands a lemonade to my dad and they both watch me and this random kid.

"So, what are we going to do now? Hayden doesn't know what he will be and then we have..."

"Hun, Hayden won't know until later, I'm probably going to tell him when he's closer to 16. As for him..."

"Hayden needs to know what's happening to him and his friend."

I look at both of them, totally confused as I'm not sure what memory this is. I keep listening."

"What are we going to tell Hayden? That's he's a warlock like me and his potential best friend might be someone that hunts him later in life?"

"WHAT! That kid, Vaughn?" I sit down on the grass and keep listening.

"Connor, we don't know what Vaughn really is yet. We know that something happened to him when he was younger, but we have to keep an eye out for him. Hayden can never know his best friend's a..."

"Oh c'mon, what the hell is Vaughn?" This is nuts, Vaughn can't be something supernatural, can he?

"Listen, we have time and right now they are both just kids."

"Yeah, but what happens when Hayden turns 16 and Vaughn goes into his fits."

"Then we take it one day at a time. Vaughn is a great kid, and we need to keep it that way."

The scene starts to fade out and I'm not quite sure what just happened. I don't want to leave this so-called memory, but it's pulling me out of this memory and then I'm done. I've entered someplace else.

"Yo Hayden, wait up." Vaughn says. It looks like we just started freshman year of high school.

"What's going on?" I say to Vaughn.

"Are you going to tell me what happened the other night?" Me, Hayden, at 14, looks over at Vaughn.

"Nothing happened, dude. Not sure what you saw."

"Dude, you started to glow and then you kind of just fell flat on your face. I thought maybe you had too much vodka."

"Oh yeah, it was totally the vodka. I don't even remember what happened." We both start to walk into the school. Vaughn, 14, looks back toward this random car. He waits until I'm gone, and sprints over to the car.

"I told you to leave me alone." He talks to a random stranger.

"You can't escape from us. We will always find you. We know what you are."

"What the hell is he?" I say, as me, 16. The scene starts to fade out yet again and I'm being pulled back to another location. I realize, though, that there's something going on with Vaughn, and I never noticed before. I'm currently falling for what seems like a long time, when I hit Waverly's lawn, in present time and I see her kissing Vaughn on the lips.

"What the SHIT!" I say.

"Fuck!" Vaughn and Waverly say at the same time.

CHAPTER 7

I'm standing in the middle of the lawn, witnessing my best friend kissing the girl of my dreams. They slowly pull apart from each other and no words are exchanged.

"Someone want to tell me what the hell is going on?" I say, anger is clear in my voice.

"Hayden, we were just..." Waverly looks so embarrassed.

"What, you've never seen two people kissing before? It's called making a move." Vaughn says, with no filter and a bit of anger in his voice.

"Well, don't let me keep you. By all means keep kissing one another while I figure out how the hell I time traveled." I'm just annoyed now.

"I can't believe you're a time traveler alongside being a warlock. Hayden, where did you go?" Waverly asks, easing the tension.

"Like either of you care. I'm going to go for a walk to clear my head." I start to make my way past them when Vaughn takes my arm and pulls me toward him.

"Stop being an ass. So, you saw us kiss, big deal. Now what, you're not going to talk to us because of it?"

"Let go of my arm, Vaughn." I warn him with my tone.

"Or what? You going to disappear again on us?" He looks dead into my eyes. "Where did you go anyway?"

"I said, let go. If you must know, I went to what looked like the past. I saw things that don't make any sense." I pull away from Vaughn's grip with force. "Oh, and to top that all off, you were there with me, Vaughn, and so were my parents."

"With you where? Where did you go?" Vaughn says, trying to

care.

"The year before he disappeared. Do you remember that summer at all?" I ponder if he will remember.

"How the hell do you think I'd remember something from that long ago?" He says.

"Forget it. Come to think of it-they were talking an awful lot about you. I guess my question for you is, what are you?"

"What do you mean, what am I?" Vaughn looks at me like I'm the one with all the issues. "I'm human, just like Waverly and yourself, at least I think you're human. Why does any of that matter?"

"Don't bullshit me. You've been acting so odd lately, and it's not because I found out that you're in love with Waverly. You've been having weird, dropped calls; you don't answer me when I'm trying to reach you. There is a mysterious car always lurking in the shadows. So, I'm going to ask you one more time, what are you?"

"Hayden, what in the world are you talking about? There's nothing wrong or different about Vaughn. Now stop being so weird and blaming him for whatever it is that happened." Waverly starts to walk toward me. I quickly put up my hand in frustration, a clear glow leaves my hands, and she can't move.

"STOP THAT! Hayden, let her go." I look toward my hands and see this clear glow.

"I don't know how I'm doing this." I glance over at Waverly who is clearly scared. "This is awesome."

"Hayden, let me go. Stop doing this, please. You're hurting me." she says, with pain in her voice.

"Ahh both of you, stop telling me what to do. You of all people should know how much I care about you, Waverly. Instead, all you do is kiss my best friend, probably to get back at me for liking you. Then there's Josh, who God knows why you are even with that loser. But why should I care, it's not like I've been in love with you or anything. But, kiss Vaughn, have a happy life. I'm just a freakin' warlock about to blow my brains out because I have no idea what I'm capable of."

"That is not true. Vaughn and I have a history, and yes, I do still have feelings for him. I'm sorry that you didn't tell me sooner how you felt. I don't know who I want. I like all of you and it's awfully hard for me to choose just one."

"WOW, that's a load of bullshit. I never expected this of you. Of all people, Waverly." My invisible grip on her neck, gets tighter. She struggles, but I'm so angry that I can't control it. Vaughn looks over at me, then back at Waverly.

"I need you to stop, Hayden. You're going to kill her. HAYDEN, STOP!" Vaughn runs toward me and pummels me to the ground. My clear glowing grip is no longer on her neck. She takes in a deep breath holding her neck, terrified of me. "What is wrong with you? Can't you see that you were hurting her?"

"Waverly, I'm so sorry. Something came over me and I don't know what happened." She puts up her hand and backs away from me.

"Don't come near me. I'm sorry that you are going through this. I can't even imagine what you're going through, but I can't be around you right now." I have no words.

"Let's go, Waverly. Hayden, I think you need some time to process what you've just done." Before I can even retaliate, they both get into Vaughn's car and drive away, leaving me in the background.

***

Waverly and Vaughn are in the car driving away. They both look at one another and quickly look away. Waverly rubs her neck, where the invisible grip was.

"Are you okay?" Vaughn keeps staring at the road, waiting for a response of some sort.

"Not really." She gives him a short answer.

"You have to talk to me or else I can't understand what you're feeling." Vaughn says, later realizing that he's being such a girl in this situation.

"Did that really just happen? Did we really just make out and then witness Hayden with a new power?"

"Are you regretting making out with me?" Vaughn ponders.

"I don't usually regret things in life. But it was wrong. We shouldn't be doing this, especially knowing Hayden's feelings, and OMG Josh."

"Oh jeez, dump his ass. I'm not just saying that because of us. I'm saying that for you. Stop stringing him along and just be done with it."

"Easier said than done. But what are we going to do about Hayden? He scared the shit out of me." Vaughn starts to reach for her, she jumps, and he backs away.

"I honestly think his emotions are attached to his powers, whatever else they may be. I'm afraid that every new affection he comes across, something retaliates and becomes scary dangerous. We have to help him, no matter how pissed we are at him." Vaughn turns right down Waverly's Street.

"You're right we have to help him. I'm afraid of him, though. What if he has the capability of killing someone? One of us? How do we protect ourselves?"

"We just have to learn what his powers are, and possibly study them to help him out. Oh, and not piss him off in the process." Vaughn can't help but laugh a little. He parks the car, they both stare at each other. Almost like they have no idea what is going to happen next. Waverly opens her car door. "Look, before you head inside, can we..."

"Talk about the moment we had?" Waverly finishes his sentence.

"Yes, if that's cool with you. I just don't want to, you know, waste my time if things don't go the way it's looking."

"Oh, so I'd be a waste of time then." She smirks and gets out of the car.

"Ugh, no, that's not what I meant. Damnit. Women!" Vaughn gets out of the car and walks to the other side and slams Waverly's door shut. "There's something here."

"There is something here, but we shouldn't even cross that path. We had our moment a long time ago, and now we just have to focus on Hayden and how we can help him." Vaughn moves in very close to Waverly, to the point where their noses are almost touching. Before Waverly can say anything else, Vaughn leans in and kisses her on the lips. She doesn't pull away. They keep kissing for a moment until a black car pulls up. Waverly pushes him away forcefully.

"Shit, its Josh." she says, wiping the saliva off her lips.

"You've got to be shitting me. He drives a black Jaguar; can you be anymore douche." Vaughn starts to laugh as Josh gets out of the car.

"Hey babe, who's this tool?"

"What did you just call me?" Vaughn's not having it with this idiot.

"Oh, you heard me. First you hang around my girl and then kiss her. Not sure she wants that." Waverly gets in the middle of them before someone throws a punch.

"Josh, stop. Yes, I kissed him, and he kissed me back. So, as far as I know, you're a complete ass and I'm done with you. So, let's just call it like it is. We're not good together."

"Oh no, you don't break up with me...I break up with you, you slut." Vaughn winds up and throws the biggest punch at Josh. He knocks him to the ground, blood gushes from his nose.

"You asshole." Josh says, covering his nose and mouth as he rapidly gets into his car, rolls the window down, and drives away middle finger up in the air.

"YOU SUCK YOU PUNK-ASS BITCH." Vaughn yells at Josh as he peels away in his Jaguar. "Show him who's boss. What a prick." Waverly just stands there staring at Vaughn.

"You just punched him. You just..." Vaughn interrupts her.

"Listen, if you're going to say that I shouldn't have punched him, then just save it. I did you a favor."

"That was so hot." She takes him in and kisses him like no other. She pushes him to the ground, and she straddles him kissing him with force.

"Wait, wait, wait. Is this really happening?" She looks at him and nods her head, yes. "We should go inside then, too many prying eyes." Vaughn says. Waverly nods and they both run toward the door and up to her room. She throws him on the bed, straddling him yet again and rips his shirt off. Naturally there's a lovely six-pack awaiting her.

"Holy shit." she says, covering her mouth as she didn't want to say that out loud.

"What, did I do something to hurt you?" Waverly laughs.

"No, no! You have abs." Vaughn smirks and kisses her again, flipping her onto her back. He takes her shirt off and stares at her. With awe he can't help but crack the biggest smile. She sits up and unhooks her bra, leaving him now in charge. They continue to kiss and strip down. He slowly reaches to her pants, unbuttons the top of her jeans, and slides them off.

"You are beautiful." They continue to kiss and more.

***

A few minutes after I saw Vaughn and Waverly peel out of here, I get so heated that I don't even realize my anger left a small hole in my front yard. I look at it and decide that there is nothing I can really do about it. I'm about to walk into my house, when I see a black car approach my front yard. Without hesitation, I walk toward it. The car gently pulls away and turns down the next street. I run after it but lose sight of it. Luckily, I got a glimpse of their license plate.

"I've got you now!" I head into the house and quickly jot down the number of the license down. As soon as I write the last number down, my cell phone vibrates. Thinking it's Vaughn, I let it ring a few more times.

"Hello, this is Hayden." I wait to hear whoever is on the other line.

"Hi Hayden, this is Doctor Gregory. Just wanted to let you know that we have your mom back in stable condition, and she will only talk to you now. Would you mind coming down to room 321. Thank you." I hang up the phone, grab my sweatshirt, and start walking toward the bus. I don't want to call Vaughn or Waverly. As I'm walking, a dark blue Acura pulls up next to me. I keep walking, not sure who is tailing me.

"Yo, Hayden." I keep walking, as I still can't recognize the voice. "Hayden, it's me, Kyne." I stop dead in my tracks because I haven't heard that name in a long time.

"Kyne, what are you doing here? I thought you left to go…" I don't finish my sentence, as I remember that we were just in his secret hideaway. Plus, pretty sure he didn't leave to go abroad like he intended to, so I didn't finish my sentence. He pulls the car over and gets out. Walking toward me, he takes his hand out and gives me a firm shake.

"Never really made it to Europe. There were some things here that I had to take care of. Plus, I didn't want to leave Waverly all alone in our house." Kyne, if you didn't realize this before, is Waverly's older brother.

"I'm sorry that your plans didn't work out. It's great to see you, though. So, what brings you on my doorstep or close to it?"

"Well, I wanted to ask you something, and don't, like, freak out." Great, another thing that I must deal with. I listen intently to what he has to say.

"So, as you know, when my parents died, I started to notice a bunch of patterns happening in this town. The one thing that I started to figure out, was your family. I know that I might be a little weird and whatnot, but I started to study the patterns of hunters and the supernatural. I noticed one day, when Waverly came over a while back, that there was something off about your house and your dad. Now I'm not an expert in the supernatural at all, but there was definitely something strange and magical about your house." I stare at him not knowing what or how to respond. Is he about to say what I think he's going to say? Does he know that I'm a warlock or that my dad was? I mean, I know all about his "supernatural" ghost hunting whatever you want to call it. But I never actually thought that he would be saying all these things out loud to me. I realize that I've been holding my breath the entire time he's been trying to explain what he thinks is happening. "Long story short, ever since I saw your dad move an object with his mind, I had to know how. I had to study the mystical and supernatural. It consumed me, until one day I stumbled into your dad. I knew he was different, and I asked him if he needed help. Hayden, I saw him get captured and taken. There was nothing I could do to help him. He trusted me with his secrets and now I need to know-are you like him?" All I can do is let out the massive air from my lungs. I think I'm about to pass out, here is Kyne, who I haven't seen in probably five years, who is telling me that he knew what my dad was and tried to help. Not only was my mind racing to the fact that, he pretty much knows what I am... but how weird is it that not only a few hours ago, Waverly had brought us down to his secret lair where we discovered what *he* is. I'm stumped, it's all a weird coincidence. My brain is going a million miles an hour, and I don't realize that my hands are bright red and starting to light up with fire. Before I can tuck them away from Kyne, he grabs my hands.

"You are just like your dad. I thought you would have been like him, but what's the extent of your power?"

"How can I trust you?" Kyne gives me a nod in agreement. "How will I know that you're not going to just tell everyone what I am?"

"You can trust me, Hayden. I'm not going to tell a soul. Plus, who will believe me that you are what you say you are?" He smiles as he lets go of my arm. "Sorry, this just fascinates me. You are by far the only warlock I can say that is still living and young. May I ask what your powers are?"

"You have to promise me that you will never ever tell anyone what I am. Promise me!" I say, with anger toward him.

"I promise, on my sisters' life. Hayden, you can trust me. I want to help you and possibly get to know what you're capable of."

"So far, I can light things on fire using my hands. I just recently developed a clear glow stopping people from approaching me. Let's see…Oh found out that I created a hole in my front yard because I got super angry." Kyne interrupts me.

"Hold up, you can create a glow?" I smile because I have someone that I can share things with and not be judged. "Okay, I'm listening, what else?"

"Oh, the most recent one, I can time travel." I wait for his response.

"You can time travel? Do you have control over it? Can you, like, pick a time and place and then bam, you are there?" Kyne is leaning toward his car, fascinated.

"I don't actually know how I've been doing it. I have no control over it. I think it's whenever I get upset, my body tells me that it's time to go someplace else. For example, I've been to the past and future. Actually, just about a few hours ago, I went to the past when I was seven. I found this weird box in my room and once I opened it, I traveled into the future. I saw some scary things that I can't even explain. Wait, now that I think of it, what the hell is wrong with me?" I let out a deep breath, that I didn't know again I was holding in.

"Hayden, you are a wonderful creature. Do you realize how

many people would kill for your powers? To travel back in time and see things unfold or to even know what the future holds. Can you tell me more?"

"I can, but I need to go see my mom. Do you mind giving me a lift?" Kyne smiles and opens the door for me. We start driving toward the hospital. Kyne parks his car and we both get out. I don't tell him otherwise, as he follows me into the hospital. I walk into my mom's room, Kyne behind me. He pulls me aside for a moment.

"Does she know what you are?"

"Yes, both my parents told me before...." Kyne looks at me and understands. My mom is wide awake and looks over at Kyne. It's the first time that I've seen her smile since my dad was back.

"Oh sweetheart, you came back?" I thought she was talking to me, but she reached her hand out to Kyne and he took it. I'm completely in shock. How is this even happening?

"I never wanted to leave you both. Hayden is immensely powerful from what he tells me." Kyne says. My mom looks over at me, shocked.

"Hayden, you already know about your powers? Oh honey, I'm so sorry that you don't have your dad here to help you in these times. I need you to be careful, you are capable of so much, I can't even begin to tell you." She slowly gets up from the bed. "Will you grab my bag on the other side of the room?" I grab her bag, not knowing what she's going to tell me. "Your dad wanted to give you this." She hands me a piece of paper, but it's blank. I pass it to Kyne, and he looks over at it.

"Is this it?" I examine it and look at my mom.

"Yes, guard it with everything you have, Hayden. It's the one thing that holds your secrets." I look over at it, it's literally an old parchment paper.

"Mom, there's nothing on here. It's blank." She smiles.

"You have to unlock it with a certain power, your dad cursed it so only you could see the words." I'm in shock. They were prepping me for some war. To think that I only knew about my powers for a few months now. I wondered what the piece of paper in my hand really meant. Kyne looked at it and then said his goodbyes, waiting by the door.

"Sweetheart, if something should ever happen to me, just be careful in who you tell things to about yourself. Kyne, helped your dad before. We were skeptical at first, but he brought more information to us. Your dad would be so proud of you. Just please be careful, as I think someone might be after you as well. Kyne, I know I can trust you, so please take care of my boy. Hayden, watch out for what might be of you know who."

I look at her, and I have no idea what she is talking about. "Watch out for who?"

"Just be on the lookout." My mom starts to close her eyes.

"Kyne, if you know so much about my family, who was after my dad to kill him?"

"I have no clue. All I know is that I was summoned to help you in any way I can. It's like I was called up for duty. I'm what you might call your sidekick." I start to laugh.

"Sidekick, I'm not some superhero here. I can't just trust you and have you followed me around. Plus, there's your sister and my best friend that already know."

"WAIT, you told my sister?" Kyne shakes his head. "She was never supposed to be involved with any of this."

"Dude, no sense in hiding things from her. She already knows about your secret door and hideaway." He slams his hand on the door. "Sorry."

"Damnit, now I have to protect her from things." I feel horrible now telling him this.

"Okay, since you are going to be my 'sidekick' I need a few things answered." Kyne walks out of the room, and into the creepy long hallway. He points to the door to the right, and we both walk in. He looks around the room, checking to make sure there's no cameras or microphones.

"Coast is clear. I guess you can ask me whatever you'd like. I do owe you that much." He says.

"You owe me a lot more than that. Okay, first question is...why were you looking into my family?" I look at him, but he doesn't seem to budge and just answers my questions, like it's nothing.

"Ever since my parents died, I felt like I had no purpose. Not a lot of people know this about me, but I did go to school to study alchemy. I know, it's a weird subject, but I was convinced that my parents' death wasn't an accident. So, I tried to study as much as I could, while taking care of Waverly. It wasn't easy, let me tell you." I had no words, I didn't know anything about Kyne, and this was my chance to find out all.

"Are you in fact a supernatural hunter? Do I have to be worried that you'll turn on me and then kill me?" I had to ask, knowing fully now that he was an actual hunter.

"Oh God, Hayden, I would never hurt you or your family. Yes, I do hunt supernatural things, but only ones that are harmful to others."

"One last question for now, and then I'd like to go home." I wait until he gives me the approval for one last question of the day. "My mom said that I need to watch out for something, or possibly someone...what does she mean?"

"I can't really come to understand that one. She thinks that someone was after your dad and that's why he was killed. So perhaps she's taking the same scenario and protecting you before it's too late." I looked toward him and all I can think about is when I suddenly jumped into the past and my dad was talking to Vaughn and me.

"Promise, this is the last thing I want to ask you." Kyne looks at me but doesn't seem to mind the 20 questions. "When I went to the past, something bothered me a bit. My dad thinks that Vaughn is something supernatural or well maybe I'm the one who's thinking about that. Do you know anything about that?"

"Vaughn, supernatural? I don't think so. I haven't really looked into him or his family at all. I mean, I know he's been really close with Waverly recently, but other than that...nothing." Just the fact that he even knew about Waverly and Vaughn becoming closer, made my blood boil. I started to just get really agitated thinking about it. Kyne started to notice that my hands were lighting up red, and that I was getting angry. He touched my arm and then the next thing I knew, I was someplace else, Kyne in tow.

"What the hell just happened, Hayden?"

"Welcome to Time Travel 101. I guess I know what triggers it now. It seems like every time I get angry, my body decides that it's time to leave this universe and enter another one." Kyne looks around, but he doesn't really understand because we're in the same exact place as we left. I open the door and walk into that same creepy hallway, which is now very vibrant. I hear a nurse calling from another room.

"Nurse Kristy, can you just come and check on this patient. It looks like we might just have a mild concussion." Without hesitation, Kyne and I walk into that same room. We look at a familiar person laying on the bed.

"Vaughn?" I say, shocked. Kyne looks at me.

"Wait, can he hear us?" Kyne asks.

"As far as I know, no one can hear me when I'm in another time or place. So, let's figure out why my other self decided to come to this moment." Kyne is beyond fascinated by what has happened, but he doesn't seem to be fazed at all.

"This is outstanding, Hayden. Not only have I been studying certain philosophies and/or witchcraft, but I never even imagined that someone would be capable of time travel without thinking about a destination or time period. Can you guess when and where this is?"

"From the looks of it, this is when Vaughn broke his leg skateboarding down the street to impress yet another girl. I remember it clearly now because the nurses couldn't figure out his blood type." Kyne walks over to the chart and looks at his medical history. "Yeah, this was the day that he did some weird move off his board and landed flat on his side. I had to call 911. But where am I now?"

"It says here, that according to his 'blood work' it says that he has no blood type. That doesn't make any sense. The only way someone doesn't have a blood type is if they're... Oh shit."

"What? If they're what?" I ask taking the clipboard from him.

"I read about this in my studies, the rarest blood type of mankind or-of any kind is called, 'the golden blood.' Hayden, it has never been found in a human before. Vaughn has it. You were brought to this moment for a reason. Think about it."

"You're right, I was in the waiting room because the doctors didn't want me in there. What the hell does all this mean, Kyne?"

"I don't know, and maybe it's time that we confront Vaughn about it." I drop the clipboard back to its holder and walk out the door.

"I tried to ask him the other day, all he did was yell at me. Then I got super angry because well, something else was going on." Kyne looks at me, and I give him the "I don't want to talk about it" look. We both leave the room and then all of a sudden, we are back in that same hallway, but creepy again.

"Well, looks like we're back to real time." I say, then Kyne walks out of the hospital and into his Acura. "Listen kid, there's a lot we need to figure out. Hop in and let's take a ride to my house. No one should be there. I know Waverly is most likely at Josh's house." Just the thought of his name makes me upset, but I must calm down just in case I transport someplace else again. We start to drive away and head toward his house.

***

Meanwhile, Waverly and Vaughn are lying in bed, naked. Waverly has the sheets covered over herself, while Vaughn does not. They both can't look at each other.

"I don't know..." Waverly starts to say before Vaughn interrupts her.

"It was worth it, if you're having second thoughts." She leans over onto her side and looks at him.

"Was it, though? Am I supposed to feel like this? We're only 17 and I just don't know." Waverly says, scared of what just happened.

"Seems like you regretted it when you clearly stated that you don't regret things. I'm not the one who started kissing on the grass. If I recall…"

"Don't be an ass about it, Vaughn. It was something in the moment and now I don't know if it was the right move. I care so much about you and yes, I do like you. We just have so much to focus on Hayden is someone that needs our help and here we are just having sex."

"Was it just sex for you? Cause I'm not trying to be all girly here, but I thought what we did was more than that. But, what the fuck do I know, I'm just, like you said, a 17-year-old who doesn't really know things."

"That's not fair, I'm trying to express my feelings and think that Hayden really needs our help." She says, moving away from him in bed.

"For the love of…can you for one hot second not think about Hayden. Are you just in love with him as well?"

"AHHH, stop putting words into my mouth. I don't know who I like. I like you both, why do I have to choose?"

"Choose! Really, so you want to have sex with both of us then?" Vaughn gets so angry that he climbs out of bed, butt naked and looks at Waverly. "Do you want this or not?" Waverly doesn't answer and gets out of bed, pulls him back in close and kisses him passionately.

"I don't want to choose Vaughn." Vaughn stops kissing her.

"You have to, you can't have your cake and eat it, too." Vaughn kisses her again, and they start to have sex. A few minutes later, they both shower and go downstairs to grab some food.

"Promise me something, Vaughn." He nods, as he shoves a piece of bread in his mouth. "We shall never, ever tell Hayden that we slept together again."

"Why, he's my best friend?"

"Seriously?" She says, with an angry look on her face.

"Alright, secret is safe with me." They both smile at one another when Vaughn's cell phone rings. He walks outside and takes the call.

"Vaughn here." He waits until he realizes who is calling him.

"Did you do what I asked?" The stranger on the other line says.

"No, and I told you I want no part of it. Leave me alone."

"You can't escape what you signed up for. It's the way we are. Get in the car." Vaughn takes the phone away from his ear and looks out toward the driveway. He sees a white SUV.

"I'm not going anywhere with you." Vaughn looks over at the SUV.

"Vaughn, get in the car, now or your girlfriend gets it!" The line cuts, and Vaughn looks over at the house and thinks of Waverly. He has no choice but to leave. He looks back again and then runs toward the white SUV. He gets in, slams the door, and the car peels away. Waverly hears something, and then runs outside as she sees the car pull away.

"VAUGHN!" She starts to panic.

Vaughn scared, is sitting in the SUV across from an unidentifiable shadow figure.

"I gave you one job, and you haven't done it. Beta, I warned you not to get attached." He hands Vaughn a piece of paper. "This is what I want done, and if you can't deliver it, then I will kill her."

"Don't you dare touch a hair on her. I will kill you myself." The car comes to a complete halt.

"You dare speak to me like that. Watch it boy." Vaughn gets

tense and doesn't say another word. The car continues to drive away.

***

Waverly is screaming and crying at the same time. She has no choice but to call the one person she can trust. Her brother. She dials his number. It rings, and he answers.

"Waverly, are you alright?" She's hyperventilating.

"Kyne, they took him. They took him." I can somehow hear every word that she is saying. I look over at Kyne, and he realized that I could hear her.

"Who took who? Where are you?"

"I'm home. Kyne, I don't know what to do. I need your help, please!" She hangs up and Kyne steps on the gas pedal.

"New power kick in, I'm assuming?" I look at Kyne and take in a deep breath.

"How are they all coming in at once? Super hearing is now in full effect." I lean my head on the side, as I take in the cool breeze from the open window. "I know who she's talking about."

"How?" Kyne stares at me. "What gives you this knowledge?"

"It's a feeling I have, and to be honest, I've had it since I was a kid. I can weirdly feel that something is wrong with him."

"Spill it, Grant, who?"

"Vaughn. He's scared, and for some reason I can feel it." Kyne just keeps driving and doesn't ask me anymore questions. We arrive shortly to his house. He gets out of the car and runs toward Waverly, who is sitting on the front steps.

"What happened, Wav?" She starts to tear up and then sees me coming.

"What's he doing here?" I look at her, hurt.

"He's with me. What happened?" I sit down near her and try to make sense of it all.

"Waverly, I know this is hard, but you need to trust us so we can help you. Kyne and I are here for you." She smiles at me and then starts to talk.

"He went out of the house to take a phone call. I went out to follow him and he sounded scared on the phone. Then suddenly, I turned my back for one minute and a white SUV peeled out. He just vanished and I'm afraid someone is trying to hurt him." She starts to cry in my arms. I know now that she does really care about him.

"We're going to find him, Waverly. I promise you." I hug her and Kyne looks at both of us.

"Hayden, can I speak to you for a second?" I get up and walk toward Kyne. "Something happened with her and Vaughn, right?"

"Yeah, I saw them kissing when I came back from the past and I'm sure he spent the night. But I don't care anymore, we need to find Vaughn." I did care, but this was not a time to get angry and I didn't want to vanish again.

"Can you control your emotions?" I look at him and nod, yes.

"Waverly, I need you to tell me everything that happened prior to Vaughn's kidnapping." She starts to talk about what happened and how she witnessed the car and saw them turn down a street. I wasn't really paying attention, as I was trying to piece things together in my head, when something odd happened. *"Hayden, help me. I'm sorry for everything I've done to you. I hate to admit this, but I'm afraid of what he will do to me if I don't do what he tells me. Look at me standing here thinking that you'd hear me. I know you're a warlock and all, but you don't have the power to hear my thoughts no matter what. You are my best friend and no matter what anyone tells me or forces me to do, I'll never harm you. I made that promise and I'm always going to keep it. No matter what! Ugh this is so pointless. Shit!!! Let me go. I told you I'm not going to get the information you need on him. Leave me alone. Harm me, do what you must, but there is no way I'm going to ever listen to him again. He's hurt me in so many ways, experimented on me and I can't take it anymore. I'm not some lab rat for him. So you tell him, that if he wants me to do anything, then he will just have to kill me first. Stop it, STOP! Okay, okay you win! Please, don't hurt her and I'll do what you say. HAYDEN HELP ME!"*

Both Waverly and Kyne see the look on my face and rush to my side before I pass out.

"Hayden, oh God, Hayden, can you hear me?" Waverly is holding my head and pushing my hair back. She leans in and plants a kiss on my cheek. Kyne just watches her, not saying a word. "Hayden, come back to me. I can't lose you, too." I slowly wake up. "Oh, thank God, don't scare us like that."

"What happened?" I say, getting up slowly.

"You passed out. Did something happen?" Kyne looks at me and whispers, "magically."

"I heard him. Kyne, I heard Vaughn; he spoke to me." Kyne smiled as he knew another power came into play.

"What do you mean, you heard him?" Waverly looks at me and then at Kyne. "Is there something I should know, more than your warlock stuff?" Kyne starts to laugh.

"He should have never told you what he was." Kyne comes to my side and lifts me up. "Could you tell where he was?"

"No, I could only hear him, but it doesn't sound good. It seems like he's being forced to do something, and he doesn't want to do it. He said, not to harm her and he will do what he's asked."

"That means what?" Waverly puzzled, gets up and starts walking toward Kyne's car. "Well, what are we waiting for! Let's go."

"Waverly, we don't know where he is. We can't just blindly search for him." Kyne says, I look at him and then back at Waverly.

"Let's go find him." I give Kyne a look as Waverly heads toward the car.

"We can't find him this way." he says.

"Yeah, I know that, but what other choice do we have. I can't let my best friend kill something to protect someone else."

"What if…" Kyne says, but I get in the car, and we start driving.

***

Vaughn is now in a tiny windowless room. "You can't keep me here. I told you I would do what you've asked." He bangs on the cement wall.

"You have to learn to obey me, no matter what. I'm your master." The mysterious man says.

"Screw you then, I don't want a master, and I never asked to be this. So, let me go." He continues to pound on the wall.

"You have no choice, you are what you are, it's in your blood and that's final. So, stop fussing around and don't ever piss me off again. Understood?"

"Yes, Dad." Vaughn sits there and then starts to fade into a black figure.

CHAPTER 8

Waverly and I are currently crammed inside Kyne's tiny blue Acura.

"Driving around is not going to bring him back, you know that, right?" Kyne says looking through the rear-view mirror at Waverly.

"It's better than sitting on our assess and doing nothing at home. I should have done more. I should not have left him. But how was I supposed to know that someone would come take him off my lawn. What was I thinking?" She takes in a deep breath, almost having a panic attack.

"It's not your fault. You can't blame yourself for something that was out of your control." I tell her, trying to also convince myself that I wasn't to blame for all of it either. Kyne steps on the gas pedal and continues driving.

"Can you hear anything else from Vaughn?" Kyne says, looking at me.

"Nothing. I can't even feel his presence. Something must be going on, that I can't feel him." I can tell Waverly is scared about what's happening with Vaughn. Sitting in silence, we seem to drive to what looks like nowhere.

***

Vaughn is lying face first in the same cell that he has been trapped in for days. He's very frail and can't seem to stand up easily.

"Are you ready to do what I ask, now?" His dad says.

"I'm not going to feed you any information on my friends. They are regular humans and have nothing to do with your stupid-ass Society."

"Don't you dare talk about that with me. This Society is part of your history, and you will respect it. It runs in the family and in your blood. Why do you think you are capable of so much?"

"Maybe because I'm actually a smart kid and don't follow your orders. AHH, just leave me alone. I don't want to be a part of this family any longer." Vaughn tries to get up, but he can't. His dad walks into the cell, lifts him up and throws him on the bench.

"Turn." He looks directly at Vaughn, but Vaughn can't seem to give him an answer. "I said, TURN!"

"Fuck you. I'm not doing a thing. Get out!" Vaughn slowly gets up and tries to punch his dad in the face. He misses and his dad punches him back.

"If you will not turn, then I have no choice to go after the ones you love. Waverly seems like a good target. Hayden, well, since he's an all-powerful warlock, I can't seem to get close enough to him...yet." Vaughn spits out the blood from his mouth.

"How do you know about Hayden?" Vaughn asks, as his dad gives him a smirk, and lifts his hand up to punch him again. "Go ahead, try your worst. Do what you need to do on me, they have no idea what or who I am." His dad smiles and then closes the cell doors again.

"They will soon. If you don't turn, things will be very ugly for you." His dad leaves and Vaughn runs up toward the cell door and pounds on it.

"You will never make me turn on command. NEVER!" He falls to his knees and cries. Vaughn has never been in so much pain. He doesn't know how he will escape his dad's realm. *Hayden, I need your help!*

***

"Stop the car." I say, as Kyne slams on the breaks. I get out of the car, possibly thinking that maybe I can somehow communicate with Vaughn.

"What's happening?" Waverly asks, looking at her brother, but she doesn't get out of the car.

"Did you hear him again?" Kyne asks, as I nod my head in agreement.

"I think it's only a one-way street. There's no way that he would respond back to me if he was human. Unless..." I look at Kyne. "Here goes nothing." I take in a deep breath and respond to Vaughn. "Vaughn, dude, can you hear me?" Silence. "I'm not sure where you are, you need to give me a clue." Still silence. Waverly gets out of the car, slams the door, and looks at me.

"What are you even doing? Seems like you're talking to yourself." She doesn't really care about me, and why would she. "What's the point in doing that. We need to find Vaughn." I start to get upset, as she's just annoying the hell out of me.

"Waverly, you need to back away." She doesn't move. "I mean it, back AWAY!" I'm yelling at her, because I know what's about to happen.

"Hayden, you need to calm down. Don't get upset, you know what happens when you get upset." Kyne says, without trying to be annoying as well.

"Both of you need to just shut up or else I won't be able to concentrate." Waverly rolls her eyes.

"Please, like you're going to save the day. All that's happened since you told us that you're a so-called 'warlock' is well, nothing. Except for your mini seizure of time travel and whatever you forced out of your freaky hands to command me." Kyne takes a hold of

Waverly and pushes her toward the car.

"Are you freakin' serious! He's a warlock, and his powers are so fresh that we have no idea what's going to happen. You can't irk him, Waverly." Kyne says, still holding onto her.

"I can do whatever I want. Why do you suddenly have so much interest in Hayden? You have barely been home to even care about me. But nooooo when you find out something about Hayden, you rush to his aid. You know what, I don't need any of your help. I'm going to find Vaughn on my own." Before she even takes a step, my clear glow is back and I'm holding both Kyne and Waverly in my grip. They are pinned to the car.

"I told you both to shut the hell up. One more word out of you, Waverly, and this grip will only get tighter. Don't test me! Kyne, we have a lot to talk about, but she's right. I don't think I fully trust you. Now, can I get some quiet here?"

"Screw you, Hayden. You've only caused trouble for all of us." Waverly starts to choke, as my grip gets tighter. Then I hear it again, *"Hayden, you need to help me. I'm not safe here. Please, I hope that you can hear me."* I start to get angry. "BOTH OF YOU JUST STOP" The pressure on Waverly now is gone, Kyne is holding his neck and they both look at one another.

"Where did he go?" Waverly looks over at her brother.

"I told you not to get him upset."

***

Meanwhile, back in the cell, Vaughn is huddled in the corner. Suddenly, a massive gust of wind appears, and I'm sitting on the opposite side of him.

"Hayden, what the..." Vaughn tries to get up, but can't move. "Dude, you can't be here. How did you get here?"

"I heard you. You were talking to me." Vaughn gets up and comes out of the shadow.

"You heard me talking to you? Is this another power? Hayden, this is amazing. But you can't be here, it's not safe." Vaughn comes up close to me. "You need to leave before he finds out that you're in here." I take a good look at him; he's covered in blood and new bruises.

"Who will find out that I'm in here? Where is here exactly? What is going on?" I have a million questions, when we both hear footsteps again.

"Shit, you need to really hide yourself. Hayden, NOW!" Someone comes up to the cell door and peers inside.

"I warned you to turn, and you haven't. We've been monitoring you. Be a nice boy and do what I've asked or we're going to kill someone you care about." The mysterious voice proceeds to taunt Vaughn.

"Empty threats, you keep saying that, but you haven't done a thing. I told you I will never turn for you and you can kiss my ass." The man on the other end chuckles. "Laugh it up, dude, but when I get out of here, I'm going to hunt your ass down and kill you." The man laughs even harder and walks away. A few seconds go by when I come out of the corner.

"Turn, what is he talking about, Vaughn?" He looks at me and takes a deep breath.

"I can't tell you. You aren't even supposed to be here. They know that you're a warlock and if they find you...Hayden, please, you have to leave me here."

"Who knows I'm a warlock? I told only you and Waverly. What did you do?"

"I didn't do a thing. Hayden, you have to trust me."

"How can I trust you. So many things have happened since. I can't even begin to tell you how upset I am. I need to get you out of here. Waverly is becoming a whole different person without you present. Her brother is paranoid, and here I am thinking that my best friend told someone about me. I just need to know something, what are you?"

"I told you I'm human." Vaughn comes out of the shadow. He doesn't hear the faint footsteps coming from the other side of the cell.

"Oh Vaughn, tell the truth now." I quickly go back into the shadows. "Hayden, you can come out. I'm very fascinated by you. Please, come out of the light so I can get a better look at you." Vaughn yells at me.

"Hayden, don't listen to him. He's just going to use you to gain power. You need to get out of here. I will explain all of this, but LEAVE."

"I'm not leaving without you." Vaughn looks over at his dad, then back at me.

"Fine, if you won't leave, then you and I will leave together." Before I can even ask him a question, Vaughn appears in the middle of the cell. "Take my hand, this may hurt and I'm so sorry about this." His dad investigates the cell, and fumbles to get his keys.

"Vaughn, don't you dare even think about it." His dad puts the key into the lock and is about to open the door.

"Are you ready?" I look at him, nodding yes. He takes my hand, turning black and into a shadow-like figure that's translucent. I squeeze tight and have a weird feeling in the pit of my stomach. I close my eyes, when I open them, we are in the middle of some street. He lets go of my hand, but I don't open my eyes.

"We made it." He says, and I slowly open my eyes. I look at him. "Don't look at me that way."

"What are you?" I do a quick circle around him, as his body still hasn't come back to being a solid figure.

"I never ever wanted you to find out about my family curse. Therefore, I needed to keep myself away from you. If some people were to find out certain things about you and your family, then they would have killed you. But now, it's too late. They know so much. I had no choice; they were going to kill Waverly."

"I asked you what you are, please don't make me repeat myself." He looks at me, afraid.

"I'm a shade." Vaughn comes back into human form. I just stare at him.

"A shade? What does that mean?" I'm honestly not even really fazed by all this, because apparently when you inherit my powers...nothing really compares.

"I'm not human and I'm not alive either." I don't really know how to respond.

"Not alive? I'm sorry, what?" I back away from him. Not because I'm afraid, but because I've never encountered something like this.

"Hayden, you have to understand this is my curse. To roam the earth as a creature of the Underworld. I couldn't tell you, but I needed to stay in human form to help." My hand flies up and my clear glow is back.

"Underworld, what the fuck, Vaughn. I tell you I'm a warlock and then all of a sudden, I find out that you're not even real. How am I supposed to process this? Tell me, did you know all along what I was?"

"No, honestly I had no idea. I told you this is my family's curse. That guy back in the cell, is my dad. If I don't do what he tells me, people I care for will die. I never wanted to get you involved. He somehow found out that you are a warlock, I'm not sure from who, but I can't protect you. Hayden, are you listening to me?"

"I'm listening, Vaughn. You expect me to believe that your dad is what...Hades, and that you are here to kill me or something? I knew something was off about you. Especially when I went back to the past and my dad was talking to my mom about you. They knew what you and your family were, and they still didn't tell me. AHHH what the hell is wrong with everyone?"

"Hayden, you need to calm down. Please, I don't want to hurt you." I laugh at him.

"You can't hurt me, Vaughn. There's nothing you can do to me. I'm a warlock and you are just a shadow that is from hell. You are hell, so back away from me or so help me..." Just like that I disappear again. This time thinking of Waverly and Kyne, I come right back to them. I slam into Kyne's car and fall to the ground.

"Hayden, are you okay? Where did you go? I'm sorry that I yelled at you." Waverly helps me up. I hold my head as Kyne comes to my side.

"What did you see?" I look at him and know that I can't tell them what Vaughn is.

"Nothing, it was all black and I was lost. I don't even know how I got back. Let's get out of here." I get into the car before Kyne can ask me questions. We start to drive, when Kyne pulls the car over.

"You went into a black hole?" I roll my eyes.

"I told you I got lost and didn't really remember where I was. Now can you just leave me be." Kyne doesn't give me a rebuttal. We keep driving back to their house. Minutes later, we pull up to the sidewalk. Waverly immediately gets out of the car and starts running toward her front door. Little did I know that someone was sitting on her steps, waiting. Not knowing who it is, I look over at Kyne and we both bolt after Waverly. She keeps running and the person gets up and starts running toward her.

"Waverly, STOP!" Kyne yells out. I try to use my mind to stop her, but I can't seem to do anything. I stop dead in my tracks and almost plant face down on the grass when I see who it is.

"Oh my God, Vaughn I was so worried about you. Where did you go? Are you hurt?" Waverly hugs him tight, as Vaughn looks in my direction. He whispers, "I'm sorry" and closes his eyes. Kyne looks over at me and then back at Vaughn.

"You went to him, didn't you?" Kyne says, glaring at me.

"Not now, Kyne. Please, it's been a day." He puts a hand on my shoulder and doesn't say a word after.

"Vaughn, would you like to come inside." Kyne says, I look toward Vaughn and back at Waverly. He looks sad.

"I think it's best that I go." Waverly grabs his hand.

"Where will you go?" She says.

"Home." Vaughn looks at me, and I look at Kyne. Vaughn starts to walk away, and Waverly runs after him and plants a kiss on his lips.

"I lo…" He walks away before she can say the L word. Waverly stays outside sitting on the front steps. Kyne and I walk into the house for a few minutes.

"Are you going to tell me what happened?" Kyne asks me.

"No." I respond.

"You still don't trust me? After everything and your mom's

word?"

"I can't trust anyone right now. I'm sorry. I need to go home." I walk out the door, leaving Kyne to wonder what secret I'm keeping.

"See you later, Waverly." I walk past her, without even caring about what happened with her and Vaughn or the fact that she was about to tell him she loved him.

"Where are you going?" She says, as she wipes tears from her eyes.

"I'm going home, I have a lot to process. I'll see you later." She gets up and walks toward me, like she's going to say something. She reaches her hand out and then pulls me in close, planting a small kiss on my cheek.

"What was that for?" I'm shocked she even did that.

"For helping Vaughn, and for you just being you." I don't know if I should be upset with her or just let this all go. I can't really win her over if she likes Vaughn. I don't say a word and walk back toward my house.

I arrive shortly, to find Vaughn waiting for me on my front steps. He looks nervous, as I approach.

"Can we talk?" Vaughn gets up and walks toward me.

"There's really nothing more that I can digest. I told you that I needed time."

"I'm sorry to say this dude, but you don't have much time. I warned you about my family and they will hunt you down, no matter what. Do you understand that!"

"Vaughn, I need you to leave."

"Hayden, I'm trying to help you."

"I SAID LEAVE!" I get so angry that my hands are now on fire and I blast a fireball right at Vaughn. He immediately ducks and turns back into his shade and vanishes. I watch as the fireball hits the ground and creates another hole in my front yard.

"Well, looks like I have to protect myself...from you." Vaughn says, coming back into human form.

CHAPTER 9

Kyne and Waverly are sitting in their kitchen, not saying a word to one another. Kyne doesn't know how to handle everything that's been happening, so he tries another approach.

"Are you in love with Vaughn?"

"I don't know, why does that even matter?" Waverly responds, with anger in her voice.

"Because you need to figure out who you care for, Wav. I know this is dumb coming from me, but you can't have them both."

"And you know about both, because?" Waverly crosses her arms in protest.

"Oh, come on Wav, it doesn't take a genius to figure out that you have feelings for both. They are both powerful, and you don't even know how to handle them."

"What do you mean powerful? I know Hayden's a warlock but..." Before she can continue her rant to her brother, someone arrives at their front door. Kyne immediately gets up, stands in front of Waverly and heads toward the door. He peeks through the hole, to find Hayden standing there. Kyne takes in a deep breath and opens the door.

***

"We need to talk." I say, pushing the door open and slamming it behind me.

"You're telling me! You say you don't trust me, but yet you're here. I think I have a right to know what's happening." Kyne looks toward me, angry. I look around the room.

"Is Waverly here?" Kyne nods and points toward the kitchen. "She can't be here when I tell you this." I make my way toward the kitchen. Waverly stands up and looks at me.

"Hi." That's all she has to say to me.

"Hi back. I'm sorry to do this to you, but can you go upstairs? I have to talk to your brother." She immediately feels offended.

"No, whatever you have to say to him, you can say to me." Kyne pulls her away.

"Waverly, go upstairs. We have things to talk about and it's not appropriate for a lady."

"Oh, screw you both. Fine, but don't think this gets you off the hook about Vaughn."

"UPSTAIRS!" Waverly gives her brother the middle finger and runs upstairs. She slams the door. I walk toward the bottom of the stairs and peek up to make sure she's not listening in.

"Okay, do you mind telling me what's going on." Kyne walks back and forth now in the kitchen.

"He's not human." Before I can keep going, he stops in his tracks.

"What do you mean he's not human? That doesn't make any sense." Kyne ponders.

"If you would let me finish, I can tell you. Jeez, between you, Vaughn, and Waverly you guys are driving me mental." I start to pace as well, but Kyne is now sitting at the kitchen table. "As I was saying, Vaughn, come to find out isn't human. He's something called a shade. Do you know what that is?"

Kyne rapidly gets up off the chair, causing it to fall behind him. He takes in a deep breath and walks toward the coffee maker. Taking in another deep breath he slowly turns around and gestures me to sit down. He pours two cups of coffee and then joins me at the table.

"So, you're telling me that Vaughn is a shade?"

"Isn't that what I just said?" I say, sarcastically.

"This isn't good. Of course, I know what a shade is. Greek mythology and all. Damnit, he can't be one of them. It's not possible. What did he tell you?"

"He didn't tell me anything, Kyne. We escaped from where they were holding him, as he turned into a black shade-like figure." I take a deep breath and wait for his response.

"Okay, okay, we can figure this out. So, you are basically telling me that Vaughn is a shade and can transport people in and out of places. Do you know that a shade is from the Underworld and is basically a ghost of someone dead?"

"He did mention something like that. But the weird part about this entire thing, besides finding out my best friend is a supernatural figure...is that he says it's a family curse. Does that make any sense?"

"Family curse? No, that doesn't make any sense. If my mythology is correct, shades are already dead and live in the Underworld. So, the question really is, is Vaughn dead and if so, does that mean his family is dead too?"

"Dude, how the hell should I know. I thought I had problems being a warlock and all, but this. My best friend is DEAD!"

"Vaughn's DEAD?" Waverly yells as she enters the kitchen.

"Damnit, Wav, we told you to stay in your room." She kicks the cabinet door closed and yells.

"I'm not a child, you can't shut me out on what's happening to the people I care about. What happened? And I swear to God if you don't tell me the whole truth I will..."

"You will what, Waverly? This is something much bigger than

your stupid-ass feelings for Vaughn. I know you both had sex, so you don't need to deny that to me. It was written all over your face when he got captured." I need to be harsh because this is serious now.

"Then please tell me what's going on? I have a right to know. Kyne, just tell me." I look at Kyne and shake my head. He looks back at Waverly and then back again at me.

"I'm sorry, we can't." Kyne responds to his sister.

"Screw you both. Fine, you want me to choose, then I will choose."

"Waverly, that's not what we are trying to say. You don't know anything." Her brother says.

"Choose, what are you talking about?" I'm very confused.

"My smart-ass brother here told me that I have to choose. I have to choose between you and Vaughn."

"WOAH, hold up. This is not where I thought the conversation was going toward. I don't honestly care right now who you want to 'choose' to be with. I'm sorry Waverly, but things are more important than feelings right now."

"So then tell me what the hell is going on." Kyne looks at me again and then I finally give in.

"Vaughn isn't human, okay. Happy?" She starts to laugh. "Go ahead, laugh it up. But we're telling the truth. Vaughn hasn't been a human since...well, I actually don't know." I tell her.

"You expect me to believe you that he's not human. Okay, then what is he? Because as far as I know, he talks, walks, kisses, and more like a human."

"Ugh Wav, too much information. Hayden is telling you the truth." Her brother gives Waverly a disgusted (TMI) face.

"Why don't I believe you. You can just be making shit up and have me not be a part of whatever this is."

"You have to understand that we are telling you the truth. Why would we make something like this up?" Getting a little pissed at her now.

"I don't know, Hayden. Maybe because you now know the truth about him and I."

"OMG just stop, I don't give a rat's ass about you and him hooking up. I'm sorry Kyne, I have more important things to figure out than her feelings."

"Waverly, please just sit down and let him explain it." She sits down without a fuss and listens to what I have to say.

"As I was saying to Kyne before you came in... We have much more to worry about. He mentioned that people knew I was a warlock and that I wasn't safe. No one was safe. Vaughn said he was trying to protect me, but I'm not sure from what." Before I can even say something else, Vaughn appears in the kitchen, actually walking through the kitchen door, in shade form. Waverly's mouth drops and looks over at both of us. I get up and throw my hand up, and Kyne sits down not knowing what to do.

"From my dad and family." Vaughn says looking at me and no one else.

"What do you mean?" I'm confused.

"The guy that came up to you and knew that you were a warlock...yeah, that's my dad. Before you question anything, no I didn't tell a soul."

"Oh, how ironic, since you don't really have a soul." Kyne says. I create a clear glow from my hands and push Kyne down back in his seat. He can't move.

"I just need to know why?" I ask Vaughn.

"Why what?" Vaughn replies.

"Why did you never tell me that you were a shade?"

"How am I supposed to say that to my best friend? Oh Hayden, by the way, I'm actually not human and I work for a secret society that hunts supernatural things and that I can phase in and out of walls and become a black mist. Yeah, fairly sure you would have freaked out." Waverly opens her mouth, but I quickly use another glow of my hand to close her mouth.

"You hunt us? Kyne, any thoughts here?" I look over at Kyne.

"Will you let me out of these mystical restraints?" I let him go, as he rubs his wrists. "A shade isn't supposed to hunt down other supernatural's. You are mainly a ghost of someone who was once a human. Vaughn, are you actually alive?"

"Yes, as far as I know, I am. This is why we call it a curse. You don't think that I did my research on what a freakin' shade was! Every day I was looking it up and trying to figure things out. Try doing that when your family is breathing down your neck. Hayden, I don't know what my family or mostly my dad is up to, but you have to stay hidden."

"So, all those phone calls, and that mysterious car?" I ask him, not looking at anyone else.

"My family. I'm what they call, Beta. My dad wanted me to get close to you when we were kids. I swear I had no idea what I was back then. Seemed like your parents did, though. All I know is that every two weeks or so, I had to report things on your activities. I didn't realize what they were looking for. Then the first time I turned, I was so scared that I asked my mom, and she looked even more scared. That's when I kind of disappeared from you and did my research. Hayden, I don't know what my dad is up to, but I swear to you that I would never ever tell anyone your secret or harm you. I would never do something to my brother."

"How am I supposed to believe any of this? When I told you that I was a warlock, you didn't even flinch. Did you already know?" I asked.

"I mean...yes and no." I look at him with a little disgust.

"You knew that I was a warlock then? How?"

"I wasn't sure, but I heard Scorpion talk about another mystical creature in the town, and well, I kind of put two and two together. I've known you my entire life and just recently was when I noticed you were becoming different. I really had no idea that it was going to be a warlock. I support that so very much. It's so cool to have any power that you want. Hayden, you can time travel."

"Be careful, Vaughn, they might be tracking you." Kyne says, without hesitation.

"They can't track me. I took the device out. I'm not a fool. But I do have to be careful. I feel like someone is watching me all the time."

"What do they want from me?" I ask.

"I'm not sure, Hayden. But you must promise me not to use your powers in public. I don't want them finding you. My dad already knows what you are, who knows what he will do to you." Before I can answer, my cell phone rings. I really don't want to pick it up, but I do.

"Hello, this is Hayden." I wait as I hear nothing on the other end. "Hello."

"Hayden, this Nurse Ariel. Your mother is doing great, and she's been asking for you. Could you come down to the hospital?" I hang up and look at everyone in my kitchen.

"Mom needs me. I have to go." I start to walk out the door. Vaughn approaches me.

"May I drive you?" I nod my head in agreement.

"You two stay here and don't do anything stupid. I will be right back." With a flick of my wrist, I let the clear glow from Waverly's mouth loose. She takes in a deep breath, and I can hear her cursing at me as we both leave. We get into the car and drive toward the hospital.

***

Kyne is sitting down again, and Waverly keeps cursing and yelling.

"Waverly, please! SHUT UP."

"Hayden just basically taped my mouth shut and you want me to shut up. How can you be so calm about all this?"

"You think for one second that I'm calm, then you clearly don't know your brother as well as you thought."

"Well, if you ever decided to stay home for more than a week then I wouldn't have this problem of not knowing you. How am I supposed to know you? Only thing I know about you is that you are a hunter. So, tell me, now that you know they are both supernatural, are you going to hunt them down and kill them?"

"Why would you even think that? Damn Waverly, I don't hunt bad things. Plus, how are you so calm then?"

"You think I'm calm...ha ha I just not only found out that Hayden is a warlock, but then just found out that the guy I slept with isn't even human. OMG ewww what the hell did I sleep with then?"

"See, this is your problem, Wav. You always bring it back to you. You realize that these two guys that you're head over heels for are dealing with so much more than your petty thoughts. Grow up and realize that there's more to the story than meets the eye."

"I'm freaking out here. Vaughn is a supernatural...what...shade? Hayden can basically create glows from his hands to shut me up. I mean did you see how quickly he mastered that? How do you know that he's a good person? For all I know, he could turn on a dime and kill us all."

"Why on earth would you think that?"

"Because he nearly tried to the other day. Kyne, he had me in a choke hold and was grinning about it. There's something dark in him and I'm afraid that now knowing about Vaughn and what his powers might be...Kyne, we need to help them both."

"I'm trying to. I'm thinking what the best possible way to deal with all this is. The only other person that I can think about who can help us, is currently in the hospital."

"Who?" She says.

"Hayden's mom." Waverly looks at him puzzled.

"What does she have to do with it all?"

"It's an exceptionally long story, but she knows about warlocks and about Hayden's powers. She married one." Waverly stares at Kyne baffled and doesn't say another word. Kyne gets up and pours himself another cup of coffee, this time putting heavy amounts of Bailey's inside.

"Great way to drown the sorrow, bro." Waverly says, and walks upstairs.

***

Meanwhile, in the car ride over to the hospital, it has never been so silent between us. Vaughn drove slowly, which is very unlike him and I just had my head out the window. We pulled up to the hospital and he locked his doors before I can get out.

"Are we okay?" Vaughn says to me.

"I'm not sure. There are a lot of things that we have to deal with, Vaughn. It's not just going to be all good in a few hours." He nods his head in agreement and unlocks the door. We start to walk toward the entrance and into what seems like a busy hospital. We both glance at each other and keep walking toward my mom's room. Right before we enter, I hear another voice coming from her room. It could be a doctor or nurse, but Vaughn gives me the same look as we try to listen in without being seen.

"This is all your fault. If you had told me what was happening, I could have helped." Another mysterious voice replies.

"Oh, right because all of a sudden you are okay with this. Seventeen years ago, you didn't have that thought process at all. You figured out I was pregnant and knew that the child could be a potential match for you. Well, why do you think he hated you. You killed him."

Vaughn and I look at each other, trying to figure out who my mom is talking to.

"Listen, if he doesn't control things then I will have no choice." The mysterious man says.

"Don't you dare touch a hair on his head. I'll die before any of that happens."

"That can be arranged." The mysterious voice chuckles. "You really think that low of me. Tell me, were you ever going to tell him that his best friend is someone he's supposed to hunt in the future?" Now I'm in complete shock. I crawl toward the door ever so slowly, to not be heard. I peek in but only see the man's back.

"Who is it, Hayden?" Vaughn says, as I shush him.

"Think it over because once the Society gets ahold of him, there's no going back. You thought Connor wasn't safe. well think again. I'm offering you my help, but if you don't want it...then so be it."

"I don't want your help. All you have brought to Connor and I was misery. Everywhere you turned, you created havoc. He had to clean up your messes. Then to top it off, you killed his best friend."

"That was an accident. I couldn't control myself. You think at that age, coming to powers is easy. You have no idea what it's like...you're human.:

"Oh, screw you. I'm so glad that you weren't in our lives after that day. Accident or no accident. Connor was beside himself. He thought that he killed that family. But now that I know the truth, you enjoyed killing them. You want me to just hand Hayden over to you, so you can what...show him the ropes. Fuck that. Damnit, you made me swear."

"Don't get all high and mighty on your horse their doll. I want to teach Hayden everything he needs to know about his powers. Connor isn't here to help him."

"DON'T you dare speak his name. He did everything I asked and left to protect his son. Probably against you and the Society. What did he get in return...killed? For all I know, you had something to do with it."

"Listen you little bitch, I have tried to be so genuinely nice to you. But that time is now over. You either hand over Hayden, or else I'm going to get very angry. You know what happens when I get angry." The mysterious man starts to choke her, and she starts gasping for air. I look at Vaughn, giving him the sign that I'm about to go in. Vaughn nods and follows me in. I put my hand up and the clear glow comes out of my hands and is around the mysterious man's neck. He starts to choke and lets up on my mom.

"You bastard, let her go or I will snap your neck right now." The mysterious man tries to turn around but can't. Vaughn then comes through the wall in shadow form and punches the mysterious man in the face. He goes down and doesn't get up. I let go of my hand and the glow subsides. Vaughn now comes back to human form.

"Mom, are you alright?" She's in shock from what she just witnessed. Words can't leave her mouth. I hug her. Vaughn walks over to the mysterious man, now unconscious, and kicks his side, turning him over.

"Uhh Hayden, we have a problem." Vaughn looks over at me and then my mom.

"What?" I say abruptly.

"It's your uncle." I look at my mom and jump off the bed and walk toward the body.

"Mom, what the hell is going on?" I look toward her again. "MOM! Why does Uncle Lincoln want to hurt me or teach me things?"

"Oh sweetheart, you heard that?" She gets up off the bed. It's the first time I've seen her out of bed. She walks toward me. "It's not safe here anymore for you."

"He killed someone. Why didn't you tell me that he had powers just like me and Dad?"

"I couldn't. He's your dad's brother, of course it's going to run in the family. He was so scary back then when he first got his powers, your dad and I were terrified that you would get those same traits. He's an evil man, and I never trusted him. You can't tell him about your powers or anything that you've discovered. Do you understand me?"

"Yes, Mom. What am I supposed to do? He knows what I am, and probably wants to kill me for them."

"He doesn't want to kill you; he wants to teach you, his ways." My mom looks nervous.

"Hayden, what's happening to him?" Vaughn looks over as a black mist comes rushing out of my uncle's body and straight into me. I fall to the ground, shaking uncontrollably. Vaughn and my mom are yelling, but I can't seem to hear them. I hear another voice instead.

"Well, hello there, son. I didn't want you to see me this way, but I had no choice. Your mom is a pain in my ass and all I want is for you to learn what I know. It's a dangerous world out there, and you have to protect yourself. If I must use force to have you cooperate, then I will. Hayden, you must know that there are two sides to every story. Join the right side." Vaughn looks at me and doesn't know what to do. My mom is holding my head.

"Sweetheart, can you hear me?"

"Dude, I know you can hear me like last time." Vaughn closes his eyes and tries again. *"Hayden, you need to snap out of the trance."*

"Let me back into my body you bastard." I say, and then I come back, and the black mist leaves my body and back into his. He wakes up slowly. I quickly create another glow and wrap it around his neck, lifting him off the ground. "You ever come near me or my friends and family again, I will do what you did to that poor family. Don't think I didn't read your thoughts when you were talking to me. It's a two-way street. Do I make myself clear?"

He chuckles even louder. "You think a little threat and a glow around my neck is going to hurt me. You are surely mistaken." He leaps toward me, knocking me to the ground. He's about to, what looks like, take some of my power when Vaughn jumps on him. Vaughn takes his arm, making it into a mist and puts my uncle in a chokehold.

"You listen to Hayden, you asshole. Or else it's not just him that will come after you. The Society will as well." Uncle Lincoln laughs even harder.

"I own the Society kid. Ha. Nice try. Catch you later, Hayden." Before anything else can happen, my uncle vanishes from the room.

"Where did he go?" I say, hoping that I can get another shot at him.

"It's too late. He knows too much." My mom says. She's fully standing and presses the button for a nurse to come in. The nurse arrives, as she kicks both Vaughn and I out of the room.

"What did he mean by he owns the Society? What's the Society, Vaughn?" He takes a deep breath as we walk out of the hospital and inside his car. Vaughn looks around to make sure no one can see us.

"The Society is what I'm part of. It's the place where all evil is cooped up. Why do you think I'm a shade...I'm not supposed to be a nice person, Hayden! We control the dead and inhabit their bodies. You really think the person you saw in the cell with me, was my actual dad? He can hop into whatever body he wants, that's dead. That's why I never know if I'm safe or not from him. For all I know, that was my dad in there posing as your uncle." I grab his shoulder to calm him down. "Hayden, this is so fucked up. You and I were never supposed to be friends because of this nonsense."

"I believe you. After what I just saw in the room there, I believe you, Vaughn. I know that you don't want to hurt me. But what does my uncle mean by everything?"

"I think, he's the head of the Society. I thought my dad was the head, but now that I think about it, he was always calling someone to get confirmation and approval. This is messed up. We need help, Hayden; we can't fight them alone."

"We need to tell Kyne and Waverly. They are the only ones that can help us." We drive quickly from the hospital to Waverly's house. We park the car and run inside, hoping that no one followed us. We're both huffing and puffing when we enter the doorway.

"What happened?" Waverly anxiously says, looking at both of us. Before we can answer, Kyne comes running down the stairs.

"It happened, didn't it?" Vaughn and I both look at Kyne.

"You're the mole, aren't you?" I say and am about to pummel Kyne. Vaughn holds me back.

"I'm not a mole. Damnit, I didn't want to tell you this." He hands over a box with a symbol on it.

"Hey, where did you get that?" I say, puzzled.

"Your dad gave it to me. He told me to keep it safe, until the right moment when it lit up."

"Lit up?" I look at the box as its glowing.

"Hayden, your hand and back are glowing." Waverly points to my finger where I had that symbol that came from nowhere.

"Touch the box." Kyne says.

"No way, so I can be teleported to another realm like the last box I touched?"

"Wait, you have the same box?" Kyne says, scratching his head.

"Yes, it's how I time traveled the first time. I touched this random box and next thing I knew I was either flying through the air in my room or being teleported someplace else." Before I even had the chance to finish, Vaughn grabs the box from Kyne, throws it up in the air. I run toward it and catch it. The box lights up red and my entire body is now glowing. I drop the box, look over at everyone and collapse to the ground.

CHAPTER 10

"Hayden, dude, can you hear me?" Vaughn seems to be yelling at me.

"Hayden, wake up!" Kyne is looking down at me, alongside Vaughn.

"What happened?" I say, still looking up toward them, groggy, and not able to pick myself up. I can't feel my body. Kyne looks over at Vaughn, and then back at me.

"We should help him up, guys, he doesn't look like he can do it on his own." Waverly yells from the background. I can't physically see her.

"Maybe if you got up off of your ass, you could come and help him." She rolls her eyes at Vaughn. They carefully take hold of my arms and drag me up from the floor. Placing me on the nearest chair, they slowly back away. I, for some reason, am not able to see straight. *What just happened? Did I pass out? For how long?*

"Hayden, are you alright?" Waverly kneels so she's directly in front of me.

"Why is everyone treating me like something crazy just happened to me?" Silence is upon everyone. "Will someone fuckin' answer me!"

Kyne looks over and comes to the foreground. Everyone else backs away, and I'm starting to see things normally again.

"Well, let's see...how do I put this." Kyne takes a big gulp. "You umm." He can't seem to spit it out.

"Oh, for the love of...You disappeared into the box." Vaughn blurs out. Then waits for my reaction. I start to laugh so hard, that I feel like I'm going to pee in my pants.

"Hold up, you're telling me that I just went into that 2 by 4 box?" I point to the box on the ground. I notice they are all dead serious. "So, give this to me slowly so I can remember what just happened."

Kyne starts to explain. "Do you remember Vaughn throwing the box into the air?"

"Yes, and me jumping to grab it." I say, still trying to piece it all together.

"So, yeah that happened, and then once you touched the box, the entire room became white and a pulse came out of the box and you were…" Kyne stops.

"I was what…Jesus, just spit it out." I'm getting very annoyed.

"You were gone. We had no idea where you went. It took us a while to figure it out." Waverly said, sounding as if she wasn't sure if she should have told me.

"What's a while?" I'm now looking at the boys. No one is giving me a straight answer. Slowly I get up and walk away from the box that is no longer glowing. I'm about to head out of the door when Vaughn's shadow figure stops me.

"You can't leave without knowing." he says, coming back into human form.

"Then tell me what the hell happened. Are you afraid of me?"

"No, Hayden, it's just that you were gone for a long time." Kyne says, and then finally blurts it out. "You were gone for a week." I laugh again.

"What do you mean, I was gone for a week?" I look toward Vaughn.

"I threw the box at you and then you disappeared. We all got thrown across the room, and when we all came to, you were just, gone. Then you know what happened next." Vaughn explains. I take a seat and look over at Kyne.

"Did the box do it?" Kyne nods his head, yes. "Then why am I keeping a box that traps me in there?" I say, thinking to myself, well duh, get rid of it.

"I think it's a sign of protection. This all makes more sense now. Therefore, your dad had the box hidden from you." I am completely confused. He continues to ramble when Vaughn comes toward me.

"How do you feel?" He says, grabbing my shoulder.

"I feel fine, honestly. Just a weird sensation, but other than that..." I look at Vaughn.

"We thought you just disappeared from us. We had no idea what was going on, we thought that maybe you went somewhere." Waverly suddenly chimes into the conversation.

"Come to think of it, I do vaguely remember something odd." They all look at me, waiting for me to say something else. But I just zone out and daze into the distance. Vaughn snaps me back into reality.

"Perhaps you should rest." Vaughn looks over at Waverly, who then escorts me up toward one of the rooms. I don't argue and walk with her.

***

Meanwhile, Kyne and Vaughn are downstairs waiting for Hayden to disappear.

"How are we going to tell him the truth?" Vaughn says, as he's looking up the stairs for reassurance.

"Oh, you mean not tell him that he almost killed you." Kyne says, angry. "You are so lucky that you can turn your humanity or whatever off and on. If you didn't notice what was about to happen, this would have been a freakin' crime scene. I don't need something else shitty happening."

"I know, calm down, Kyne. You're right though, I'm very lucky that he didn't kill me. What was that?"

"I'm not sure, but I do have a feeling." Kyne says. He pours himself a glass of whiskey and offers one to Vaughn. They continue talking.

***

Waverly is now sitting next to me on the bed. She looks over at me but seems afraid to touch me.

"You're scared of me?" I can tell by looking at her.

"Honestly, yes. I've been afraid of you ever since the glow came out of your hands. But I know that you would never hurt me or any of us...until."

"Until what, Waverly? What happened? Please, just be honest with me for once." I look at her with my puppy-dog eyes, hoping that she will tell me what occurred in the week that I was in this so-called box.

"Promise me that you won't freak out."

"I can't promise you anything, so just tell me." I sit up from the bed. She hesitates. "Waverly!"

"You almost killed Vaughn." My entire body becomes white and I'm starting to float from the bed. "Hayden, please you need to calm down." I can't hear her, I'm getting this weird feeling in the pit of my stomach and then out of nowhere, I fall back onto the bed. "Hayden, are you..."

"I'm totally fine, really. What were you saying?" I look at her confused face. "What now?"

"I just told you that you almost killed..." She couldn't say it a second time.

184

"Killed whom? Seriously, why is everyone keeping things from me? Ever since this box came back, things have been weird." She reaches over and touches my hand. I don't pull away for some reason.

"Everything is going to be alright. I promise. We are all here for you. You just need to get some rest. Lay down and I can go make you a cup of tea." Before I can even respond, she's out the door, where I can hear her going down the stairs. I close my eyes looking up at the ceiling fan that keeps going around and around in circles. I start to doze off. Suddenly I jolt from the bed, or what it would seem like, when I notice the room is pitch black. I can't move my legs; I'm just sitting in the middle of someplace. Everything is black and I'm a bit nervous.

"Guys, can you hear me? Where am I?" No one responds to me. I slowly try to get up. I can feel my legs now and start to walk when I hit a wall. Rubbing my fingers on my forehead, I reach my arms out to see where this so-called wall is. *Did I lose my sight, is that why I can't see anything here? Where is here?*

"Hello, is anyone out there? HELLO?" I try to walk along, using the wall as guide, but nothing seems familiar. It's dead silent and I'm afraid that I might have teleported someplace dark. "Vaughn, Kyne, Waverly?" Still no answer. "If anyone can hear me, I think I'm trapped somewhere." I keep walking along the wall and notice that each side I come across, is a corner. Staying in one corner, I glide myself down to sit. If you could see me, I look like a little kid who just saw a ghost. I start to think of the possibilities of me being trapped here for a long time. I begin to hyperventilate when my clear glow starts to appear from my hands. The smile on my face says it all. I lift my hands to guide me around.

"Now, let's see where I am." With my glowing hands, I start to walk along the edges of this black hole. I make it to one of the corners, when suddenly everything starts to move around me, and I'm being tossed in every which way. Almost like I'm trapped in a room that moves. I slam my head hard on the floor, or maybe it's the ceiling. The movement stops and my clear glow is gone. I'm back in the darkness. Suddenly I start to see another light, coming from what looks like the ceiling. I look up and am blinded by the light. The light gets brighter and brighter and I'm weirdly back in Kyne's kitchen, lying on the floor. I slowly start to get up and realize that everything is frozen. I'm the only one capable of moving.

"Vaughn?" Fairly sure he can't hear or see me standing in front of him. But I see him blink, which is very odd. I do the same for Kyne and Waverly, but they are like statues. Vaughn starts to move.

"Hayden, why can't I feel anything?" I look at him puzzled.

"I have no idea what is going on. One minute I'm upstairs with Waverly, and the next I'm here. What's going on?"

"What do you mean you were upstairs with Waverly?" Thought maybe his jealously was coming through, but looking at his face, he genuinely had no idea what I was talking about.

"I went upstairs to lie down after you guys told me about the box. Then Waverly came back down to grab me some tea." I look around and realize that Waverly is nowhere near the kitchen and Kyne is looking at some research book. "Did I miss something?"

"Umm, Hayden, not to burst your little bubble...but you've been missing." Okay, I've already heard this before.

"Right, I've been in the box for a week you said." He looks at me so very puzzled. But then I realize just where I went...into the box with the corners and that I somehow traveled back in time to when

I was in the box. But why would I want to go back into the box?

"How did you..." Before I can answer, something happens to me and then everything goes black again. This time, it's like I was transported someplace. I look around but I have no idea where I am.

"Did I just teleport, or am I just talking to myself, yet again?" I say to myself, but then I hear a response.

"No dude, you are definitely not talking to yourself." Vaughn says, in shade form.

"Where are we?" I look at Vaughn and he looks afraid, and I've never seen him this way.

"Shit," is the only thing he says to me before I see something in the distance. "Quick, hide." Vaughn comes back into human form and we're hiding alongside what looks like a creepy black rock and something that resembles death.

I whisper to him, "Ooh shit, are we in..." He places a hand over my mouth before I can finish my sentence.

"Don't say it out loud, I'm not sure what will happen. I've never been able to come here. Hayden, I think you teleported us here."

"How though, the last thing I remember was a black room, then in Kyne's kitchen with you, and now the Under...."

"I told you never to speak it, especially here." I knew we were in the Underworld; it was scary looking and super damp. But the question really is, how did I get here? Also, side note, IT EXISTS!

Something in the distance starts to move. We both hear voices and peek our heads out to look. A shadow figure is talking to something that I can't quite make out.

"Sir, what are we supposed to do with Vaughn?" says this mysterious figure. I glance over at Vaughn, but he's eagerly listening.

"What do you mean by that?" The shadow figure replies.

"Just saying, we know that he's not really one of us, so should I...like...kill him?" The shadow figure takes a hold of its neck and lifts him in the air.

"You ever utter his name out loud to me or threaten him again, I will kill you right here and make sure that you never can possess another soul. Do I make myself clear?"

The mysterious figure is having a hard time breathing. "Yes, sir." The shadow figure lets him go, and he takes off like a rocket.

"Trying to get good help these days is like searching for a needle in a haystack. That is the right term, right?" The shadow figure says, as another person approaches.

"Correct, that is the term. Now, we do have a little matter of upstairs and the boy. Do you want to discuss that, or should I avoid getting my throat slit?"

"Now, now Shane, there is no need for you to not speak your mind. I trust my little companions. But yes, there is the matter of Hayden and his goonies. Vaughn, I will have to deal with on my own." They both continue speaking when I notice Vaughn is back in shade form.

"Where are you going?" I whisper to Vaughn.

"I need to get a closer look at who he's talking to. Just stay here and I'll be right back." Before I can rebut, he takes off, leaving me.

"Great, I'm in the Under...shit, can't even say it. What the hell am I supposed to do? Oh, I said hell, ha. Concentrate, Hayden. Maybe I'll just say, powers, activate?" Maybe I thought the wrong thing, but my hands start to glow, and my body turned a bright red color. I'm not sure how I'm doing it. Something inside me gets

weird. Vaughn sees what's happening, but it's too late. Shane, the mysterious person, grabs Vaughn.

"We were just talking about you, what are the odds?" Shane says. Cracking a smile, jagged teeth are shown.

"Ugh, please, do me a favor and don't ever smile." Vaughn says, as Shane drops him on the ground.

"Sir, your beloved son has arrived. What shall we do?" Shane says to his master.

"Leave him to me." Shane walks away, leaving Vaughn and his dad alone. "Son, where have you been? I can't believe you finally made it to your real home. How do you like the new decorations? Too tacky?" He keeps talking, I can see Vaughn is somewhat nervous, but my glow has disappeared and I'm back behind a rock, but closer.

"What do you want from me? I already told you I don't want to be a part of your stupid ass Society." I get a little nervous for Vaughn after that statement. His dad just starts to laugh.

"Oh son, no one is forcing you to be in this Society. If you want out, then just say the word. But naturally, you will be stripped of your shade and then who knows what will happen to you." Vaughn starts to walk away, when his dad grabs him by the shoulder and pulls him in close. "Now you listen to me. If you don't do what I've asked, then there will be some very harsh consequences. Don't make me use Shane."

"What will Shane even do, he seems like such a pussy anyway." Vaughn smiles at his dad. Shane comes flying alongside them. "What the shit!"

"Pussy, is that what you called me? What is that even?" Shane starts to ponder; Vaughn's dad rolls his eyes.

"Shane, I think it's time that we active Plan B." His dad now returns the smile to his son. "How does that sound, Vaughn?"

"What's Plan B?" Vaughn stupidly looks over at me.

"Shane, will you fetch me whomever is lurking behind us, and bring them forth." Vaughn struggles but gets free from his dad's grip. Shane heads toward me when I hear Vaughn in my head. *"Dude, I don't know how you teleported us here, but get us out before he finds out you're here. Please, he can't know that you are here."*

I hear him loud and clear, but before I can even think about teleporting, something grabs a hold of my arm. Shane has a massive grip on my shoulder and drags me toward Vaughn's dad.

"Oh Hayden, so good of you to join us." Shane interrupts Vaughn's dad.

"Can I do the honors, master?"

"NO! Sorry, where are my manners. Hayden, this is Shane, Shane, meet Hayden...the warlock."

"He's a warlock? Why would you ever bring him down here? You know what they can do. It's what happened with the last one." Shane abruptly says, before being silenced.

"What last one? Are you talking about my dad?" Vaughn's dad laughs in my face.

"Good God, no, not that abomination. He was talking about your uncle, naturally. None of that. Since I have you both here, I'm quite sure that a certain someone would love to speak to you." Vaughn's dad disappears.

"Hayden, you have to get us out of here before it's too late." Vaughn yells. Shane flies toward Vaughn, knocking him down.

"Don't you dare touch him; I will kill you, whatever you are." I yell out. Shane starts to laugh as I glance at his disgusting-looking teeth. "What are you?"

"How can you not know what I am? What is wrong with people these days?" Vaughn shakes his head, and points toward what looks like another tunnel. I look as well, but I'm still curious about what this Shane creature is. It's not every day you see something supernatural. Well, besides me and my best friend. Come on, we live in a small town of Vermont.

"Then tell me what you are?" Shane lets Vaughn go and comes closer to me. I can smell the stench of death on his breath. His teeth are rotted and gross looking. He cracks a smile, extending his wings.

"I am, the one and only, Fury." I crinkle my nose because I've never heard of that before. Shane can tell.

"Seriously?" Shane says, as he starts to soar above us. "I'm a legend in Greek mythology." He continues to chat when I see Vaughn running toward me. He grabs me as we head toward the tunnel.

"He's a fuckin' Fury, I'll explain once we're out of here. I'm sorry, dude. This is all my fault." Before I can even answer, Shane catches on and swoops down grabbing me. I can't even hear what Vaughn is saying. Shane continues to laugh and then drops me. I start to fall rapidly. The next thing I know, I'm back on the ground and in Vaughn's arms.

"I didn't know you could do that." I applaud him as he puts me down.

"Neither did I." Vaughn looks at me, then back toward Shane. "We need to get out now. He will kill us." We start to run when I notice my hands are getting hot and I'm glowing. I can see Vaughn looking at me.

"Hayden, don't." I'm so confused, why is Vaughn saying that? "Hayden, watch out!" Shane comes at full force and without thinking, I bundle up energy within my hands and throw a massive ball of red fire toward him. He screams and crashes to the ground. We dart toward the tunnel in hopes that there's a way out. We're not sure where it may lead, but anywhere is better than here. The tunnel is damp and dark.

"That was awesome, dude. Who knew you could make fireballs from your hands?" He smirks.

"I had no clue. Everyday there is a new power that comes out. I'm kind of digging it." I say, as we continue down the tunnel. Finally, in what seems like ages, we come to a bright light. Vaughn walks through and I quickly follow. We both look around puzzled, not quite sure how this was even possible.

"How? WTF!" Vaughn yells out. He keeps looking around.

"How are we back? It's like we just did a full circle." I look at Vaughn, who now has a terrified look on his face.

"You can't escape the Underworld. You thought that going through a tunnel would lead you outside? Wow, Hayden, I thought you of all people were smarter than that." my uncle says, with a hint of sarcasm in his voice. "Vaughn, pleasure seeing you again."

"Can't say the same." Vaughn says, as my uncle flicks him across the hall.

"Do that again, and I will snap your neck. Now, Hayden, have you thought about my offer?"

"The offer you made to my mom about 'teaching' me to be the best warlock I can be? That offer? Yeah, no thanks. I'd rather not know what I'm capable of, than have someone evil teach me shit." Uncle Lincoln comes remarkably close to me and I don't have time to react.

"Look what happened to your dad when he disobeyed me. Do it again, and, well, you shall see what happens. I'm willing to cooperate with you, Hayden. Don't make me use force. I'm not an evil person."

"Says my own relative who is trying to kill me." I back away slowly.

"I don't want to kill you. Trust me, if I wanted that, you'd be dead already with your dad." The mention of my dad and knowing he killed him makes me incredibly angry. My body is on fire and bright red. "Oh, I'm liking this power. Tell me, what do you call this?" Before he can even ask another question, I hurl a lightning ball toward him, and he quickly moves out of the way. "See, if you let me teach you, I can show you how to use that power properly. All you have to do is take in a deep breath and let out all the anger you have. It will kill your opponent easily."

"Thanks for the advice." Sarcasm in my voice. But naturally, I do just that. I take in a deep breath, concentrate on my target and then let out a huge ball of lightning. I'm too late however, as my uncle grabs Vaughn and places him in the direct line of fire. I scream at the top of my lungs, just as the bolt is about to reach Vaughn. I let out a massive pulse and run toward Vaughn. This time, everything is in slow motion. The bolt hasn't caught up to Vaughn. I grab hold of him and the light in the room gets very bright. I let go of my breath and we're suddenly back in Kyne's kitchen. We land hard on the marble floor, as I notice the lightning bolt coming toward Vaughn.

"Fuck, it came with us. Vaughn, look out!" Before I react, there's another pulse and it flings me across the room, knocking me unconscious. Kyne gets up off the floor, looks toward the ball of light, looks at my body on the ground, hands glowing, and then looks toward Vaughn. The ball of light is just about to reach Vaughn. Vaughn quickly realizes what's happening and transforms into a shade. The ball goes through him, causing a massive hole in the kitchen wall, and he collapses to the ground.

"Vaughn, what the hell was that? Are you alright?" Kyne says, lending him a hand. "And where have you been?"

"It's a long story, but thank goodness I am, what I am." He takes hold of Kyne's hand and gets up. Waverly comes running toward him and into Vaughn's arms.

"I was so worried, where did you go?" Vaughn looks at Kyne, and then back at Waverly.

"Someplace, that no one will ever go again." She's about to say something when Vaughn plants a kiss on her lips. Kyne looks away.

"What was that for?" She says, looking only at Vaughn.

"For helping me through these weird times, and still caring for me."

"I'll always care for you." she says, hugging him again.

"Okay, enough of the lovey-dovey crap. Did Hayden try and kill you?" Kyne looks over at my unconscious body.

"Well, to be fair, it wasn't on purpose. He was aiming for his uncle and it just kind of went toward me instead. I've never seen him do that before. Not sure what it was." Waverly looks totally confused. "It's something we have to keep from Hayden. He can't know what happened."

"What do you mean he can't know what happened? What happened?" Waverly chimes in.

"We tried to escape, and his lightning bolt almost killed me."

Everyone's in the kitchen, shocked. Waverly glances at the massive hole in her kitchen. She points but, doesn't say a word because I'm starting to wake up.

"Oh man, my head. What the...? Vaughn, are you here?" I say, still looking up toward them, groggy, and not able to pick myself up. I can't feel my body. Kyne looks over at Vaughn, and then back at me.

"We should help him up, guys, he doesn't look like he can do it on his own." Waverly yells from the background. I can't physically see her.

"Maybe if you got up off of your ass, you could come and help him." She rolls her eyes at Vaughn. They carefully take hold of my arms and drag me up from the floor. Placing me on the nearest chair, they are slowly back away. I, for some reason, am not able to see straight. *What just happened? Did I pass out? For how long?*

"Hayden, are you alright?" Waverly kneels, so she's directly in front of me. I begin to realize, that I've already had this conversation. This is very odd. I play along, until I'm upstairs with Waverly and she's about to go grab some tea.

"Hold on, I don't need any tea. Can I ask you something?" She smiles and comes back into the room, sitting down on the bed next to me. "Do you think I'm crazy?"

"What, no, why would you say that?" She says.

"I think I might be going crazy. I feel like I've had this exact moment before when you were telling me about Vaughn and then grabbing me tea." She looks at me so confused.

"If anything, I think you are brave. You find out that you're a warlock and you are so calm about it in the end. If that were me, I'd be freaking out." She lets out a laugh. Our eyes meet and she takes in a deep breath. "Listen, there is something I have to tell you."

"I already know, Waverly, it's alright." I sigh.

"What do you think you know?"

"That you're in love with Vaughn. That's totally okay. You can love whomever you want. Don't let me get in the way of that." She comes extremely close to my face.

"No, you don't understand, I think...I think I'm in love with b..." She doesn't get to finish her sentence, when I see a black hole in the corner of the room, where the box is.

"Umm Waverly, back away slowly." She sees the same thing and screams. Something comes out of the black hole and closes. Standing right in front of both of us, is the Fury.

"That was a trip. Hayden, nice to see you again. Next time don't leave clues to where you go. I can always follow. Vaughn on the other hand, is harder without his tracker. But shh, master doesn't know I came." I rapidly get out of the bed, and gently shove Waverly away.

"Waverly, get away from him." She huddles in the corner, petrified.

"Well, well, well. Waverly Coutler, I presume. It's so very nice to meet you in...well...you get it. Tell me, what's it like to be in love with not one, but two guys at once? It's the only gossip I get down below." I just want to kill this creature. Waverly is terrified and backs away. She hits the bureau, causing the lamp to come crashing down. Vaughn and Kyne hear it and run upstairs barging into the room.

"Waverly, are you okay?" Kyne says. No words came out of her mouth; she just points in my direction. Shane starts to laugh uncontrollably.

"Kyne, wow, it's been a while. How are the folks? Oh wait." Shane keeps laughing. "How long has it been?"

"What the f!" Kyne backs away toward the door. "Vaughn, take Waverly downstairs, NOW!" Vaughn doesn't ask questions but is about to take her downstairs. I give one wave of my hand and slam the door, locking it, keeping them all in. I can't take anymore chances with my friends' safety.

"There's no need for that, Kyne. We are all familiar here." Waverly's face is as white as a ghost, and Vaughn looks over at me puzzled. Wondering I'm sure, how he found us.

"You don't belong in these parts," Vaughn says, without hesitation.

"The nonhuman getting all antsy." Kyne backs away. "Don't be so afraid of me, Kyne, I'm not going to harm you...yet." He says.

"Hayden, even though our encounter was brief, I've heard so many great things about you. Give my regards to your dad, after all, he is the one who freed me." Now I'm pissed, as I'm pretty sure this creature knows my dad is dead.

"He would never let you out. No matter what." Vaughn starts to turn into shade form, but then decides not to show it all off.

"What are you?" Kyne is trying not to look overly terrified, like his sister.

"Oh, my apologies. You can call me, Shane. Does that help?" He keeps talking. Sometimes you wonder what goes on in these creatures' heads. Waverly walks forward.

"Hayden, fight him." Shane laughs at her. I try so hard to get loose of his hold on me. I need to figure out how he even got through the portal.

"I didn't ask for your name, I asked what you are?" Kyne is still trying so hard not to be terrified of this creature.

"He's a Fury, Kyne." Vaughn doesn't even worry or flinch at what he is.

"I'm so impressed with you, Vaughn. Now shall we get down to business?" He keeps talking. I look toward Vaughn, as we are trying to figure out our next steps.

"Vaughn, we need to banish him. How did he even find us? Talking to Vaughn in my head.

"Hayden, you need to focus on something positive. He's a Fury and sucks on your guilt. Stop thinking about what you are guilty over and banish him." Vaughn grabs a hold of me and starts to shake me. "Think fast, Hayden before it's too late." Kyne is on the other side of the room, holding onto Waverly.

"Hayden, think of your mom." Kyne chimes in. Waverly is still silent in the corner.

"You people need to stop telling Hayden what to do. The kid has a mind of his own. Maybe I should just get rid of him for good." Shane says. "Although master wouldn't like that very much."

"Don't you dare touch him!" Waverly finally blurts out. She runs up to me and whispers something in my ear. I'm shocked that she even thought of this. The box...I know what to do next. I can see everything that is happening but can't fully react to it. Shane's wings expand, knocking down the walls around the room, and a gust of wind comes rushing in from outside.

"Before things get a little out of hand...Vaughn, they know what happened. Before you go asking me what, I think you know. I'm the most powerful Fury down there and I can't seem to figure out what this source of power is from Hayden. No wonder master wants to harness him." Shane keeps talking, when suddenly, I push him out with my mind.

"Get out of this universe, you asshole." I yell and the next thing I know, I'm covered in sweat and there is no sign of Shane.

Everyone is staring at me, but Vaughn. Waverly comes running toward me and gives me the biggest hug. Kyne just smiles, and whispers, "what the flecking fuck." Vaughn is now looking out the window.

"I have to go, Hayden, thank you." Vaughn looks at me. "Never think of your guilt ever again. You understand me?" I look over and nod in agreement. "I have to figure out what's going on. I'll be back, promise." Vaughn turns into a shade and disappears from the room.

"What the actual f!" Waverly finally blurts out. "I feel like I'm in an episode of *The Umbrella Academy*. And I know you've all seen that show." She takes in a deep breath. "A few months ago, I woke up in bed thinking how much I hated going to school. The fact that my brother was never around, my parents were dead, and the only thing I had to look forward to, was seeing you and Vaughn. Now I find out that, Hayden, you are a freakin' warlock, my brother hunts ghosts or whatever, and Vaughn is not even HUMAN! He's not human. Hayden, you create glow from your hands that can probably kill me. Kyne, I just can't even with you. Now we have a supernatural creature, Fury, or whatever in our house. How is anyone supposed to be normal and calm after all this? I'm sorry, am I the only one freaking out here that we just saw a Fury? What is HAPPENING?!" Waverly is hyperventilating, as she sits down, putting her head between her knees and taking huge breaths. Kyne walks over to her, but she pushes him away and then walks out the door, slamming it behind her. Kyne is now left with me in this room, we have no idea where to even start.

"She has a point, Hayden." Kyne looks over in my direction.

"How was I supposed to know that I was a warlock? No one told me anything to even hint to that fact. You don't think this all freaks me out? Here I am, with enough power to probably kill someone and create a giant hole in my front yard. Not to mention that I find out my best friend is a shade, and then you pop into my life. Waverly is having sex with a shade." I stop abruptly and start laughing. "I've gone mental. Literally, I have so much guilt inside of me that I don't..." I take in a deep breath.

"He knew everything about us, Hayden. It terrifies me and now I know what the box contained." Kyne holds the box up. "Your dad had two boxes, doesn't that sound a bit odd?"

"Don't even talk to me about odd right now. But go ahead, continue with your theory, you seem to know more than any of us."

"You possessed a box that allowed you to harness your time travel abilities, correct?" Kyne waits for my answer.

"Well, yes, I guess that is correct." I let him continue.

"Right, so that box was meant for you to find in your room. Which, I'm assuming is where you found it. So that means the box that he gave to me was the one he wanted to keep hidden and safe from you. Does that make any sense?" I look at him, and for once I do understand it all.

"My dad kept one box for me, and the other for all other evil things. It makes sense that the box I touched, when Vaughn threw it, was the one that was never meant to be opened." I say, with confidence.

"Meaning with everything that happened, you unleashed this Shane creature and now we have to figure out how to put him back." Before I can answer or correct him on his facts, Vaughn comes back into the room.

"Guys, we've got company. Where's Waverly?" Kyne and I look out the window and then rush down the stairs. We take hold of Waverly's arm and run toward the basement.

"Quick, get inside. It's protected and they won't find you here. Quickly!" Kyne opens the secret room and forces all of us in. Vaughn looks toward all of us.

"Let me help." He shuts the door, leaving me, Kyne, and Waverly inside the secret room. It's dead quiet, nothing can be heard or seen from either inside or outside this room.

Vaughn heads up the stairs. Before he can even change into a shade, a huge gust of wind knocks him down, making him fall down the stairs to where we are hidden. I can hear their conversations, thanks to my new power.

"Vaughnny boy, you can't escape us. Think of all the good you can do with us. Don't make me ask you where Hayden is. I know you know where he is. Now, be a peach and fetch him for me. I can't have you two wander off like that again on me," Uncle Lincoln says.

"Screw you! Why would I help someone like you? I told you to leave us alone and if you ever came near Hayden..." Vaughn's threats, weren't that accurate.

"Ha, oh come on! Is that really the best you can do? I know he's here, so you give him this little message for me. Tell him that if he doesn't come willingly to the Society, that I will kill his precious mom. You hear that, Hayden. Just because I can't see you, doesn't mean I can't smell you. I'm the head of this freakin' Society, I have powers that you can't even fathom. So, I'm asking you one more time, reveal your location, or your mom gets it." I take a big gulp and Kyne looks over at me.

"You can hear something? What's going on?" Kyne says.

"He's going to kill my mom if I don't go willingly?" I say, not looking back at Kyne.

"Who is saying those horrible things?" Waverly looks over at me, worried.

"My uncle. He's in the room right now with Vaughn. Shit, shit, what do I do?" I'm pacing back and forth.

"You know it's a trap?" Kyne looks over in my direction, knowing that I know what he means. "You can't let him take you, Hayden. He knows all about you."

"Actually, he doesn't. That's why he wants to control me. He wants to know what my powers are and what I'm capable of. If I have the upper hand…"

"Then he will kill you." Waverly says, loudly. "Hayden, you can't do this. This is like every movie out there. Dangle the bait in your hands, and you just go for it. It's not smart." Waverly does have a point. Also, realizing that she's very keen on certain genres of movies.

"What am I supposed to do? Listen to this conversation that only I can hear and do nothing?" I have no idea what to do. "Vaughn is out there risking whatever he has, to not let the Society get me. That's twice today he's saved me."

"So, don't let that go to waste. Don't fall for your uncle's bullshit. Don't let him take you just like that." Kyne says, with confidence. "Wait it happened, twice today?" I ignore him.

"Hayden, if you can hear me…don't listen to your uncle. I will get your mom to safety. But promise me that you won't do anything rash. Stay in there with Kyne and Waverly. When I tell you to move, then move! Promise me." Vaughn demands.

"I promise." I respond to Vaughn.

"You did it again, huh?" Kyne asks, looking at me.

"Yes!" I answer with a smile. Waverly just looks at both of us but doesn't question it.

Uncle Lincoln is still in the room. I hear him punching Vaughn and threatening him.

"Beta, Beta, I had high hopes for you. What am I going to do with you? Maybe I should just crush you right now, so Hayden can hear it. Then I will take your real body and kill it for good."

"My real body? What are you talking about?" Vaughn is doubled over in pain. He spits out blood and then looks up toward my uncle.

"Oh, you poor soul. You thought that you are inhabiting your real body? This is some sucker who never made it." My uncle laughs.

"Liar, you are lying." He laughs even harder.

"Just ask your dad what really happened." He laughs and then looks over in the direction of the secret room. "Hayden, you have 24 hours to do what I ask, or else your mom is toast. Got it?" With a snap of his finger, he vanishes from the room. Vaughn lets out a deep breath and collapses on the floor.

"It's safe, Hayden." He mumbles to me, spitting out more blood.

"Kyne, let us out." I point at the door.

"He's still out there." Waverly says, but Kyne knows that it's safe. He slowly opens the door. Waverly runs toward Vaughn; he pushes her aside.

"I'm sorry, I didn't mean to do that." Waverly understands. "Hayden, we have to get your mom to a safe place." I help Vaughn up and we bro hug it out.

"Thank you for having my back." We smile at each other. "Kyne,

Waverly, it's time to cause some damage."

A few moments go by while we gather ourselves after the traumatic occurrences.

"So, about your door?" Vaughn says looking at Kyne.

"What about it?" Kyne responds. I know exactly what Vaughn is trying to ask.

"How did you make it so it's soundproof and more?" Kyne smiles and then goes into a whole spiel.

"So basically, what you are trying to say, Kyne, is that someone made this door." I ask the questions, that others seem to want to know.

"Well, yes and no. I mean, it was here in the family and well...Idk. Why does the freakin' door matter?"

Vaughn takes in a deep breath, sits down, and groans. "Because that door makes it so he can't see us, no matter what he is. Which means that we need to lure him back into that room. Hayden, you and I can communicate and then hide your mom in the process."

"Yes, I like that plan. The only thing I'm worried about is, how are we going to get my mom to safety before my uncle gets to her?" I tell Vaughn. Kyne and Waverly look at me and back at Vaughn.

"Distraction." Kyne says. "I'll grab your mom with Waverly, and you need to go back to where you saw him last."

"No, that is not an option. You have no idea what it's like down there." Vaughn starts to pace. "We need a better plan." We all start to ponder but can't seem to think of anything that comes to mind.

"I've got it." Waverly blurs out. We all wait eagerly for her to tell us the master plan.

"Well...we're waiting." Vaughn says, rudely.

"I'm the bait. I'll go grab your mom and then you guys can create a diversion." She continues to talk, not noticing what is happening in the background.

"Waverly...Waverly, stop talking!" Vaughn yells at her. Kyne does the same.

"I can't believe he left. He just left, and now we don't have a plan." Kyne paces the room.

"Obviously, we know where he went, so what are we waiting for?" Waverly rolls her eyes and walks out the front door. The boys don't say anything and follow her. Kyne gets behind the wheel of his car and drives toward the hospital.

"Today marks a new age. The age in which adults have a purpose in life. We are the new society, one that can bear the right to get what they want..." Uncle Lincoln says, giving his speech to what looks like 1,000 followers. He's standing on a podium looking down at his disciples. "We might always have some obstacles in the way, but we will always prevail. To kill and always to kill. Am I right?" He continues his speech. I peek around the corner and look up toward that podium. I can't even believe my own eyes. I'm watching my uncle give a speech to his evil cult and standing next to him is Shane, the Fury. Why I came back to the Underworld, is a question I have to ask myself over and over. They would know that I went to the hospital to save my mom. I couldn't just sit there anymore and watch my friends take the bait for me. I had to do this on my own. I crept closer so I could get a better vantage point. Before I move any closer, I'm pulled back hard on the dirt floor.

"Are you mental?" Vaughn says. I smile because I'm actually happy to see him. "I knew you would come here, and not go to your mom. What were you thinking?"

"I just couldn't take you all coming up with a plan and whatnot. I just had to get out of there. Plus, how did you know that I would even come here?" Vaughn smiles.

"Dude, I know you by now. Plus, the one place that you wanted to come back to was here. Listen, we really can't be here. What was your big plan?"

"I don't know. Ahh, I don't know, Vaughn. I just know that whatever my uncle is planning, I want to know it before..."

"Before what, he spots us and tries to kill us yet again. Listen I don't know all my powers just yet, but they can probably take my shade away. Do you want that?"

"No, of course I don't want that. I just need to know what he's planning so I can beat him." I say and look out toward the podium. Everyone is starting to move and walk away. Looks like my uncle was done with his speech. Vaughn looks up and my eyes follow.

"Well, well, well, we meet again. Can't stay away, can you?" Shane says, laughing. "What brings you down here? Ohh let me guess, you heard about your uncle's offer and now you have come to make amends!"

"Shit, how did you spot us?" I look toward Vaughn then back at Shane.

"Seriously?" He responds. Vaughn has had enough, takes my hand, turns into a shade and we disappear. We reappear outside of my house.

"See, this is why I told you we could never go back down there. Who knows what they are capable of? Damnit Hayden, you can't just do that. You can't just use your power and go wherever you want." Vaughn starts pacing again, I know that he's nervous.

"I'm sorry, dude, but I feel like I was given these powers for a reason. It's so dumb to not use these powers. What am I supposed to do, just sit here and pretend that everything is alright? My mom is in danger, and my best friend is scared to face the demon downstairs. Waverly and Kyne...dude, where are they?"

***

"Okay, so Vaughn, I think that if we both go to the hospital, we can grab her from the room and then perhaps, if you say my door works, put her in there." Kyne says, while driving toward the hospital.

"Vaughn, I think it's rude that you don't respond. We're trying to come up with a plan." There's no answer, Waverly turns around and looks at the back seat, to find Vaughn no longer there. "Kyne, STOP!" Kyne slams on the brakes.

"What? I could have crashed the car. What is so important?" Kyne says, without looking back.

"He's gone. Vaughn is no longer with us." Waverly says, pissed off.

"What the...he shaded, didn't he? Son of a... I can't be the babysitter here. First Hayden disappears and now Vaughn." Kyne is very frustrated. He gets out of the car and slams the door. Waverly follows.

"Listen, we need to finish the mission. We have to save Hayden's mom before his uncle gets to her. She needs us," says Waverly as she tries to calm down her brother.

"The mission? Are you serious right now? Seriously Waverly, sometimes I don't understand what goes on in your head. For example, you like two dudes at the same time. Like, make up your mind already." Kyne is on a rampage.

"Oh, don't even start with me. You have no right to tell me who

I can like. I don't give you shit for all those other girls you had after Mom and Dad died. There I said it." Waverly walks away from the car.

"Waverly, get back here this minute. I order you." Waverly stops dead in her tracks.

"You order me? Screw you, Kyne. Do you even know what I had to go through when you up and left me? You left me alone for years, not knowing if you were safe. Mom and Dad died, and I didn't know why and then you just vanished. I was a kid, Kyne, a kid." Waverly starts to tear up.

"I'm sorry, Waverly. I'm so sorry." Kyne hugs her. "I never meant to leave you like that. I didn't know how to tell you that Mom and Dad were murdered." Kyne keeps hugging her. She pushes him away.

"What do you mean they were murdered? Kyne, what have you been holding back from me?" Tears are streaming from her eyes.

"The reason I left was because I think there was something off about their deaths, so I was looking into it when..." Before he can finish, Vaughn and I reappear.

"Hey gang." Vaughn says, nonchalantly. I just nod and throw my hand up to say hi, instead of saying it.

"Where the F have you both been? One minute we're driving and I'm talking to you, trying to figure out our next move. Then I turn around and poof, you are gone. Hayden don't even get me started on you. You just up and teleported without filling us in. Damnit, I feel like everything I say, just goes in one ear and out the other." Waverly takes a deep breath.

"Are you done?" I say out loud. "All this bickering back and forth is driving me insane. Thank God I can teleport out of here. Waverly,

I don't know what went up your ass, but stop being a whiny bitch. There, I said it! Now if you can stop talking and let me explain, then we can get on with this." I inhale deeply and see the look on everyone's faces.

"Where has this Hayden been, I dig him. My dude!" Vaughn says, as he high-fives me. Waverly rolls her eyes.

"Alright, Hayden, what's the plan?" Kyne just looks in my direction, because clearly, he doesn't have a plan.

"The plan is to get my mom out of the hospital and back into Kyne's secret room. Therefore, she will be safe." I keep talking, but then I see the look on everyone's faces. "Okay, what? Did I disappear again and then come back?"

"Hayden, you're fading in and out." I look down at my body and see what they're talking about.

"Great, just another thing I have to worry about." Vaughn smiles from ear to ear. "What are you grinning about?" I'm not enjoying this.

"If you can control fading in and out, then you can grab your mom without being detected." Vaughn does have a point.

"That's a brilliant idea. Alright, now Hayden, just practice as much as you can." Kyne looks over at me and he can tell I'm not pleased.

"You want me to harness this new power, today, so we can go grab my mom before he does?" I start laughing. "All you people are idiots. I can't even control my teleporting power, and now you want me to harness this one?" I can't stop laughing and I don't know why.

"Waverly, you haven't said a word. Care to share what you are thinking?" Kyne looks at her sister.

"Oh, my apologies, I was told not to speak. So therefore, I'm not speaking." I stop laughing and look at her.

"Get over yourself, Waverly. Loosen up. What happened to the girl I hooked up with?" Vaughn clearly has no filter.

"Everyone is ganging up on me, not sure why or what I did for it." She starts to walk away. Kyne nods to us and follows her.

"Waverly hold up. I'm sure it's not a huge deal, but maybe the guys are just having a hard time with everything. Just think about it. Hayden lost his dad; Vaughn is a shade, and his dad is the head of some evil secret society. Not to mention Hayden's uncle. Plus, you and I are not normal much either. I'm a supernatural hunter and you have been trying to live a normal life. I get it, I'm having a hard time, too. You think it was easy for me to be a parent at 10. Or find out that warlocks exist and that I had to team up with one. Not to mention, I knew things that I probably shouldn't. I'm sorry, but you are not the only one going through a hard time. So please, come back to the group and let's sort out our next move. Deal?"

"I'm sorry, I didn't realize everything would hit me in this way. I love you, Kyne. You're the only family I have left. Let's go help the boys."

Waverly and Kyne head back into the circle, as I try to come up with a plan. We all smile at each other and get back into Kyne's car. We've got the perfect plan. We start to drive for a few minutes when I tell Kyne to pull over. I get out of the car, closing the door behind me.

"Okay, everyone good with the plan?" I say, as I peek my head into the car.

"You bet your ass." Vaughn responds, giving me the thumbs up. Kyne and Waverly nod their heads in agreement.

"Okay, meet me there in roughly 20 minutes. Don't be late, or this won't work." I smile, and then disappear.

"Are we sure his plan is going to work?" Waverly asks, as she's only looking at her brother.

"We have no choice. Here, take this, don't shoot it until it's time." Kyne hands the gun to Waverly.

"Are you kidding me, I'm not shooting this rare pistol. Give it to Vaughn." Waverly passes the gun to Vaughn, but Vaughn doesn't take it. Even though it's one of his favorite pieces, he can't take it. "Vaughn, take it, please!"

"I can't take it. I'm not human, therefore I can protect myself. You are the one that will need it if in case Hayden and I aren't here. Just trust yourself with it. It will work, don't worry." He pushes the gun back toward her. Kyne goes back into the car to get the last-minute items on my list.

"Listen, I need to tell you something before it's too late." Waverly grabs hold of Vaughn's arm. She pulls him in close. "I adore you, even after I found out what you were. But there's something that I don't know how to tell you."

"You're in love with both of us." Vaughn says. Waverly just looks dumbfounded.

"How did you..." She says.

"I'm a dude, I know when I'm not fully in the picture. Plus, Hayden is my best friend and I know how much he cares for you. But I also care for you, too. Even though lately I haven't shown it. I'm just not sure this can ever be something real. I mean look at me, I'm not even fully human. How do I know that things won't be different? You'll always have a place in my heart Wav, but right now...it's just not the time." Vaughn takes in a deep breath. "Look at me being the one all mussy and stuff. Ugh, I hate that. Maybe I'm not human after all."

"No, Vaughn that makes you human. I totally understand everything. I'm sorry that this has been a wild ride for all of us. I care so much about you. I hope that once things settle down, we can actually have another conversation about this." She smiles and then walks away from Vaughn.

"You guys alright?" Kyne says, as he resurfaces from the car.

"All good, got the tools?" Vaughn asks, Kyne nods in agreement. "Good, let's go!" They all make their way toward the hospital.

***

I'm currently in the basement of the hospital. Or rather the lovely morgue in which all this creepiness started. The lights start to flicker, and I'm not sure if it's my powers or my uncle vastly approaching. I push the swinging door open, making sure that no one hears me. The hospital is empty and I'm a little worried that something has happened already. Tiptoeing through the creepy hallway, I spot a dark figure. It might have been the same figure I saw months ago. I hold my breath and close my eyes to concentrate. I listen closely to every room with my super hearing and spot my mom. It's extremely quiet and there's no sign of nurses or doctors. Letting all the air out of my lungs, I start to harness my new power and fade out. Here I am walking the hallways, and I'm actually invisible. How long can I hold this... well, that's the main question. A large gust of wind comes from the hallway, and I'm knocked on the ground. My head slams on the floor hard, and I start to fade back into view.

"Hayden, I'm so impressed. You harnessed a new power without any guidance. You have to teach me the ways." Shane rapidly approaches me. Lifting me up with his nasty-looking claws.

"What, so now my uncle needs a henchman to do his dirty work? What, are you his little lap Fury?" I try to stay calm; I've learned to do that from Vaughn.

"What did you just say to me you little punk. I'm a damn Fury, I can do whatever I want. I want to kill you right now." Shane's grip on me gets tighter.

"But you can't, Uncles' orders. You can't do a thing to me." I smile and I know that irritates him.

"Oh, I can't do anything to you, but your precious mom...that's another story." He smiles, showing his ugly jaded teeth. I try to get away from his grip. Thinking about my mom and how she's in danger, I take in deep breaths. I close my eyes and start to fade out once again. Shane does a double take. I set myself free and run down the hallway quietly, as to not be heard.

"Get back here you little shit." Shane expands his wings, flying away and leaving the roof of the hospital building fully exposed. I slow down as I approach my mom's room. I'm huffing and puffing but I need to slow my heart rate down, as I don't want her to know what's happening. I take in deep breaths, and slowly open her door. Pushing it open ever so slowly, I notice she's not on the bed but instead is looking out the window. She turns around and looks right at me, startled. I've come back into view.

"Hayden? What on earth is going on? Why is the sky black and what are you doing here?" She slowly looks away from me and back at the window. I walk toward her, being cautious, and look at the same window. She's right, the sky is black and I'm not sure why.

"Mom, I need you to listen to me." She turns around and sits down on the chair. I can see how miserable she is. But I also notice something odd about her. She's got bruises on her neck and arms. I slowly make my way to her, making sure that I'm not invading her space. "What happened to your neck?" She looks at me, dumbfounded. "Mom, can you hear what I'm saying?" I kneel toward her so she can see my face. "It's me, Hayden." She doesn't respond. I stand back up and move away from her.

"Hayden, is that you? Can you tell your dad that I'm going to be late for dinner? He will be worried sick about me. Oh, and make sure you tell your uncle that we can't make it to his new business gathering." I look at her and have no idea what's happening. She's mumbling all these weird things and I don't know if she's under some sort of spell or just having visions from the past. I take her hand and stroke it.

"Mom, I need you to listen to me very carefully. You are currently in a hospital, where you've been for several months. We were in a car accident, and well, Dad didn't make it. You and Dad have been together on and off because of what he is. He came back here to help me out with my new powers, and now something is after me...well, more like someone. I'm not sure what he wants from me, but I have to protect the ones I love. So, Mom if you can comprehend what I'm trying to say to you, please, you need to come with me." She looks at me, gets up from her chair and walks toward the hospital bed.

"I have to gather all my things and then we can go. Hayden, your uncle was just here. We have to leave now before he comes back." I'm not sure if she's telling me the truth or something that happened a while back ago. I don't argue and gather her things up. We're about to head out the door when I'm blasted across the room, hitting the glass wall hard. I hear it start to crack. My mom drops her stuff and backs away toward the wall. I see her being lifted by some magical force. I try to catch my breath, but I can't seem to. I'm also pinned to the ground, and incapable of moving anything.

"Trying to pull a fast one on me, did you now, Hayden?" I hear the familiar voice but can't see him. I see my mom being suspended off the ground. "You see, Hayden, this is what happens when you don't do as I asked. All I wanted was for you to join the Society where I can teach you everything you need to know about your powers. But instead, you decide to do the one thing that I told you not to do. So, what am I supposed to do with all this? Your mom is useless without your dad. She can't be protected, and now she will pay the price for what you've done." My uncle continues to threaten me, but I don't give in.

"See, the problem with all your threats is that you have no idea what I'm capable of. It's the only reason you want me to join your Society. You don't know who I am, and that kills you. You can't kill me, because then you can't have what you want. You can't really harm me because then you can't have the powers that I have. You have no leverage. Sure, my mom is something that will always be my weakness, but then what? So, go ahead, tell me what you are going to do to me now?" My uncle stares at me, somewhat baffled.

"You bring up a good point there, kiddo. Let me make it quite simple then." He walks into the room, looks over at me, then back at my mom. "You always were the loving type, even after finding out what we were. I loved you so very much, but in the end, you chose him. I didn't take it very well at first, but now with him out of the picture, I thought we could rekindle things. But you insulted me and treated me like the brother you hated. Therefore, this is something I wish I didn't have to do." Before he finishes his sentence, he takes in a large deep breath, a red circular glow appears around his body, and with one fluid motion he lets the red glow go. It pulses toward my mom and with a swift motion of his hand, he snaps her neck. She falls to the ground, motionless. My entire body goes still as I look at my mom's motionless body on the ground. My fingers start to turn bright red followed by my body. It gets windy inside the room, like a tornado hit only this one spot. My eyes roll back and are white with rage. I start to glow a bright red and white color, as my body is floating in the air. That's when I create a massive lightning bolt and with all my might, throw it at my uncle. He's not fully prepared as the tremendous lightning bolt hits him hard. I yell at the top of my lungs, letting all my anger go with the bolt. I see it hit him as he crashes through the wall and into the hallway. I run toward my mom, grab her and teleport out of the hospital.

Meanwhile, Vaughn and Kyne enter the hospital through the front door, minutes before my uncle arrives in the room. Also, minutes before my mom's accident.

"Kyne, there he is. How do we approach this?" Vaughn says, looking up and down the hallways and finding it odd that no one is here.

"We stick to the plan. We know that he's here to do something horrible to his mom. We just have to trust that Hayden doesn't lose it. And that our plan really works." Kyne takes a gulp, hoping in fact that I don't lose my shit.

"What if he does lose it, and this plan is useless? Then what?" Vaughn seems a bit nervous, but we stick to the plan. Waverly in the meantime is outside guarding the entrance, just in case. We thought that with her inside that my uncle could possibly harm her as well. She agreed to stay watch.

Vaughn and Kyne tip toe toward the room that I'm in and try not to be seen by my uncle. Vaughn approaches the door and peeks in. He sees me talking to my mom and doesn't understand why she's mumbling about the past. Vaughn looks over at Kyne and then back toward me. I spot him and give him the nod.

"Are you sure this is a good idea?" Kyne says, while placing a hand on Vaughn's shoulder.

"Yes, if all goes to plan, Hayden will piss of his uncle and something drastic will happen. It must work, Kyne. It has to!" Vaughn smiles at Kyne and slowly turns into a shade. He enters the room, while my uncle's back is turned. He's giving the speech to me. My mom is still pinned against the wall, but she notices Vaughn. She blinks, making it known that she knows Vaughn's here to help. I glance toward them both and close my eyes ever so slowly. It is then I give the hateful speech to my uncle. In the background, I see the grip on my mom get looser. Vaughn, in shade form approaches my mom.

He whispers to her, "Hey Mrs. G. It's me Vaughn. I'll explain everything later. I need you to do exactly as I tell you. Nod if you understand me." She nods her head in agreement. Vaughn looks at me one last time. I take in a deep breath and continue my rant. Kyne is in the doorway now; I see his fingers are crossed, hoping that this plan works. Kyne goes into the hallway and back toward the main entrance. The sliding doors open and Kyne walks toward Waverly.

"It's almost time. You know what to do when you see me running, right?" He tells her sister.

"I've got this. As much as I don't want to do this, I have to...for Hayden's sake." She says, as she takes in the biggest breath and doesn't let it out."

"Breathe sis, you've got this. Remember one thing…" Kyne looks directly in her eyes. "I love you and don't miss." Waverly smirks in his direction, and Kyne is back through the sliding doors and into the hallway. He can hear everything that's happening in the other room.

Vaughn does one last take at my mom.

"Mrs. G, take in a deep breath. This is going to hurt really badly, and whatever you do, don't scream." She doesn't argue, takes in a deep breath and closes her eyes. Vaughn's shade gets darker and enters my mom's body, inhabiting her. I can see that my mom is in severe pain, and I know this because it happened to me when Vaughn decided to teleport us out in shade form. Vaughn is now inhabiting my mom's body. Uncle Lincoln, now insulted, starts to talk to my mom and how much he loved her and all that crap. He starts to form his red glow and I know that something awful is going to happen. But for some reason, I had already predicted this happening. I must react in a way that will make it believable. He then snaps her neck, and for a split second I forget that Vaughn is protecting her inside his shade. That is when I retaliate and shove my uncle through the wall and into the hallway.

"Vaughn, now." I say, as I watch Vaughn leave my mom's body. She's motionless in the corner, unconscious. I pick her up. "I owe you big time." Vaughn winks at me, as he's back in human form.

"Go, it will be clear and safe at Kyne's. When she wakes up, I'm sure she will have a million questions." My mom and I teleport out of the hospital.

In the hallway, Kyne sees my uncle crash through the wall and smack into the side corridor. Kyne makes sure that my uncle is still down and not moving. He runs toward the sliding door, and signals Waverly.

"It's time. You've got this." Kyne takes a step back and stands outside the sliding doors. Waverly makes her way inside, to where my uncle is still lying on the floor. She stands at the end of the hallway and takes a deep breath. My uncle slowly moves and gets up from the floor.

"Stupid piece of shit. At least I got rid of the one thing he loves." My uncle looks up toward Waverly, who is holding Kyne's supernatural gun. They are now standing facing each other, like in a Western gun fight. "Or so it would seem."

"Don't you dare move." Waverly says, as the gun in her hand is shaking.

"Ha, what is that you are holding? You know that guns won't hurt me. I'm a powerful warlock, you stupid bimbo." Waverly doesn't pay attention to his snarky remarks. She pulls the safety as it clicks.

"OH, look at you. So brave, maybe I should kill you as well and see what Hayden will do. He's not even here, he fled like a coward." He smiles in her direction, but Waverly doesn't return the gesture. "Are we playing the no speaking back again. I do like this. So, tell me just one thing Waverly Coulter, what is going to happen when you end up losing both the loves of your life?" Waverly lowers the gun ever so quickly, but then regains her strength.

"You can't make me falter with your stupid words. You have no idea whom I love and in fact, you know nothing about me." She responds with a heavy tone in her voice.

"On the contrary, I know a ton about you. After all you did meet them both when you were little. Neighbors and all. But what was it that got you to love both Vaughn and Hayden...maybe it was because they're not human?" He keeps rambling. Waverly can't take it anymore and closes her eyes. "You don't have the b...." Before he can finish the sentence, Waverly pulls the trigger and watches the bullet hit my uncle in the gut. He starts to laugh.

"I do have the balls to pull the trigger." She smiles and then backs away into the darker part of the hallway.

"You thought that a measly bullet was going to harm me? You are surely mistaken. You can't harm..." He stops talking mid-sentence, looks down at his gut, which is now gushing blood. "What the..." He falls to the ground, cupping his hand over the bullet wound and passes out. Waverly comes creeping back into the hallway, glances at my uncle and then runs toward the sliding door. Her hands are shaking uncontrollably.

Hyperventilating she approaches her brother. "Kyne." She gulps. "I did it." He runs in Waverly's direction and plants a massive kiss on her cheek.

"Is he...?" Kyne looks at Waverly and then peeks down the hallway.

"I'm not sure. I did what you told me to do. I pulled the trigger and then aimed. He was laughing at me, then fell to the ground without a sound." Kyne smiles and hugs her. He rapidly walks down the hallway to make sure that, in fact, my uncle was down for the count.

"Umm Waverly...where is he?" She looks down at where my uncle's body was.

"I swear, he was right here. I shot him, look at the blood." She's very nervous now. "I don't understand."

"Shit, I do. Supernatural bullets or not, he's so powerful that one shot is not going to harm him. Sis, we have to go...NOW!" Kyne takes Waverly's hand and they run to the car. Vaughn reappears, just in time.

"Did you get it done?" Waverly can't react, words can't seem to leave her mouth.

"Fuck, we had a minor setback. Get in the car." They all pile into the car and drive toward Kyne's house.

"What was the minor complication, guys?" Vaughn is very impatient at this point. "Hello!"

"I shot him, and I saw him fall to the ground. There was blood and everything. I ran to get Kyne and then something must have happened in the process of that. He was gone, just left a pool of blood." Waverly then cupped her face with her hands, ashamed.

"Sweetheart, look at me." Vaughn says, as he grabs her face. "You did everything that you were supposed to do. Trust me, it's extremely hard to have someone hold a gun let alone pull the trigger. I'm so proud of you. This is not your fault. We didn't predict this happening." Vaughn kisses her on the lips. Kyne keeps driving, paying attention but not fully.

"Everything okay on Hayden's end?" Kyne asks, as he swerves to avoid a stupid chipmunk. "Stupid creatures."

"I'm hoping that everything worked. It happened just as he planned. It's very intense and weird at the same time." Vaughn plants his head on the window, peeking out.

"Remind me again how Hayden knew this was all going to happen?" Kyne anxiously waits for Vaughn's response.

"He just had a weird moment back at the house. He told me that he saw something that hasn't happened yet. He just told me to trust him and do what he asked. I did. I wasn't sure if they were going to turn out the way he wanted. But we all stuck to the plan, and some of it worked." Vaughn still looks out the window.

"Are we sure that it all worked? Is Hayden's mom alright?" Waverly asks, touching Vaughn's arm.

"Yes, she's fine. We will know more once we get there." Vaughn closes his eyes and listens to the hum of the car. No other words are exchanged.

***

I teleport into Kyne's basement with my mom in tow. She wakes up to realize that we're no longer in the hospital. Before she can say anything, I give her the biggest hug.

"Sweetheart, are you alright?" She pulls me away from our hug. "What happened back there?"

"I'm so happy that you are safe. There is no time to explain, I need to get you to safety. Please, Mom, get inside this door." I open the secret room in Kyne's basement and push her in. She resists me.

"I need to know what is happening before I get into some room that I have no idea what it's used for. Explain yourself!" I start to tell her everything that has happened since we last spoke. How Kyne's been helping me. Vaughn is a shade, and how his dad is partnered up with this so-called Society. How Uncle Lincoln is the puppet master of the entire show and how things have just gone out of control. I also mention to her my powers and how I seem to be getting one every day. After a few minutes pass, she glances at me. Not in shock, but in amazement.

"Your dad and I always knew there were some things off about your uncle. He was a villain from the start. Did you know that he loved me at one point and wanted to fight your dad for me? It was insane. Oh honey, I wanted to explain everything to you before. Your dad came home to protect you from him. He knew that you would inherit both of their powers but didn't know to what extent. It was everything he hoped for, he wanted to teach you his ways. I wish he were here to see how amazing you've become. But there is something I must tell you..." She sits down inside Kyne's secret room. I keep looking up to make sure that my uncle doesn't appear.

"What?" I wait patiently for her to tell me.

"Your dad noticed something about your genes when you were little. You have enough dark magic inside you to harness. You have to be careful on how you use your powers." She keeps talking to me, but all I hear is that I have dark magic inside me. "You must promise me," she says, but naturally I don't hear what the promise was.

"What did you say?" She doesn't repeat her statement. "Sure, I promise Mom." I wish I heard what I was promising her. But right now, I needed to get her into a safe place. She agrees and I close the door, locking her in. "I love you, Mom." I place my hand on the hidden door and walk up the stairs into Kyne's living room. Patiently, I wait for the others to arrive.

Kyne, still driving home, looks ahead of the street and does a double take. He looks behind him, and sees Vaughn and Waverly sleeping. Waverly's head is on Vaughn's shoulder. Kyne smiles and continues to drive. He turns right down his street and screams. Waverly and Vaughn jump up.

"What's going on?" Waverly yells. The radio turns on in the car.

"Clever girl you are, Ms. Coulter. But don't think you can get away from me so easily. You might have wounded me, but in the end I always prevail." The voice on the radio terrified everyone in the car. Waverly's face turns another sheet of white. Vaughn turned into shade form and Kyne's staring into blank space, not paying attention to the road. Uncle Lincoln appears in front of the car. Kyne doesn't have time to react and step on the brakes. He turns the wheel hard to the left and the car smashes into the nearest tree. Kyne's head is saved by the air bags, but blood is gushing from his nose. Vaughn has disappeared and Waverly's head went through the back-side window, and she's hanging out of it. Blood is everywhere. Vaughn appears back in human form and slowly opens Waverly's door.

"Waverly, can you hear me? Oh my God, Wav, please respond to me." Silence. Vaughn starts to tear up. He makes his way toward to the front door and opens it slowly. "Kyne, dude, are you alright?"

"Shit, what the hell was that. I saw him for a split second and then I couldn't control the car. Are you alright? OMG-Waverly?" Kyne tries to turn his head but can't. "Tell me she's, okay?" Vaughn doesn't answer but shakes his head. "HELP HER!" Vaughn watches as Kyne gets out of the car slowly. He looks at Waverly and starts to scream. Vaughn lifts Waverly out of the car, but she's still unconscious.

"Never underestimate what I am capable of. Do you understand me?" Uncle Lincoln approaches. Vaughn is about to turn to shade form when his dad appears out of nowhere and inserts a massive needle in his neck. Vaughn falls to the ground, taking Waverly with him.

"Children, they never do listen. After all the things I've done for this boy." Vaughn's dad smirks as he looks at his son.

"Take him away, I have unfinished business with Waverly." Uncle Lincoln approaches Waverly's body and lifts her up. "Wake up, sweetheart." With a cool breath from his lips, Waverly wakes up. Without any time to react, he covers her mouth, so no one hears her scream. Kyne doesn't have the strength to react. He just lies on the ground looking at what is happening.

"You think that you can outwit me? Well, think again, because now I will do what you have done upon me." Waverly's eyes widen in fear. Uncle Lincoln throws her body to the ground. She hits the pavement with such force, she starts bleeding from her elbows and knees. There's a faint crack, as her arm breaks.

"Hayden, if you can hear me, we need your help. Waverly is in trouble. Please, I hope that you can hear me." Kyne tries to reach me.

***

I walk outside waiting for the gang to get back. I know that my mom is in a safer place. Twenty minutes pass by and I'm getting a bit worried. I start to pace back and forth when I hear something faint in the distance. I'm not sure what it is, but I stop and listen even more. That is when I hear Kyne's voice and immediately teleport to him. I'm not sure what was more terrifying, seeing my mom's neck get snapped or seeing Waverly bleeding all over the pavement with my uncle beside her using his power to keep her down. Kyne sees me, smiles, and passes out. I quickly approach the car, trying not to be seen by my uncle. I don't see Vaughn anywhere and I'm not quite sure what to do.

"Vaughn, dude, where are you?" I hear nothing in return. I keep trying and still get no response. I'm in panic mode now. As I continue to reach Vaughn, I don't notice my uncle creating an electric pulse. I've never seen it happen in real life, only in comics that I've read. I'm in awe and can't seem to react to it in time. My

uncle releases the electric pulse at Waverly who takes the full force of it. She's thrown through the air and into the middle of the street. Blood is now pouring from her eyes, nose, and mouth. I'm pretty sure she broke something else. I'm petrified, as I can't move an inch. I see my uncle start to create another electric pulse. This time I can fully move and react.

"Don't you dare harm a finger on her ever again." Without thinking I mimic the electric pulse and with all my force, hit him hard with it. He reacts in time and both our pulses collide, creating a giant electric current that is pulsing black. With all my strength I hold the pulse toward him, not to harm anyone else in the process. As I'm doing this, I notice Waverly moving in the distance. She distracts me and I lose some of the electric pulse and my uncle throws it back at me. I hit the pavement with a thud. Vaughn's dad appears in the distance, he takes one look at me and then back at my uncle.

"Lincoln, it's time to go." He says to my uncle. "We have him." I don't understand.

"I'm not finished here; I need to be done with this once and for all." Vaughn's dad approaches him.

"This is not how it was supposed to be. You know this, he has a greater purpose to us. Leave it be." Before my uncle can react, I get up and run over to Waverly. Vaughn's dad looks at my uncle and then back at me again. "See you very soon, Hayden." Only Vaughn's dad disappears.

"Before things get any more complicated, Hayden, there is something I must tell you." I give him the middle finger. "That is no way to treat me, son."

"Stop calling me son, you have no right to. You killed my dad!"

Uncle Lincoln starts to laugh.

"Your mom never told you, huh."

"Told me what?" I hold on to Waverly tightly as he approaches me.

"That I'm your real dad." I don't believe a word that comes out of his mouth.

"Liar! All you've been telling me are lies. Why should I believe you, I know it's not true!" I ponder. He can't be telling me the truth. There's no way.

"Well, I guess now you don't have any proof of that, since your mom is dead. But just ask yourself, how do you harness all the same powers as I do, when you know for a fact that your dad didn't have these powers. Just think about it, son." He laughs and disappears. I'm left there with Waverly in my arms.

She mumbles. "He's lying to you. There is no way you are his son. Don't believe a word he says." Waverly's coughing up blood.

"Shit, we need to get you to the hospital." I grab her and start to carry her. Kyne, now awake, crawls toward me.

"Heal her." I look at him and can't help but laugh a little.

"What! I can't just heal people. She needs to be taken to the hospital." I keep walking away from the car and I'm about to teleport her to the hospital.

"HEAL her! I've seen you do it, just think about it and then do it. Please, Hayden. She won't make it and you know that she's bleeding internally. Help her." I scan her body, because now I have that ability and I can tell from what Kyne is saying that she won't make it.

"How do I help her? I don't know how to heal people. If I could, I would have with my dad."

"Your blood, Hayden." I don't know what he means by that.

"I'm not some vampire who can just heal people from them drinking my blood." Kyne smirks at me, and I know that he's not joking. I guess maybe my blood will help her. I bite down on my wrist and watch the blood ooze out. I shove my palm to her mouth. Her eyes open and without hesitation, she starts to drink it. I'm in awe as I have no idea how this is even possible.

"Hayden, your dad and I did a study a while back about DNA and how in your bloodline, your blood is pure. You not only have the power to heal people, but you also have the power to destroy the world." I'm taken aback by his comment, and I push away from Waverly, who now looks a thousand times better.

"You decide to tell me this all now? So, am I in fact my uncle's son too?" I see the look on Kyne's face and know that he has no idea what I'm talking about.

"I know nothing about that, but I do know that you are capable of a lot of things. Scary and great. That is why I know you can heal people. Thank you for healing my sister." He walks toward Waverly, grabs her, and walks her back to the house. We all go in silence as we approach Kyne's front door.

"Where's Vaughn?" Waverly notices that he's missing.

"They took him, Wav." I stop in my tracks.

"Who took him?" I say, not sure why he's so calm.

"His dad." Kyne for some reason is keeping things short and sweet. We enter the house, and everything is silent. I head toward the kitchen, grab a towel, and dab it with water. I start to clean up Waverly's face.

"Thank you for saving my life." She takes ahold of my hand. Kyne looks over and walks out of the room. "I didn't know what was happening. I was so scared, Hayden. I thought he was going to kill me right there and then. Vaughn was gone, and I couldn't even see Kyne. I was stuck, I couldn't move and all of a sudden, I was flying across the street and hit the pavement. I'm pretty sure I broke my arm and leg. I couldn't see anything, and I thought this was how I went. It was terrifying." She continues to speak when she looks at me. I haven't said a word since she started. I have nothing to say to her, I'm just lost and confused. I'm also thinking about my dark path or how I could possibly be my uncle's son. I know that there is only one way to find out the truth. I look into her eyes and kiss her cheek. She smiles.

"I have to go do something. Will you be alright here?" I place my hand on her cheek.

"Yes, come back though. I have to tell you something." She takes the towel from me and mends to her own wounds. I make my way downstairs. Taking in a deep breath, I stand in front of Kyne's secret door, afraid to open it. Finally coming up with the courage, I open it with force, to see my mom laying down, not moving. Terrified, I run to her.

"Mom!" She opens her eyes and sits up.

"I'm okay, sweetheart. Are you?" She grabs my face, looking at the bags under my eyes. Because, yes, I haven't slept much.

"My friends have been in a terrible accident. Caused by, you know, and Vaughn is now back with them. I have to save him." I continue to talk to her; she just plants a kiss on my cheek.

"Take in a deep breath. Everything will be alright. From what you've told me about Vaughn, he's capable of anything. I know what he is. I've known for a while and I'm sorry that I didn't tell you. It's just that some secrets we had to keep from you..."

"Ah Mom, that is not why I'm down here. There's something that I need to know. I need the truth from you and only the truth. Promise me?"

"Of course, sweetheart. I promise, just like you promised me." I smile, even though I have no idea what I promised. I'm hesitant to even ask her the question. "What is it, hun?"

"Am I Uncle Lincoln's son?" I look at her intently, waiting for her response. She looks at me, scared.

"Why would you say that?" She says, with a hint of nervousness.

"Because he told me that I'm his son, and of course I didn't believe him. Connor was my dad, and he will always be my dad." I nod my head, convincing myself.

"Connor will always be your dad. He loved you and only wanted the best things for you." Now I'm a little confused, is she telling me that Connor is my dad?

"You didn't really answer my question, Mom. Is Lincoln my dad?" She stands up and forces herself toward the wall.

"Don't be upset with me. There was a time in my weak moments when your dad and I were having a ton of issues. It wasn't my proudest moment." My jaw drops and I stare at her.

"Just spit it out Mom. Yes or no, it's a simple question." She starts to tear up and fidget with her hands.

"Yes, Lincoln is your dad. I'm so sorry honey. It was the worst possible mistake of my life. But I love you so much and I would never trade you for a second. Connor was your real dad and always will be. Do you understand that?" She walks toward me, but my glow comes back. I hold her in place, and with great anger I shove her to the wall. She hits it hard. I hear her groan.

"You lied to me my entire life. You've lied since the day I was born. You would have never told me that I was a warlock until it was convenient for both of you. You never told me that you and Connor teamed up with Kyne to solve these weird supernatural occurrences in our town. Oh, not to mention that you and Connor had inklings about Vaughn being a shade. What else did I miss, Mom? Are you going to tell me next that I can destroy the world too?" She cries and turns her head away from me.

"You promised." She takes a deep breath, trying not to look at me.

"What exactly did I promise, Mom?" I yell at her. "Tell me!"

"You promised that when and if you found out the truth, that you wouldn't lash out on anyone." I laugh in her face.

"Promise broken. You think that any kid who hears that his dad is a phony and that the one person who is his dad, is trying to kill him and his friends is a good thing? You know nothing of my powers, I've seen what I'm capable of. Past and present. So tell me, what gives you the right to keep this massive information from me?"

"I am your mother, and I have every right to protect my child. That is enough!" She yells back at me. I get incredibly angry, and my glow gets brighter and tighter around her neck. "Hayden, stop it. I can't breathe. You're hurting me." My grip gets tighter when I hear something from the distance.

"Hayden, STOP!" It's Waverly at the door, yelling at me.

"Stay away from me, Waverly, don't make me hurt you." She notices my eyes are a darker shade of black.

"You've already hurt me. Hayden, look at me." She screams at me. "LOOK AT ME."

"WHAT." I yell back, releasing the grip on my mom's neck.

"I know that what you just found out is horrible. And before you go choking me…I heard it when I came downstairs to see what the yelling was all about. You think you're the only one with issues. I found out that my parents were murdered. Kyne told me the other day. I wanted to kill him for not telling me and for disappearing from me. But in the end, I know that he was protecting me for a reason. Your mom did the same thing. You think she doesn't feel the same when she did what she did. We all make mistakes, Hayden. That's what makes us human. Your mom was trying to protect you. So please, don't make this all her fault. Show her that you actually understand what she's going through." I listen to her and realize that she does have a point. But I'm so upset with my mom it makes me more irritated.

"That's what makes us human, you realize that I'm not human at all. The two people that you claim to love are NOT human. I'm a freakin' warlock who can snap your neck in two seconds. Vaughn can vaporize and take someone else's body. In fact, I'm pretty sure that the person I grew up with my whole life, is not even the same person. Different body and everything. Who is Vaughn? I'm actually glad that he's back down there." Waverly and my mom look at me with disappointment.

"I can't believe you would say something so cruel about the people who care about you. Hayden, you must realize that we are just trying to help. Your mom included."

"Maybe you have to realize that I don't need or want your help. Maybe I'm better off being the villain of this story."

"Don't ever say that. You are not your uncle. You are the best thing that has ever happened to me. Do you realize that?" Waverly pushes me. "Do you?" I come extremely close to her, but she doesn't back away. "I'm not afraid of you, Hayden. I love you."

"No, you don't. You love the thought of me. It's Vaughn that you're in love with." She comes even closer, enough to have our lips touch.

"I love you, Hayden Grant. And I'm perfectly happy with loving you and Vaughn. Do you?" I don't know what to say. All these things are rushing through my head.

"Just stop! Stop saying that you love me. Stop telling me that I'm not an evil person. And for the love of God, stop telling me what to do. All of you need to leave me alone." Before I know it, I fade out and think of someplace else to go. I teleport out of the room.

***

Vaughn is back in the 2x4 cell that he was locked up in before. His dad approaches.

"Hi kiddo. How are you holding up?"

"Screw you. You drugged me and brought be back here against my will. What do you want?" Vaughn spits at his dad, as he opens the cell door.

"I want you to kill Hayden, like I asked all these years." His dad smiles.

"I will never, ever kill my best friend. You and this stupid Society can shove your feet up your asses. I'm not doing anything for you." Vaughn's dad starts to smirk and lets out a tiny laugh.

"Oh kiddo, it's too late for that. See, the lovely needle I injected in you will soon take hold. You will have no choice but to do as I say. That's the power I will always have over you. The minute you see Hayden again, you will want to kill him. OH, I can't wait to see how this all unfolds. For now, hang tight and make sure you eat. Kisses." Vaughn's dad closes the cell door behind him and locks it. Vaughn rushes to the door and kicks it.

"I hate you!!" He screams and tries to transform into a shade. His dad comes back.

"Oh, and by the way. Your powers won't work for another 24 hours. Toodle-oo." He laughs in the distance and fades out.

"I fuckin' hate you. You hear me! I can't stand the sight of you." Vaughn slams his fist against the wall, causing it to bleed. "Damnit."

"Sucks, doesn't it." I pop into the cell. Vaughn jumps in shock, not knowing who's there. I come into the light. He lets out a deep breath of relief.

"Are you trying to give me a heart attack?" Vaughn comes closer to me, but I back away from him. "What are you doing here?"

"Does it matter?" I look at him, with no emotion. "Maybe this was meant to be. You kill me after all and transfer my power to him." I come back into the light; he can see I've been crying.

"What happened, Hayden?" He sits down on the tiny bench in the cell. "I'd never hurt you; you must know that."

"No, actually I don't know that. I'm so sick of people lying to my face. Tell me something, Vaughn...would you have ever told me that you were a shade?" Vaughn looks away briefly and then back in my direction. "Answer the question."

"Honestly, I was going back and forth in telling you. I didn't want my best friend knowing that I was freak and possibly not even remotely human. So no, Hayden, I leaned more toward not telling you. Why do you want to know this suddenly?"

"I'm tired of people using me. My mom lied, you lied, Waverly is lying, Kyne is a walking lie detector and the only person that hasn't lied to me is my dad." I take in a deep gulp, and I start to glow. This time a different color all together. Vaughn notices and slowly backs away from me.

"What do you mean your dad was the only one that didn't lie to you? He's the one that lied to you about everything. Connor would have never told you about your powers. You said that yourself."

"Connor is not my DAD!" I yell, and my entire body glows a shade of black. Vaughn backs away even more, falling to the ground.

"He will never be my dad, never."

"Dude, you're freaking me out. What is happening to you?" Vaughn stays on the ground.

"What's happening to me? I'm finding out the truth and how everyone I care for, doesn't want to tell me the truth. So, now it's my turn." I'm extremely angry.

"What does that mean? Hayden, we all care about you. You're my brother and I will always be here..." Vaughn gets up, but something happens in the process. His entire body turns into a shade, a different color shade. Almost grey and purple. Seconds later, he comes back into human form. He comes closer to me. "But sometimes you have to eliminate the threat. In this case, you are the threat, Hayden. I can't wait until you are out of our lives for good." I look toward him, realizing that this might in fact be the real him.

"See, I told you. This is who you are. You are a killer, and right now you want to kill me. Am I wrong?" I say, not moving a muscle.

"Correct, pain in my ass. Loving Waverly when you know she doesn't deserve you. So, let's make this easy, shall we?" He comes running after me, but I fade away standing just outside the cell doors.

"I'm not that easy to kill, Vaughn. Do me a favor, stay put like a good solider. I have some business to take care of." I disappear.

"Little shit, I will get you." Vaughn sits back down and then comes to again. "What the hell just happened? Oh shit."

Back at the Coulter residence, Waverly is sitting near the secret door, looking at my mom.

"Are you alright, Mrs. Grant?" Waverly is hesitant to approach.

"That was a great little speech you told him, hun. Are you really in love with my son?" She says, coming closer to the door.

"Yes, but I'm also in love with his best friend. I don't know how to explain it. Why can't I love them both? Everything I said was true. I'm so sorry that you had to keep that secret for this long. You must feel like shit?" Waverly cups her mouth, as she can't believe she just said that to my mom.

"It was the worst secret I've had to keep. I would have gladly told Hayden about his powers, but telling him that Lincoln was his real dad, would have broken him to pieces. Look what happened. I'm ashamed of myself for even thinking about that. We have to help my son, if he goes down this path, there's no telling what might happen." She walks out of the room and starts making her way up the stairs to the kitchen. Waverly follows her. Kyne is in the kitchen, making some coffee.

"What are you doing up here? You have to stay down there for your safety." Kyne says, as he pours a cup of coffee into his Star Wars mug.

"Kyne, listen to me very carefully. Hayden knows the truth." Hayden's mom waits for Kyne's reaction. "If we don't stop him, things won't turn out very pleasant." Waverly looks over at Hayden's mom and then back at her brother.

"Wait, hold up!" Waverly looks at her brother. "You knew that Lincoln was Hayden's dad?" She puts her hands on her hips.

"Yes, Connor told me the night he was leaving for good. I had to keep the secret, Wav." Kyne looks ashamed.

"It's not his fault, Hayden's mom interjects. Connor and I decided that if someone was going to know, then it would be the one person who was helping us."

"Helping you with what exactly?" Kyne looks toward Hayden's mom. "Well...."

"Do you remember when I told you that our parents were possibly murdered?" Kyne's eyes widen.

"Yes, a little too late, but yes," she says, rolling her eyes,

"I think Lincoln killed our parents. It was the night that Connor "thought" he killed that family. Well, that family was us. He thought that his powers were too much and that he couldn't control them. Come to find out that it was Lincoln all along and his goons." I look over at Hayden's mom.

"And you knew this?" She nods her head. "So, were you ever going to tell me?" Waverly looks devastated.

"You were too young when all this happened. I was trying to piece things together. I teamed up with the Grants. That was when I found out what Connor was. Waverly, you have to believe me." Kyne doesn't know how to approach his sister.

"Omg, Hayden was right. All you people do is lie. Kyne, you are the one person who I can count on. But come to think of it, you've never been my brother. I've been on my own for years. I can't look at you anymore." She starts to walk away. Kyne grabs her and pulls her in close.

"Listen to me, sis. Right now, we have to set things aside and save Hayden." Waverly doesn't seem to care and shoves her brother out of the way. Mrs. Grant comes in closer to Waverly.

"I know you are hurt; we all are right now. But if we don't save

Hayden, bad things will happen." Hayden's mom says, scared.

"Bad things, like what?" Waverly looks over at them both.

"End of the world, bad." Kyne and Mrs. Grant say at the exact same time.

Waverly looks over at them and can't decide if she believes them or not. She takes one look at Mrs. Grant's face and realizes that this is a serious matter.

"How do we find him and save him?" Waverly asks.

"He will go to the one place his dad is." Hayden's mom says, and we all know exactly where that is.

***

"Today, we come to celebrate the news of great power…Ugh, no, that sounds too vague. How do I word this, so I don't come across as a dick? Oh wait, not like that matters. Norman, come here," Uncle Lincoln states, as he's prepping for yet another speech.

"You called for me, sir." Norman approaches.

"What is the status with your son?" Lincoln doesn't look toward Norman.

"I think it worked; Vaughn has turned into my little puppet." Vaughn's dad, Norman says.

"Very good, now all we need is…" Uncle Lincoln is interrupted.

"Me." I look at him from a distance.

"Well, didn't expect you to be here. Oh, and I see we've become a shade darker." Lincoln smiles, happily.

"What can I say, you find out the truth and things come more into perspective. Isn't that right, Dad?"

"Ohhh, my boy, you found out the truth. I'm so happy to hear that." Norman looks over at Lincoln, in shock.

"Hold up, Hayden's your son?" Norman says, hesitantly.

"That is correct, he just needed to learn the hard way. Now that you know, what are you planning on doing with that information?" Lincoln walks over toward me.

"I plan on joining you. After all, this world is corrupt and I think it needs a little re-do, don't you think?" I laugh, with a hint of evil in my voice.

"I'm so proud of you, that I could cry right now." Lincoln walks toward me and gives me a big hug. I hug him back. Norman looks over as we hug, with a very worried look on his face.

In the distance, Shane, the Fury, comes full speed wings out toward me. I turn quickly around, my eyes are blood-shot and without thinking, a laser beam strikes from my eyes and hits Shane. Shane yells and crumbles into pieces.

"Ladies and Gents, Hayden Grant." I don't even flinch as I just killed a Fury without any effort.

"What's next, Dad." I smile and look over at Norman, who is puzzled. "Tell your son, that he doesn't scare me no matter what body he is in. He's no longer my friend and you can do what you please with him. But I will tell you one thing, he will not be killing me ever. I will kill him before any of that happens. Understood?"

"Hayden, I would never have him kill you..." My hand flies up and my clear glow is back, holding Norman up in the air.

"What did you say? Don't lie to me." I see Lincoln smiling and happy as a clam. He claps his hands in joy.

"Sir, all I meant to say is that I will not let him harm you. I promise you that." I let Norman down. He plops on the ground and runs away.

"Coward. Why is he your right-hand man?" I ask, rudely.

"Long story. Now, where were we? Ah yes, today's lesson is

harnessing your ability to destroy. Are you up for that?" Lincoln laughs, and I laugh with him. I'm totally on board.

Norman runs away as fast as he can toward Vaughn's cell. He stops in front of the bars, and peeks inside.

"Vaughn, are you there?" His dad says, waiting for him to surface.

"What do you want, haven't you caused enough trouble?" Vaughn doesn't come into the light.

"Son, I know that I've been the worst dad in the world. I deserve everything you have to throw at me. But you have to listen to me very carefully." Norman doesn't hesitate and unlocks the door, walking inside. "Hayden has turned." You can tell Norman's voice seems nervous.

"Hayden has turned. Into what?" Vaughn comes into the light.

"The worst version of himself. What he doesn't realize is that he has more power than Lincoln. Damnit, Lincoln is his dad. Hayden not only carries good but carries an extreme amount of darkness. If he can't be controlled, then I fear the worst." Norman is nervous for sure. Vaughn has never seen him like that before.

"Why are you all of a sudden on the good side?" Vaughn approaches his dad.

"I need you to help me fix this. As you are under my control, I will reverse the spell and make it so you help him and not kill him."

"Oh jeez, thanks Dad. So now you want me to save him from himself?" Vaughn looks over at his dad. "What do I need to do?" Norman tells Vaughn what he needs to do. They don't hug, but Norman sticks yet another needle in his arm.

"What the fuck was that for." Vaughn yells.

"To reverse the spell. Son, I'm counting on you." Norman

abruptly takes the needle out.

"I don't have a choice, seems like I have to do the unthinkable to save my best friend." Vaughn takes in a deep breath. Norman leaves the cell door open and disappears. "Great, I have to sacrifice something I love, for the one I care for instead. Shit."

Waverly, Kyne, and Mrs. Grant are about to leave the house when Vaughn fades in. His shade is back to the normal color, but only I knew that.

"Holy shit, Vaughn. I was so worried about you." Waverly comes running toward him. They both hug and kiss. Mrs. Grant looks very confused and Kyne just rolls his eyes, but he's happy to see Vaughn again.

"I'm afraid I come bearing bad news. Hayden's turned and we have to save him." Mrs. Grant looks at everyone and back toward Vaughn.

"I was hoping this day would never come." Mrs. Grant says. Vaughn looks toward all of us and does something that they would never expect. He knocks Mrs. Grant out and takes her away. He fades back moments later.

"What the shit...Where did you just take her?" Kyne says, looking around the room.

"Your secret room, she can't be a part of this. Kyne, can I have a minute with Waverly?" Kyne throws his hands up and leaves the room. "Waverly, this is going to be very hard on both of us." She looks at Vaughn, clearly not understanding. "You and I can never be. Do you understand that?"

"What? Why are you suddenly saying this now? I love you, Vaughn." She's startled, as they just had a conversation about fixing things.

"I can't have you and be who I am. I need you to understand all this. You and I were never supposed to be. It was great while it lasted, but with everything going on, I physically can't be with you ever. Hayden is the one that loves you, and always has." Vaughn tears up a little.

"No, I don't believe you. Stop lying to me. You care about me, and you wouldn't be saying all this unless something was wrong. What happened?" She takes hold of Vaughn's hand, but he pushes her away.

"Waverly please, it's over. You and I are over. Walk away before I get angry." She doesn't walk away. Vaughn turns into a shade and fades away leaving her alone. She cries and huddles into a ball. Kyne walks into the room, covering his eyes, just in case. He opens them and sees her crying on the floor.

"Waverly? Sis, talk to me." He falls to the ground and hugs her.

"It's over Kyne. It's over." She wipes the tears from her face.

"What's over?" Kyne looks outside and sees Vaughn looking back. "Oh, Waverly, I'm so sorry. He doesn't deserve you." She doesn't respond and just cries in his arms. A few minutes pass when Vaughn enters the room again. Kyne walks over to him and punches him in the face.

"What were you thinking? Doing that at this moment?" Vaughn squares his jaw.

"Yup, I deserved that. But I had to, you don't understand." Vaughn hesitates. "I have to give up something I love to save the one I love." Kyne ponders and then realizes that he's talking about saving Hayden.

"Shit, I'm so sorry. You have to tell Waverly that." Kyne says.

"No, she can't know. She and I were never meant to be anyway. I care about her, but Hayden is the one that's always been in love with her. So, it's time for me to save my best friend." They don't argue and walk up to Waverly. "Are you ready?" She looks at Vaughn, giving him the finger.

"To save Hayden, yes." She says, pushing past Vaughn and holding Kyne's hand. "Let's do this." All three of them are on the front steps, when a dark cloud approaches. Falling from that cloud, me, and Lincoln.

"Going somewhere?" I smile, as I stare at my former friends.

"Hayden, what? You look different" Waverly says to me. I laugh and flick my wrist, she goes flying across the grass and lands hard, unconscious. Kyne comes running toward me and my clear glow pulses, creating a wave that aims for Kyne. It hits him and I crunch on his vocal cords. He tries to escape my grip but can't. He falls to the ground moments later, unconscious like his sister. Vaughn is the only one left. "I'm going to make you disappear for good."

"Try your best, you would never kill your brother." Vaughn takes a massive step toward me. I get angry. Lincoln starts to create a vortex and jumps inside of it. He pulls his hand out, for me to take it. I hesitate and look at my best friend. I smile, but then yell to him.

"Don't follow me." With all my might, I teleport with my uncle, but somehow Vaughn follows. We're in the middle of the woods. Uncle Lincoln is there with his minions, and I'm standing on top of this mound. Looking down, I see Vaughn.

"I told you not to follow me. What don't you understand?" I yell down at him.

"I will never give up on you, Hayden. We are family!" I laugh. My body starts to create a wind vortex. As I'm standing in the middle of my creation, Vaughn is trying to come toward me. I push him away will all my might, knocking him to the ground.

"It ends NOW!" I yell and let the vortex inside me release. I close my eyes, letting the anger and rage out of my body. I've created a massive hole in the middle of the woods. Vaughn starts to move again and sees what I've done. He turns into a shade and approaches me on the hill.

"What were you going to do? Kill me and then create a giant hole?" Vaughn puts a hand on my shoulder.

"Get your hand off me." I zap him off me, his hands start to set fire. He turns into human form.

"You can never come back to this. Your mom needs you right now. We all need you. I broke it off with Waverly for you. Do you get that? You are the most important thing in my life, Hayden. Best friends don't come so easily. So, I'm asking you, please don't go down this path."

"I'm glad you ended it with her. She was a little slut anyway. No one wants that. Maybe this is another lie you are feeding me. I know what happens to you both in the future. Well, it's over now. This place needs a do-over, and I'm the only one capable of that. Back away from me, or so help me I will kill you. Shade or no shade," I say, as Vaughn looks at me in shock. He thought that maybe his words could help me, but they can't. I've turned to the darkness, and now it's time for me to end it all. I see Kyne and Waverly running in the distance, with what seems like an object.

"Hayden, please." Waverly screams. Kyne is running besides her holding something in his hands. Before I know what, it is, the sky turns black as my emotions get stronger. Everyone looks up and then back at me. I'm creating a black hole in the ground that seems to have access to the Underworld. Without hesitation, I lift a tree from its roots and throw it into the pit.

"Take another step, and I will do the same with you all." I stay put, but Kyne moves closer. He looks at Vaughn and Waverly and mumbles something to them that I can't quite make out. Waverly's face says it all, though. She starts to cry. Without noticing, Kyne approaches me, with the box in his hand.

"You did this to yourself, and now I have no choice." Kyne opens the box, and mumbles random words. Words that I've heard before.

"Totum iter revertemur." Kyne yells. The box turns bright red, opens and without a flinch, I'm being sucked inside. The wind picks up, and Waverly is struggling to hold on. Vaughn approaches her and holds her into place. Their eyes meet and they hug one another. Kyne lets go of the box, and they all watch me descend inside. Moments later, the sky turns blue. Lincoln is missing, and standing up on the hill is a figure, no one has seen in a long time.

"Mr. Grant? Vaughn says, shocked.

"Connor?" Kyne, and Waverly say simultaneously.

www.ingramcontent.com/pod-product-compliance
Lightning Source LLC
Chambersburg PA
CBHW070459300726
48975CB00007B/2235